TOM KENNEDY

TOM KENNEDY

JOHN RAE

This edition published in 2013 by:

Thistle Publishing
36 Great Smith Street
London
SW1P 3BU

ISBN-13: 978-1-909869-32-5

For our Grandchildren

Jamie	*Hannah*	*Francesca*
Naomi	*Michael*	*Sam*
Brownwyn	*Lucy*	*Katie*
Brodie	*Cameron*	*Jude*
	and Jimmy	

PROLOGUE

I met Dom Peter Quinn at Tyne Cot one summer afternoon in 1969. We were both on an excursion from Bruges to the battlefields and cemeteries of the First World War, ending the day at the Menin Gate for the ceremony of the Last Post. I was then a junior lecturer in the department of War Studies at King's College, London, teaching an undergraduate course on the history of warfare and running seminars for post-graduates on aspects of the First World War. My students were on vacation and my wife, Mary, had taken our two young daughters to spend a month with her mother in Connecticut so I was seizing the opportunity to visit those places – Ypres, Passchendaele, Langemarck – that had been part of my imaginative landscape since I was a boy.

My interest in the First World War was not inspired by the poems of Wilfred Owen and Siegried Sassoon but by an obscure German book called, in its English translation, Storm of Steel, which I found in my father's library and read at the age of twelve. The author, Ernst Junger, wrote about his life as a young German officer and storm troop leader on the Western front. What appealed to me was that, despite enduring the same horrors as his English enemies, he could still write with conviction about duty and chivalry and honour.

It was typical of my father that he should have such a book on his shelves. In a curious counterpoint to his daily life as a general practitioner in Wandsworth, he was fascinated by war and especially by the romance of war, by dramatic moments and heroic deeds. When he was there at my bedtime, which wasn't often, he would sit on the end of the bed, put aside Winnie the Pooh and tell me stories of battles long ago. I loved these occasions because I thought he was giving me his undivided attention and because he was a born storyteller with an eye for the telling image. My favourite, and his too I suspect as he repeated it often, was his description of King Gustavus's white stallion careering riderless across the battlefield of Lutzen, breaking the brave hearts of his Swedish soldiers who knew then that their king was dead.

The romance of war is not something that appeals to me now but the essence of my father's stories and of Ernst Junger's book was that in war the individual counts. That is something I still believe to be true despite so much evidence to the contrary. Nowhere is the individual soldier so lovingly remembered yet made to seem so insignificant than at Tyne Cot Cemetery on the western slope of the Passchendaele Ridge, the largest British military cemetery in the world.

We arrived in the late afternoon and the westering sun reflected dazzlingly from the rows of white headstones and the long white memorial Wall of the Missing. I was shading my eyes, not looking for any name in particular on the wall, just noting how some names were already fading while others – Baxendale, Bellringer, Bowman – were as sharp as the day they were cut. It was as though it was the elements that would decide which names would live for ever more. It was then that a quiet English voice at my shoulder said: 'The Royal Fusiliers suffered very badly.'

I turned and, seeing who it was, asked him if he had known any of these men. 'I was attached to their brigade,' he replied and, anticipating my next question, added with a smile, 'Chaplain to the forces, 4th class.'

He had been sitting alone on the coach. Though he must have been in his late seventies, he looked lean and fit in his black habit and his well-creased, well-weathered face suggested a life spent in the high Alps rather than in a cloister. I asked him where he was from and he told me he came from Downside Abbey near Bath in the west of England. Later, as other members of the group were making their way back to the coach, I saw him standing in front of one of the white headstones with his head bowed. I would have liked to have seen whose grave he was visiting but there was no way of doing so unobtrusively.

At a quarter to eight that evening, our group was waiting under the great arches of the Menin Gate in Ypres when a party of children arrived and their teacher asked us in perfect English whether we would be kind enough to make way for them to stand in front.

'They are from a residential school in Ghent,' she said in reply to Father Peter's question. 'They have all been deaf since birth.' All the while, she was communicating with the children whose eager faces followed her signals, then looked at Father Peter with smiles and giggles and finally turned to where the members of the Ypres Fire Brigade, each carrying a silver bugle, were assembling nearby.

At five minutes to eight, the traffic was stopped and the buglers marched out in single file to take up their position with their backs to the Menin Road. On this road, our guide had informed us, British and Dominion soldiers had marched out of Ypres on their way to the Salient, many never to return. As they left the town, they always passed the same message back from platoon to platoon: 'Tell the last man through to bolt the Menin Gate.' Was that, I wondered, what the teacher was now telling her excited children whose eyes were shining with anticipation of a ceremony they would not be able to hear?

At eight o'clock precisely, the buglers sounded the Last Post. I had made up my mind that I would remain detached from the emotion of the occasion but one glance at the deaf children and my defences crumbled. They were staring intently at the buglers as though there was a chance that if they concentrated hard enough they might catch the faintest echo or vibration of the notes that fell and rose and fell again in such sad cadences.

'I'm afraid the sight of those children straining to hear the Last Post was too much for me,' I confessed to Father Peter as we walked back towards the coach. 'For me, too,' he said. 'There was something about them that connected with the ceremony in a way that was not true of the rest of us.' I was not sure what he meant and I allowed my imagination to play on the fanciful idea that the deaf children could hear the sound of the guns from the distant past.

'Their deafness is a terrible affliction,' he continued when we both took our seats on the coach. 'Yet there were times when men in the trenches would have regarded it as a blessing. Under prolonged bombardment, some men were struck deaf and dumb, while others could not remember who they were and took out their identity discs to see if the name was familiar.'

So began a conversation about the war that, three years later, ultimately led to my becoming the custodian of the strange and tragic story of Tom and Katherine Kennedy.

Father Peter was staying with the Benedictine Sisters in the Beguinage, a short walk from my hotel. Anxious not to allow our brief acquaintance to end when we returned to Bruges, I asked him to join me for dinner. He said he would be happy to do so as he had told the Guest Sister that he would not be back in time for the evening meal. There was a small restaurant near the convent, which was inexpensive and off the tourist routes. We agreed to meet there at 9.30pm.

The restaurant was run by a young couple: she the cook and he the waiter. They greeted Father Peter as a friend and I could not resist asking if he sometimes slipped out of the convent for a meal. 'Only when someone is kind enough to invite me,' he said. We chose a table by the window overlooking the canal and ordered Flemish stew and a carafe of red wine. When the wine was brought, I poured two glasses and asked Father Peter what we should drink to. 'To chance meetings,' he suggested. I raised my glass. 'To chance meetings.' We drank and I decided this was the moment to ask him whose grave he had been visiting.

'He was a private soldier in the Royal Fusiliers,' he answered without hesitation. 'You were looking at the names of some of his comrades. I promised his widow that I would say a prayer at his grave whenever I came to Tyne Cot. The Abbot gives me permission to come every three or four years because these were the men I knew.'

The infantry brigade to which he had been attached had suffered heavy casualties in 1917 in the early stages of the battle of Passchendaele. When his battalions went into the line, he went with them, saying his office in odd corners, arranging a time and place to celebrate Mass for the Catholic soldiers and hearing confessions before the battle. He preferred to go over the top with the first wave so that he was there to give the sacraments to the dying but the colonel sometimes asked him to stay behind to comfort the wounded in the advanced dressing station and to bury the dead.

When I made a comment on the difficulty of being a chaplain in the heat of the battle, he shook his head. 'The real difficulties arose when the men came out of the line,' he said. 'The CO always wanted a memorial service for the men who had been killed but the survivors hated it; they had lost friends and comrades and the last thing they wanted was a church parade. It was the colonel's decision but the chaplain who took the flak.' His use of Second World War slang sounded odd, as though his memory had slipped a generation, but the strength of his feeling was unmistakable. The frustrations of fifty years ago had unexpectedly surfaced.

For a short while, our conversation turned to contemporary topics – the Vietnam War, Civil Rights in Northern Ireland, the restlessness of youth across the globe – but he had not done with the past. 'The young men of Europe were restless then, too,' he said. 'Later they blamed the old men but in 1914 it was the young men who wanted to go to war. We felt the mood even in the monastery.'

He had taken his final solemn vows in 1912 at the age of twenty-one and was twenty-three when the war started. He knew many of his friends from school and university would be among the first to volunteer.

'Was that why you became a chaplain?' I asked.

'No, it was a practical decision,' he explained. 'The army was short of Roman Catholic chaplains and it was easier for a religious to go than a parish priest. One day I was a monk and the next I held the rank of captain in the British army.'

'A strange transformation,' I said.

'In some ways it was,' he agreed. 'Although the male world of the officers' mess is not so different from that of the monastery. The real problem was returning to Downside after nearly four years in the outside world where I had been my own master. In those days, monks were expected to be more secluded from the world than they are now and I wasn't sure I was prepared to accept that degree of seclusion and obedience any more.

'There was a Benedictine monk at Quarr Abbey on the Isle of Wight who held some sort of reserve commission in the French army. In August 1914, he was called up and left for France. He too served for four years but not as a chaplain; he was the commanding officer of 'La Division de Fer', the crack division of the French army. I met him at Quarr in the 1920s. He was busily digging the vegetable garden. When I asked him about his strange transformation, he replied that the day he returned to Quarr and to the monastic community had been the happiest day of his life.' Father Peter paused before going on. 'I envied him. I didn't find it that easy. I couldn't shake off what had happened in the war just like that.'

We sat for a long while over our coffee and a second carafe of wine, mulling over the strange transformations that war brought about in people's lives. All the time I sensed that he had so much more to tell me but did not yet know me well enough. When he asked about my plans for the future, I did not think it was just polite interest but more like one of those English unofficial soundings for a job, the exact nature of which is never mentioned.

We walked together across the bridge to the gate of the convent where we shook hands and said goodnight. He would be glad to return my hospitality if I ever wished to visit Downside. I assured him that he would always be welcome at our house in Putney.

It was late but I was in no mood for sleeping so I took a round-about route back to my hotel walking along the bank of a canal thinking about Father Peter returning to the monastery at the end of the war. The contrast between his monastic life and his war experience was less dramatic than that of the monk from Quarr but I found it more intriguing. Something, a particular event or long exposure to the bitter cynicism of men for whom the idea of a loving God had become a mockery, had caused him to doubt his vocation. It was now fifty years since he had decided to return to Downside, yet there had been moments in our conversation that evening when I sensed that, for him, the First World War was not history but unfinished business.

Over the next two years he stayed with us in Putney on three occasions. As I came to know him better, I appreciated what an unusually balanced and well-rounded character he was, at ease in the world outside the monastery yet never giving the impression that he regretted returning, however difficult that may have been. When on his first visit, he played so unaffectedly with the children that Mary told him he should have married and had a family of his own, he shook his head. He was the youngest of thirteen children and knew the joy of a large and happy family but he had chosen to seek joy in a different way, by responding to the call of love from the Father in Jesus Christ.

His memories of childhood were entirely happy, the worst being the daily dose of cod liver oil, and he realised how fortunate he had been in his upbringing. His father was a successful coal exporter and the family home was a large house in Belsize Grove in North London. Both his parents were from long-established Roman Catholic families; his uncle was a monk at St. Augustine's Abbey nearby and his father, as a Papal Chamberlain, was given the privilege to have Mass in the house. It was taken for granted that the daughters would be educated in a convent and the sons in a monastery, so when Peter left Downside School at the age of eighteen and in the same year entered the novitiate of the monastery next door, the family was delighted but not surprised.

I asked him how he could have been sure at eighteen that he had received God's call. He had not been sure, he replied. His entry to the novitiate had been like an arranged marriage planned when he was a child but, as can happen in an arranged marriage, he discovered years later that this was after all the love of his life.

We liked him for his honesty and simplicity and we looked forward to his visits during which, usually over supper when the children had gone to bed, different aspects of his life unfolded. Before taking his solemn vows in 1912, he spent three years at Benet House in Cambridge where his provisional commitment to the Benedictine Rule did not prevent him taking part in undergraduate life. He had driven one of the long line of hansom cabs in a famous mock funeral, escorting to the railway station an undergraduate who had been rusticated. Even now he was excited by what he called the 'brisk intellect and hopeful spring' of Cambridge life before the First World War.

Like my father, he was an excellent raconteur with an eye for the telling image and the ironies of history. He was presented to the Kaiser in 1914, eight weeks before the start of the War. He was staying in the German Benedictine monastery of Maria Laach on his way to Rome when the Kaiser and his sister paid a visit. For the Kaiser, a magnificent figure in his Jaegar uniform accompanied by glittering generals in highly polished top boots, the Abbot took the unprecedented step of postponing Vespers, providing instead a sumptuous buffet in the garden. When Father Peter was presented simply as 'der Englander', the other monks having been introduced by name, the Kaiser was highly amused and, turning to his generals, repeated 'der Englander' as though it was the best joke he had heard for many a day,

Father Peter was happy to talk about his experience as an army chaplain but we soon realised that certain doors would remain closed. When Mary pressed him on why he had returned to Downside in 1919, he replied in purely practical terms. The Abbey and the school had wanted their monks back as soon as possible after the Armistice because the boys were being taught by expensive non-Catholic laymen.

For fifteen years, he taught history to the senior boys and religion to the juniors. Then in 1934, out of the blue, the Abbot sent him to Beccles, one of the Abbey's livings in Suffolk. There he enjoyed the role of parish priest, though he was now dependent for his everyday needs on the generosity of his parishioners. He sometimes went several days without a cooked meal, the large church, the priest's house and the primary school all having strong claims on the parish's uncertain income. He thought of volunteering again in 1939 – he was only forty-eight, younger than some army chaplains in the First World War – but the Abbot insisted he should return to Downside as Novice Master. Since then he had done various jobs in the monastery, including a short spell as Prior, and now he was in his own words just an elderly monk who found it hard to genuflect and wrote occasional articles for the Downside Review.

Early in 1972, we heard that his health was deteriorating and that soon he would be too frail to travel or even receive a guest at the monastery. When I was due to speak at the annual conference of civil war enthusiasts at a hotel near Worcester, Mary quickly suggested that I should call at Downside on the way. Two days before, I telephoned the monastery and was told that, although Father Peter had been poorly and was confined to a wheelchair, he would be delighted to see me.

It was the day before the start of the summer term at Downside School and the grounds of the school and the abbey were fresh and trim. A motor mower was putting the finishing touches to the lawns and the air was sweet with the scent of newly mown grass and blossom. A groundsman directed me to walk round the side of the school buildings and then to the west end of the great abbey church where I would see in front of me the door of the monastery.

The bell was answered by a young monk much the same age, I thought, as Father Peter had been when he decided to become an army chaplain. I told him that Father Peter Quinn was expecting me.

'Are you a relative?' he asked.

'No, I'm a friend.'

'I'm very sorry,' he said. 'Father Peter died last night.'

Although I had only been in Father Peter's company on a few occasions, my immediate sense of loss was acute. I had anticipated finding him weak and had already abandoned hope of ever again spending a long evening in conversation with him but I had been too preoccupied with my own affairs to consider the possibility that he might be close to death.

About a month later, I received a letter from Dom Patrick Bolton, the Abbot of Downside, telling me that Father Peter had planned to ask me to read a manuscript he had placed in the archives. Unfortunately, the manuscript could not leave the monastery but arrangements could be made for me to read it at Downside and to stay in one of the monastery guest rooms if I wished to do so.

I would happily have gone straight away to read what I assumed was an account of his experience as an army chaplain. Since the 50th anniversary of 1914, many books on the Great War had been published but none, as far as I could recall, written from the point of view of a Roman Catholic chaplain at the front. Yet it was a busy time of year for me. I was teaching an undergraduate course and my lectures continued for another three weeks. I knew from previous years that this was the time when my PhD students would be more demanding as they worried about finishing their research before the money ran out.

So it was not until early July that I drove to Downside again and, carrying an overnight bag, stood at the monastery door and rang the bell. This time the door was opened by the Abbot himself. There was no mistaking his authority though he wore no badge of office unless it was the small wooden cross that hung on his chest. His pale, ascetic features and severe expression were in marked contrast to the popular image of a jovial monk and I recalled that Father Peter had said of him that he was 'a good man and a fine scholar but shy and rather austere'.

He led the way along a Victorian cloister to his office, a large high-ceilinged room whose windows looked out on the green banks of the monastery garden on which stood a life-size wooden sculpture of Christ on the Cross. He sat behind his desk, inviting me with a wave of his hand to sit opposite him. Dispensing with polite enquiries about my journey, he came straight to the point. The manuscript was in the box on the desk in front of him, my guest room was ready, I would be welcome at any of the daily offices in the Abbey church and meals in the refectory, there was a list of times in my room. He leaned forward to place his fingers lightly on the box and said, 'When Father Peter knew he was dying, he wrote you a letter. You will find it at the top of the box.'

'I was very sorry to hear of his death,' I said. The Abbot's expression softened. 'He was my Novice Master when I entered the monastery nearly thirty years ago,' he said. 'He warned us of the hardships and difficulties of the life we were seeking but in such a way as to inspire our deep affection.'

My guest room was on the first floor of the east wing of the monastery above the refectory. I drew the unlined curtains against the evening sunlight, sat down at the table and opened the box I had brought with me from the Abbot's office. Father Peter's letter dated 15 April 1972 was in his own handwriting. It opened with his expression of sadness that he might not have the chance to say goodbye in person and apologised for not asking me sooner whether I would be willing to read the manuscript.

The letter continued: 'The manuscript is an account of the events leading up to the death of Private Tom Kennedy during the Battle of Passchendaele in September 1917 and of his widow's determination to discover the truth about the circumstances in which her husband died. It was Tom Kennedy's grave I was visiting when you and I met at Tyne Cot Cemetery.

'Katherine Kennedy wrote the manuscript for her son, Brodie, who was born after his father's death. She wanted Brodie to know his father, what sort of man he was, what hopes and ideals he had and why he met such a tragic end. So the manuscript is both a memoir of a young man who lost his life in the war and a mother's appeal to her son to understand his father.

'I met Tom Kennedy during the war and I met Katherine soon after the war. Katherine and I have been good friends ever since, so I know a great deal about their story and the way in which the manuscript was written. Katherine wrote the first part of the manuscript, which covers the period from her first meeting with Tom in July 1914 until the end of the war, soon after the events she is describing. She kept a diary throughout the war years and she also had many letters to draw on, some of which she has woven into her narrative. I am sure she must have used her imagination as well as her diary and her memory but I have no reason to think that the details of her story are not true.

'The second part of the narrative, which describes her attempts to discover the truth about Tom's death, she wrote as she went along, completing her task in 1935 when she was satisfied she knew all there was to know. It was then that she asked me whether her manuscript could be kept in the archives at Downside Abbey until the time came when it would have to be shown to Brodie.

'I was the parish priest at Beccles in Suffolk at the time but I arranged for the manuscript to be put with the confidential papers in the archives at Downside and there it has remained ever since. Three years ago, in 1969, Katherine sent me what she called 'The Last Chapter', which brings the story up to date. This is now part of the manuscript.

'For reasons that will become clear to you, Katherine does not want Brodie to read her manuscript, or indeed to know of its existence, in her own lifetime or for some years after her death. She has asked me to help her find someone who can be trusted to hand over the manuscript to Brodie on her behalf. I would have offered myself but I am the same age as Katherine and I am unlikely to outlive her. The present Abbot, Dom Patrick Bolton, has read the manuscript and understands the problem but says the monastery cannot take on this responsibility, so it has been left to me to identify a person who would be willing to give the manuscript to Brodie Kennedy when the time comes to do so.

'I believe my meeting with you at Tyne Cot that summer afternoon was providential. I can imagine your scepticism, my friend, as you do not believe in a God who intervenes in human affairs but you must admit that meeting a young man I knew instinctively I could trust and who had a professional interest in the First World

War was, from my point of view, a godsend. Do you remember how we drank a toast to 'chance meetings'? I should have told you then that, for a Benedictine monk, what appears to be chance may be part of God's design.

'I have spoken to Katherine about you and she has agreed that I should ask you to read her manuscript. I wish I could have asked you in person but my strength had ebbed faster than I anticipated. When you have read the story of Tom and Katherine, would you please consider whether you are willing to take on the responsibility of giving the manuscript to Brodie? If you decide not to do so, you must not think that in any way you have let me down but I must ask you to regard the contents of the manuscript as confidential to yourself alone.

'If on the other hand you are willing to do this, please tell Father Patrick. He will be able to put you in touch with Katherine. I am sure you will want to meet her and I know she is looking forward to meeting you. If only you and I could have sat late into the night with our carafe of wine as I would have loved to know what you, who have grown up in such a different world yet have a deep understanding of our war, think of Tom and Katherine's story.

'I send my love to you and to Mary and the children and my gratitude to you all for your friendship and kindness. I face the end of this life with a quiet mind, never losing hope in the mercy of God.

Yours very sincerely in Christ,
Peter'

I put aside his letter that was so different from what I had expected and turned to the manuscript, keeping an open mind on whether I would be willing to do what Father Peter asked. As I started to read, the bell was calling the monks to Vespers and I noted the time as 5.40pm.

CHAPTER ONE

When I came off night duty that morning, I decided on the spur of the moment to enter the café on King's Parade instead of going straight back to my digs in Jesus Lane. I was unusually wide awake after an awkward encounter with matron when, as I was leaving the ward, she had asked whether I would be attending the meeting later that day which was to be addressed by the Commandant of Queen Alexandra's Imperial Military Nursing Service and I had replied in a rather offhand way that I was not interested in being an army nurse. I was 23 and had trained at the London Hospital in Whitechapel under Eva Luckes, the most famous and formidable matron of the time, so I was not afraid of displeasing the matron of Addenbroke's. Yet the encounter left me unsettled; one bad reference could blight a career.

There were no free tables. A young man, with his dark, untidy head bent over a book, was sitting alone at a table that could easily accommodate two but I was not inclined to join him. He looked rough and out of place among the middle-aged clientele who were occupying the café in the university vacation and the last thing I needed just then was to have to make conversation with an uncouth stranger. Better to walk down to the river and enjoy the freshness of the summer morning.

At that moment, the young man raised his head and, seeing me looking at him, frowned with such undisguised hostility he could not have made his reluctance to share his table more clear if he had put up a sign. Provoked by his rudeness, I squeezed between the backs of the chairs and, arriving at his table, sat down before he had a chance to object. Without saying a word, he returned to his book.

Closer inspection confirmed my unfavourable impression of him. He had not shaved that morning or put a brush to his black hair. He was wearing a jacket and waistcoat but a shirt with no collar. Under the table, I glimpsed his navvy's boots. It was obvious that he was that not unfamiliar figure in Cambridge: a well-educated young man who wished it to be known by his appearance that his sympathies were with the working class. He was not only ill mannered, he was acting a part.

To anyone who observed us closely that morning, we would have appeared less like strangers than lovers who had quarrelled, our pretence of being unaware of each other's existence was too transparent. Only when I ordered a pot of tea and the waitress brought my order on a round tin tray, placing each item on the table with elaborate slowness, did he acknowledge my presence. With the resigned air of a parent humouring a child, he asked me, 'And do you think there is going to be a war?'

His eyes were dark and his voice had a deep, caressing quality but his patronising manner was infuriating. Without giving me a chance to answer his question – for how could a mere nurse have an opinion that was worth hearing – he said, 'England will never go to war with Germany; war between civilised countries is unthinkable.'

He went on to give me his views on the international crisis but if he thought I was impressed he was mistaken. I was waiting for an opening to bring him down a peg or two. When he mentioned the name of the newspaper for which he worked in London, I was glad to be able to say I had never heard of it.

'It's one of the few papers you can trust,' he assured me and launched into an attack on those newspaper proprietors, especially Lord Northcliffe, who were determined to push the Liberal government into war. He was trying to dazzle me with his talk of politics and press barons and I was intrigued but only as a gambler might be when he sees his opponent overplaying his hand. How seriously he took himself. How blind he seemed to be to the bad impression he was making.

When he announced too loudly that Germany was 'the engine of European civilisation', causing some heads to turn, I thought it was time for me to escape. To interrupt his monologue I picked up his open book and saw on the cover 'The Green Helmet and other Poems, W.B. Yeats.'

'It's the latest volume of his poetry', he said.

He had been reading a short poem which began:
I had this thought a while ago,
My darling cannot understand
What I have done, or what would do
In this blind bitter land.

I liked Yeats' poetry but chose not to say so. Instead, I finished my tea and pushed the cup and saucer away.

'Perhaps, we could meet here next week at the same time,' he said. He worked in London during the week but came down on Friday evening to spend the weekend with his father in Grange Road. He was so swarthy he could have had gypsy blood and he was so obsessed with his own opinions he had not bothered to ask my name. Why should I waste time on him?

'If you like,' I replied but with less indifference than I had intended. I told myself that I found him more amusing than annoying. I could tell he was interested and I thought that I was not, or at least that I was still free to choose, but when I had returned to my digs, in the brief twilight before I fell asleep, I was wondering what my family would make of him.

The Reverend Canon Andrew Lovegrove, my father, was Rector of Kirkby Lonsdale, a market town in the beautiful valley of the River Lune in what was then the West Riding of Yorkshire. His Rectory at the church of St. Mary the Virgin had been our family home for the last eleven years. Although he voted Liberal and supported Mr Asquith, the Prime Minister, he was a model of male conservatism, suspicious of change and stubborn in defence of his daily routine. As a parish priest, he was thought to be rather aloof, his sermons lacking the common touch, but he was a kind and loving father who never gave a hint that he was disappointed to have no son unless it was in the occasional reference to his grandfather who, at the age of 14, had fought at the battle of Waterloo.

My mother, Elizabeth Lovegrove, was tall and fair and claimed Viking descent. She was such an independent minded woman with advanced views on many subjects that I sometimes wondered how she and my father had conducted their courtship. On the importance of a good education for girls she was adamant. When we moved to Kirkby Lonsdale, she went at once to see Miss Williams, the headmistress of the Clergy Daughters School in nearby Casterton (the school once attended by Emily and Charlotte Bronte though much changed since their day) to negotiate a reduction in fees for my younger sister, Amy, and myself. It was our mother who also encouraged us to pursue a qualification and a career when for most mothers the priority would have been to identify a suitable husband.

My mother managed my father with great skill, indulging his idiosyncrasies and making a point of protecting his daily routine. She never openly contradicted his arbitrary decisions, preferring to wait until a moment arrived when she judged he could be persuaded that the course he had rejected out of hand had merit after all. He had at first refused even to discuss my wish to train as a nurse in Whitechapel, where in living memory Jack the Ripper had terrorised the female population, but my mother had returned to the subject a few weeks later when he was basking in the unusual compliments with which his sermon at Matins had been received. Mother took the opportunity then to remind him that I would be living in a nurses' hostel and that the matron of the London Hospital was so well respected as an authority on nurses' training that she was consulted by Mr Asquith's government.

When my father gave way, he did so with good grace which enabled him to claim some of the credit if things turned out well. He attended the ceremony when I qualified and introduced himself to Matron Eva as a father whose cherished ambition for his daughter was that day being fulfilled. On the day I left home, it was he who accompanied me to Carnforth to catch the London train and made me promise to write to my mother every week.

I liked to share with my mother my opinion of the people I met but as I did not know the gypsy's name or he mine and did not wish to imply even to myself that our meeting had been of any consequence, I made no mention that week of the young man who wore navvy's boots and read Yeats.

The following Saturday morning it was raining. As nurses, we were not allowed to carry umbrellas so I pulled my cape tightly round my shoulders and hurried along Trumpington Street towards King's Parade. I thought I could just as easily walk passed the café as go in but it would provide shelter and if he happened to be there I would join him. This time, though, I would not let him do all the talking or take himself so seriously.

He was sitting at the same table. 'I thought you wouldn't come,' he said, getting to his feet. 'I thought I must have put you off.'

He had shaved and brushed his hair but still wore no collar and tie. He offered to take my cape and, when I had unbuttoned it, lifted it off my shoulders and carried it to the coat stand by the door. When he returned and sat down opposite me, he asked my name. We looked at one another, more directly this time, and I knew then there was a chance, I refused to put it any higher, that one phase of my life was ending and another beginning.

His name was Tom Kennedy. He tried to come to Cambridge most weekends, he said, because his father was a widower, though recently the pressure of events had made that difficult.

'The pressure of events,' I echoed solemnly.

He smiled but continued in the same serious vein. 'We are determined to stop England being drawn into a war that would be none of our business.'

'We?'

'The Independent Labour Party, the Trade Unions, most of the Liberals, all men of goodwill.'

'And women?'

'Yes, of course.'

'But there isn't going to be a war,' I said.

'What makes you so sure?'

'Because the Kaiser is on a Scandinavian cruise,' I replied.

He was not, I wanted him to know, the only person who read the newspapers. Nor was he the only person who was trying to make sense of the crisis that seemed to be sweeping the continent in the wake of the assassination of the Archduke in Sarajevo. At the Clergy Daughters School, Miss Williams had not allowed newspapers in the building but from our late childhood, our mother had encouraged us to take an interest in what was going on in the world. Though it might have come as a surprise to Mr Tom Kennedy, I knew exactly where Sarajevo was on the map.

'He is rather handsome,' I finally wrote to my mother. 'And not as ill-mannered as my first impression of him but he assumes that because I am a woman I must be educated by him in politics and diplomacy. We shall walk to Grantchester next Saturday if the weather is fine and then to Grange Road to meet his father who is a professor at the university but of what I have yet to discover.'

For the next two weekends, we spent as much time together as my duties at Addenbrokes would allow. Tom was in love and made no attempt to hide it. I was falling in love but used various pretences to keep him guessing. Then on the first weekend in August, Tom stayed in London to take part in a rally in Trafalgar Square addressed by the Labour leader, Keir Hardie, calling on England not to become involved in the war that was breaking out on the continent. I still have one of the handbills that Tom distributed with its bold heading, "Stand Clear England". Two days later, when the German army marched into Belgium, most English people, including my father, thought we were honour bound to go to Belgium's aid. The war between civilised countries that Tom had been so sure was unthinkable had come to pass.

I was not unduly worried at first by Tom's opposition to the war because none of us had the slightest idea what going to Belgium's aid would mean but when the first British casualties were reported, I, like many other people, decided that 'being in, we have to win'. I hoped Tom would come round to this point of view but he argued more passionately than ever that the people of England

and Germany had no quarrel with one another and he quoted with approval George Bernard Shaw's advice to the soldiers of both countries that they should shoot their officers and go home.

It was Tom's opposition to the war that made me admit to myself that I was in love with him. If there had been no war, I would probably have gone on playing a game for some weeks, sure of his love for me and pretending that I was still making up my mind but the increasing public hostility towards anyone who did not support the war forced me to recognise that the time for games was over. I loved Tom just as he was and I knew that if he asked me to marry him I would say 'Yes' but I saw much more clearly than he did that his attitude to the war could become a threat to our future happiness.

We continued to meet in Cambridge every weekend, walking arm in arm to Grantchester, sometimes in silence, sometimes talking of poetry, too much in love to let the war intrude but there were occasions when Tom could not contain his frustration with the way history had taken a wrong turn.

'It's the wrong war against the wrong enemy,' he suddenly burst out as we were walking along the Backs one Sunday morning in early September. When I raised my eyes to heaven, he seized both my arms so I could not resist and kissed me on the mouth in front of the passers-by. 'We have so much to learn from one another,' he said as he released me. 'Germany can teach us efficiency and we can teach them tolerance.'

I could not help laughing. His passions tumbled over one another and for a man who believed that reason could solve all problems he could be very impetuous.

It did not take me long to work out where his admiration for Germany came from. Tom had never been to Germany but his father had. Grant Kennedy was professor of Greek Literature at Cambridge and, so I was told, the most brilliant classicist of his generation with the possible exception of Gilbert Murray at Oxford. The Kennedy Library in the university's classics department is named after him. As a young man he studied at Gottingen and this gave him a lifelong admiration for German scholarship. When war threatened in 1914,

he signed with others a letter to The Times arguing that Germany
was the leading nation in the Arts and Sciences and that war with
Germany in the interests of Tsarist Russia and Serbia would be 'a
sin against civilisation'.

I got on well with Tom's father from the start. Although Tom
had warned me that his father was an unemotional academic who
was happiest alone in his study with his classical texts, the professor,
a tall distinguished man with a fine head of white hair, greeted me
warmly and we quickly established an easy friendship, partly playful,
partly conspiratorial, in which we recognised one another as poten-
tial allies. And as I watched father and son together on our visits to
Grange Road, I thought it was Tom who was holding his emotions
in check and his father who longed for a closer relationship.

It took me some weeks to discover that Tom's ambivalence
towards his father had its origins in his mother's death. Tom was
just thirteen when his mother died. This cruel loss at a critical point
in his young life, a tragedy for which he had not been prepared
and which his father's stoicism did not help him to understand,
plunged Tom into a premature adolescence so that he became truc-
ulent and rebellious before his time. The precocious child who had
read all the volumes of Macaulay's History of England at the age of
12 and who was expected to take the top scholarship at Winchester
College in a month's time, locked himself in his room and refused
to come out until his father had promised he would not have to go
to a boarding school.

Tom was sent to a private day school in Cambridge but at the
end of his first term the headmaster wrote to Professor Kennedy
to say there was little point in his son continuing at the school
'as he seems to regard formal education as a waste of time'. For
three years until Tom was sixteen, his father engaged a succession
of young graduates who needed an income to educate his son at
home but Tom worked only at those things that interested him. He
read widely in history, biography and poetry and ignored the rest.
When he told his father he wanted to live in London and become a
journalist, his father was relieved and arranged for Tom to stay with

his wife's younger brother, who had a small house in Finsbury and worked for a publisher in Soho Square.

Living apart, father and son were on better terms. The professor gave his son a small allowance and Tom came home at the weekends to keep the relationship in reasonable repair. From time to time, Tom's father suggested that Tom might consider obtaining a university degree, journalism not being in his opinion an occupation for a first class mind. Yet Tom's dislike of formal education was as strong as ever and he told his father he preferred to make his own way.

By 1914, he had made only modest progress. When Tom and I met he was 23, the same age as myself, and a junior in the London office of The Daily Citizen, a short-lived left wing newspaper whose secretary and business manager was Clifford Allen, the Cambridge-educated socialist and pacifist.

When I had discovered this much about Tom's life, partly from Tom's father and partly from Tom himself, I could not understand why someone of his ability was satisfied with a junior position on an obscure paper. His answer was that he shared the paper's socialist ideals.

'You don't approve?' he asked sharply. He was angry that the war was making a mockery of the brotherhood of man.

'I'm in love with you, not with your politics,' I replied.

'But you would rather I supported the war.'

I thought he might be looking for an argument to vent his frustration. We were standing on Clare Bridge in the fading light of one of those autumn afternoons when, after a fine clear day, the sky would remain a distant blue long after the lamps had been lit.

I said quietly, 'I wouldn't love you any more, Tom, if you enlisted tomorrow.'

We had known each other for three months and we both realised that our love had reached a point where it could no longer make light of the fact that we held very different views about the war. I despised the jingoes in the popular press and was ashamed of the women who handed out white feathers to young men who had not volunteered. Yet, like my father, I believed England had been right to go to Belgium's aid and I could not share Tom's admiration for Germany, especially after I read the first reports of German atrocities.

Tom seemed to enjoy defying the patriotic mood. He had just written a piece for The Daily Citizen condemning the anti-German riots in the East End and saying he would rather be at the mercy of the German army than a drunken London mob. My father did not read The Daily Citizen but sooner or later someone would tell him that the young man who was walking out with his daughter was the same Tom Kennedy who was in the pay of the Kaiser.

In my letters home I had been circumspect about Tom's attitude to the war. When Tom had said he wanted to meet my father and mother, I had pleaded the impossibility of being given leave by matron but now I decided that such a meeting might convince Tom that if he wanted to propose marriage, he would have to compromise his opposition to the war.

Matron at Addenbroke's was suspicious when I told her I had changed my mind but she gave me permission to go home for the weekend to talk to my parents about volunteering as an army nurse. I left a note for Tom at his father's house and made the long journey north, arriving at the Rectory late on Friday night. On the Saturday morning, before I had had a chance to talk to my father about Tom, there was a knock on my bedroom door and my sister, Amy's, called saying, 'Wake up, Katherine, your Heathcliff is here.'

He must have caught the mail train from Euston to Carlisle that stopped at Carnforth and then hired a fly to bring him to Kirkby Lonsdale as there were no early trains on our branch line. When I dressed and came downstairs, he was standing in the hall with my mother and father and all three of them looked up expectantly as though they had been waiting all this time for me to make the introductions.

My mother said, 'Katherine, Tom is here to ask your father if he may propose to you.'

I could tell from his look of triumph that Tom thought his mad dash to claim my hand very romantic. He was smiling at me like a naughty boy eagerly seeking approval because he had brought off a brilliant coup and I could not help responding. I loved him but after a night in the guards van he looked more than ever like a gypsy vagabond and his timing was bad because his arrival had interrupted my father's sacred routine of a leisurely breakfast with The Times after early communion.

I never knew for certain what Tom and my father said to one another when the door of the breakfast room closed. According to Tom, they discussed his reasons for opposing the war calmly and agreed to differ. According to my father, Tom gave the impression that, although he had at first strongly opposed England's involvement, he now had doubts because he realised that England's enemy was not German scholarship but German militarism. When my father pressed him to do something for his country at this time of crisis, Tom agreed to consider driving an ambulance in France as some young men who had initially shared his opposition to the war were doing.

It may have been a misunderstanding or Tom may have deliberately conceded too much to obtain my father's blessing. When a few weeks after our engagement was announced, Tom and his friends in the Independent Labour Party launched a campaign against compulsory military service, my father was sure that Tom had deceived him. Yet Tom argued that the threat of conscription changed everything; whether or not the government had been right to go to Belgium's aid, compelling men to fight and kill was always wrong and had to be opposed on principle.

Whatever interpretation was put on their discussion later, on the day they emerged as good friends and I believed Tom had indeed agreed to modify his views sufficiently for us to be married. Wanting to be alone with him and to give him the opportunity to propose, I suggested a walk along the riverbank to the Devil's Bridge but we got no further than the top of the Radical Steps before it started to rain and we were forced to take shelter in the church. I had anticipated that, after his dramatic appearance that morning, he would propose in a suitably romantic setting – on the Devil's Bridge perhaps, which Bonnie Prince Charlie crossed with his Highland army or on the slopes of Barbon Fell where my hair would fly in the wind but not here in the old familiar surrounding of my father's church.

To distract him, I showed him the stained glass windows for which the church was famous. We were standing in front of the altar looking up at the East window and I was explaining that the lily in the pot was a symbol of the annunciation and wondering whether he knew what the annunciation was, when Tom turned to look at me and asked, 'Will you marry me, Katherine?'

'Even the Angel Gabriel is on one knee,' I said.

Tom knelt on one knee on the altar step and asked a second time, 'Will you marry me, Katherine?'

I replied, 'Yes, Tom, yes I will.' Placing my hands on either wide of his head, I drew him towards me so that his face pressed against my body.

I might have married a quite different person and had a quite different life but that is true of all married couples and no one can say with certainty that they made the right or the best choice. All I know is that I was in love with Tom and Tom was in love with me and we desperately wanted to be together. Like many young couples at the time, whether or not they were likely to be separated by the war, we wanted to be married as soon as possible and we had our eye on the last week in January.

However, in November, Tom joined two other young members of the Independent Labour Party, Clifford Allen and Fenner Brockway, in calling on all young men of military age to resist any attempt to compel them to fight. The organisation they set up was called the No Conscription Fellowship. Although Tom and his friends were doing nothing illegal, the popular press denounced them as 'unpatriotic' and 'wont-fight-funks' whose real aim was to bring about England's defeat that would pave the way for a Marxist revolution.

Tom had never been a Marxist but the slur stuck and was repeated in the local newspaper. That was too much for my father. In a small town like Kirkby Lonsdale the Rector's family was under constant scrutiny and the news that the Rector's daughter was engaged to be married to a man who was shirking his duty and plotting revolution caused even loyal parishioners to express their disapproval. They crossed the road when they saw my mother coming and they placed white feathers instead of coins in the collection bag.

It was easy for Tom to laugh at such provincial pettiness – he told me that Fenner Brockway had been given so many white feathers he was making them into a fan – but my father could not ignore local hostility. He had never been a popular Rector, people still compared him unfavourably with his charming, outgoing predecessor, but he had gradually won the respect of the town and he feared that, at a stroke, the respect would be lost if he was not seen to disapprove of my marriage to Tom.

My mother was splendid. She refused to be ashamed of Tom or cowed by the spiteful patriotism of some of the parishioners. She liked Tom's independent spirit and she realised before I did that his opposition to the war was inspired not by his admiration for Germany but by his love of all that was best in England. She was my ally and understood better than anyone why I was impatient to be married – she had married my father when she was eighteen and by the time she was my age already had two children – but in a letter to me in early December she begged me not to defy my father and marry Tom without his blessing.

Tom and I needed no one's consent to marry but I told him I could not ignore my mother's plea. Confident of his powers of persuasion and, I think, genuinely surprised that his role in organising the No Conscription Fellowship had alienated my father, he suggested we should go to Kirkby Lonsdale together to remove any misunderstanding once and for all.

Tom's second visit to the Rectory started well. My mother had insisted it should be over Christmas as she was sure the two men would observe a Christmas truce which would enable them to restore a level of trust and respect before there was any argument about the war. For forty-eight hours her plan appeared to be working. Tom and my father shook hands without hesitation and any awkwardness they may have felt was dispelled by Mrs Bickersteth, the cook my mother had inherited from the previous Rector.

There had never been any discussion about whether Mrs Bickersteth should stay on; she came with the house like a ghost but there was nothing ghostly about her physical presence. She was a large, ruddy-faced woman in her fifties whose long association with the Rectory encouraged her to be free with her comments. 'I know what they're saying about you in the town, Mr Kennedy,' she said as we sat down to supper and she moved round the table with a tureen of home-made vegetable soup. 'But I don't care if you're the Kaiser's cousin as long as you're not a Smart Alick who will let Miss Katherine down as soon as you've had what you wanted.'

It could have been more delicately put but it expressed my feelings exactly. My father saw the funny side; he was used to Mrs Bickersteth's interventions. 'Mr Kennedy is not the Kaiser's cousin, I can assure you,' he told her. 'So don't go spreading that rumour because there are people in this town who will believe it.' So the tension eased and Mrs Bickersteth departed for the kitchen with the air of a woman who had done what she had set out to do.

I could not recall a Christmas in Kirkby Lonsdale without snow but Christmas Eve was a clear, cold day with bright sunshine. Tom and I abandoned lunch and walked for four hours along the banks of the River Lune, across the fields and up onto the fells. It was a long climb to Fox's Pulpit but I wanted to show Tom the place where the founder of the Quakers had preached to a thousand people on the barren hillside.

As we climbed, we talked about our lives after the war. We were full of optimism, I remember, sure that we would soon be married and hopeful that the mounting expense of the war would force the nations to make peace in 1915. Over a million men had volunteered in response to Kitchener's call. Most were single men as it was generally accepted that a married man was not under the same obligation to enlist, a distinction that was not lost on my father, but these men were still in training and with any luck would not be needed.

When we reached the rocky outcrop on which George Fox was said to have stood, I told Tom this was where he should have proposed knowing full well what his response would be. He kissed me for a long time and then we clung to one another, our eyes streaming in the wind. Far below, on the Upper Valley, a few isolated homesteads were the only sign that we were not entirely alone in the world.

'Why do you want to marry me, Tom?' I asked.

'Because I want you all to myself,' he replied.

Laughing, I told him that was not the right answer but he just kissed me again and this time so hungrily I knew it was time to go. On the way down, Tom reminded me that he was the only child of an only child of an only child. I asked him how many children we should have.

'Five or six,' he said merrily.

We returned to Kirkby Lonsdale in the late afternoon dusk. As was customary on Christmas Eve, a brass band was playing carols outside the Fountain House and a large crowd, many of whom knew me by sight, was blocking the entrance to the churchyard. Fearing a demonstration against Tom, I wanted to turn back but he took my hand and drew me after him through the narrow channel the crowd made for us. Whether it was the festive spirit or the fast fading daylight that protected us from abuse I did not know but I was relieved when we arrived safely at the front door of the Rectory.

For Christmas Day, Mrs Bickersteth cooked roast goose, black pudding and gimlet pie to be washed down with rum punch and ginger wine. Every year my father and mother invited two elderly couples who would otherwise have been on their own to share the family's Christmas lunch. As it happened, both the couples invited this year were due to be taken to the workhouse in Kendal on Boxing Day where the husbands would be separated from the wives even though both couples had been married for over forty years. They came dressed in their Sunday best. Although they joined in the singing at tea-time and laughed a little at Mrs Bickersteth's ghost stories that were the same every year, the shadow of the approaching separation hung over them. When it was time for them to go, they stood with heads bowed and holding hands to receive my father's blessing. I glanced at Tom. His eyes were blazing not with pity but with anger and I could guess what he was thinking.

The Christmas truce broke down on Boxing Day. Over breakfast, Tom could not refrain from telling my father that Christian charity, however well intended, was no substitute for social reform. I should have recognised that this was only a stalking house for the real disagreement between them. From the church's failure to demand a change in the workhouse rules that treated the poor in a way the better-off would never tolerate, the discussion, still calm and reasonable in tone, moved on to the church's response to the war.

Tom asked whether my father had read the Bishop of London's sermon printed in The Times comparing Germany's invasion of Belgium to Ahab's seizure of Nathan's vineyard. My father, speaking slowly, replied that he had and that, although he found the imagery rather colourful, he agreed with the Bishop that at this time of national crisis 'volunteering is a Christian duty'.

I looked across the table at my mother. We were both trying to think of a way of diverting this conversation but Tom's riposte was too quick.

'No one takes the Bishop of London seriously,' he said. He dresses up in his Territorial Army uniform and preaches like a recruiting sergeant.'

'At least we know whose side he is on.'

My father's remark ripped away the mask of polite disagreement but I blamed Tom just as much. He knew what he was doing. Afterwards he admitted that he had deliberately led my father on because that was the only way to force his true feelings about our marriage into the open but he had not foreseen the bitterness of the exchanges that followed.

My father accused Tom's No Conscription Fellowship of betraying the men at the front and Tom himself of using marriage as a way to avoid doing his patriotic duty. Tom accused my father of thinking like the Jingoes in the gutter press and of having doubts about our marriage only because he was afraid of local opinion.

At last the momentum of their quarrel appeared to be slackening but when it flared up again I lost patience with them both. 'For God's sake stop arguing,' I said, so forcefully that they both looked at me in surprise as though they had forgotten I was still at the table. I had never raised my voice with either of them before but, after a brief anxiety about how they would react, I was glad I had done so. I loved my father and I was in love with Tom but I was a person in my own right, not just one man's daughter and another man's fiancée, and at that moment I wanted nothing more than to be independent of both of them.

Tom was the first to recover. He said, 'I'm sorry, darling, but your father and I are not going to agree about the war.' I looked at my father and could see in his eyes the sadness of the conclusion he had come to. 'I am sorry, too, Katherine,' he said. But I cannot give your marriage to Tom my blessing. I think it would be for the best if you broke off your engagement.'

'I will never do that,' I said and, placing my napkin on the table, stood up and left the room. I was not a child to run upstairs and slam the door of my bedroom so the sound could be heard throughout the house, though I was tempted to do so. I put on an overcoat and went outside. Too late for this Christmas, the sky was heavy with snow.

After a short while, my mother followed and caught up with me as I was standing on Church Brow. We walked a little way in silence and then, 'I have an idea to put to you,' she said.

With characteristic foresight she had planned for just this situation. If I volunteered as an army nurse and went overseas for six months or a year, it would give everyone time to take stock. Separation would be painful at first but it would help me to be sure that Tom really was the man I wanted to marry and it would give Tom time to reflect on whether his opposition to the war was more important than our happiness. If Tom and I agreed to postpone our marriage, my mother was sure that my father would not try to insist the engagement should be broken off.

I did not need persuading. My mother's compromise was the only way of escaping from the dilemma of having to choose between Tom and my father. If I defied my father, our close-knit family ties would be broken, perhaps forever, and my mother would be hurt most of all. Tom might argue for defiance at first, that was his nature, but he would come round when he realised that postponing the wedding was the only way to save our marriage.

There was another factor in my decision, though I cannot be sure that I was conscious of it at the time. I was a patriotic young woman who wanted to see Germany defeated and I was excited at the prospect of playing my part in the war.

Tom was in his room, putting his things into his valise for his departure at midday. 'I have made my peace with your father,' he said and the note of resignation in his voice gave me hope that he had already accepted some sort of compromise was inevitable. When I explained to him why I had to go away, he understood and, however much he hated the idea of not seeing me for six months, he realised that defying my father was not a choice open to him.

'You haven't changed your mind about marrying me?' he asked but as an after-thought and I knew that he did not expect or need an answer. I stood at the window while he finished his packing. If it snowed before noon, the one Boxing Day train to Carnforth might be delayed.

'What are you thinking?' Tom asked. 'That if you hadn't come into the café that morning you could have had your pick of all the dashing young second lieutenants?'

I turned to him and smiled. 'Yes, darling, that is just what I was thinking.'

It would have been easier for us if I had gone overseas straight-away but, despite the well-publicised shortage of qualified nurses in France, Queen Alexandra's Imperial Military Nursing Service insisted on sending me on various courses, including one month in the Military Hospital in Aldershot, so that I would be familiar with the army's way of doing things. When at last I was given an embarkation date, it was not until 13 April 1915, three months after

I had sent in my application to the Secretary of State for War. Tom and I met in Cambridge at the weekends whenever possible but it was a difficult time in our relationship because we both wanted our separation to be over and done with. We were restless when we were together and unhappy when we were apart.

Then at the beginning of March, Tom's paper, The Daily Citizen, ceased publication – its radical views did not appeal to enough readers in the climate of war – and Tom decided to devote himself full-time to the No Conscription Fellowship. He would not be paid but he was living rent-free with his uncle in Finsbury and his father agreed to an increase in his allowance.

I had told Tom I was in love with him not with his politics but in the early months of 1915, as hatred of the enemy pervaded every aspect of our lives and talk of peace was labelled treason, I realised that I was being dishonest with myself if I thought that I could keep separate my feelings for Tom and my support for the war. I did not want him to work full-time for the No Conscription Fellowship because that marked him as an out-and-out opponent of the war, which would further alienate my father and might be held against him when peace came. I was puzzled and sometimes angry that he did not take seriously the consequences of what he was doing.

I never met Clifford Allen, the chairman of the Fellowship, but I understood from Tom that they were not close. They were both determined to prevent conscription but Allen was an uncompromising pacifist, which Tom was not, and had a touch of the fanatic, which Tom disliked. With the Fellowship's secretary, Fenner Brockway, Tom had quickly established a friendship. They were both pragmatists whose sense of humour enabled them to laugh at their critics in the popular press. I met Fenner with Tom on two occasions before I went overseas. They were like schoolboys together, plotting their next move in the cat and mouse game they played with the authorities and flattered that they had come to the notice of Scotland Yard's Special Branch which meant from time to time they were followed by a plain clothes policeman.

Frankly, I was glad to hear them say that, despite the attention of Special Branch, they did not believe their campaign was having an impact at Westminster. Asquith was content to let the recruiting figures dictate policy. If enough men volunteered, conscription would be unnecessary; if they did not, public opinion would accept that the single men who had not volunteered would have to be compelled. The No Conscription Fellowship's campaign appeared to be irrelevant. At the end of March, the Fellowship had only 350 members, not enough, Fenner said, to frighten the mouse under Asquith's chair. I kept the thought to myself but I hoped that while I was away the Fellowship's campaign would fizzle out for lack of support.

On the day of my departure, Tom came to Waterloo to see me off and I think he was as relieved as I was that the day had come at last. As a Queen Alexandra Nursing Sister, I had had to sign on for a year but I assured Tom that my contract would allow me to come home on leave in six months time.

There were twelve of us, including the matron in charge, travelling on the troop train to Southampton, all wearing our distinctive uniform of a long grey dress that almost swept the ground and a scarlet cape. In the army, we were known as 'QAs' or collectively as 'the Grey and Scarlets' and I was proud to be a member of such a famous corps.

The station concourse was packed with soldiers and their loved ones, the officers wearing well-cut tunics and riding britches, the men carrying rifles and so burdened with all their kit they could hardly move in the crush. For all Tom's contempt for convention, he was self conscious to be a man of military age in civilian clothes so I took him by the hand and drew him after me to a space where we could say goodbye.

Tom kissed me and held me tightly in his arms. 'Write as soon as you can, darling,' he said. All around us, goodbyes were being said, bravely, tearfully, cheerily, until mercifully the train left on time. From the platform, where some people were already walking away, Tom waved and I waved back until the train gathered speed and I lost sight of him.

As QAs, we travelled in the officers carriages but there were no reserved seats so in our compartment there was a mixture of nursing sisters and young subalterns. The second lieutenant sitting opposite me had watched me waving goodbye to Tom and was still looking at me with a slightly puzzled expression. I thought he was probably wondering at the reversal of roles, the man staying at home in England and the woman going to war.

CHAPTER TWO

5 Myddleton Square
Finsbury
London

20 April 1915

Darling Katherine,

You have only been gone one week and, like a man at the start of a long prison sentence, I count the hours but dare not think about the days and weeks and months till you return. The fact that France is closer than Kirkby Lonsdale only makes it worse because now when I am desperate to see you, I can't jump on a train. My consolation is that missing you has made me realise how dishonest poets are; it is not the heart that feels the pangs of love but the stomach. When I long for you, that is where the ache is, so unless I am an emotional and anatomical oddity or Cupid aiming at the heart fell short, the poets are wrong. You can see why. Stomach is an unattractive word and difficult to rhyme.

Write soon darling to tell me everything you are doing and what the hospital is like so I can follow you round the wards to make sure the soldiers are not taking liberties. A beautiful nurse in a base hospital is bound to have admirers and in the dark early morning hours when jealousy is endlessly inventive, I imagine that I have joined the army and been wounded just seriously enough to be sent to your base hospital and when you see me you cannot believe your eyes and we fall in love all over again. If only it could be like that but this sticking to one's principles is wretchedly unromantic business.

The weekend after you left I spent with my father in Cambridge and a curiously unsettling weekend it was. On Friday evening my father proposed that we should dine in college. I have dined with him in Trinity before though not since the war started because, I assume, he was embarrassed by the fact that I had not volunteered. It is common knowledge that the fellows of Trinity are bitterly divided over the war, which makes it all the more surprising that my father should risk having me as his guest at high table.

I sat next to a young don who has decided to abandon his medical research and join the Army Medical Corps. I could not have had a more agreeable companion. His name is Edgar Adrian and he has the humane, enquiring mind of the true scientist, a contrast to the narrow pedantry of some of the classical dons. He spoke openly about the divisions in the college, adding that, unknown to the Master, a Trinity undergraduate is the secretary of the Cambridge branch of the No Conscription Fellowship. This is a piece of information I should keep to myself because even in Cambridge there are 'pacifist hunters' who, like the witch hunters of old, make it their business to identify shirkers. When I explained to him why any form of service would compromise my opposition to the war and why, if conscription comes, I shall have to resist, he said, 'That will be a hard road to follow' but I could not tell what he thought of my arguments. We were separated after dinner and when I left with my father he had already gone. He is a man I have never met before and may never meet again but it matters to me that I may have failed to convince him of my sincerity or my logic or both.

Have I convinced you? I mean, of my sincerity? We have always known that we held different views about the war but what chance did war have? We were in a world of our own, our 'land of heart's desire'. Yet if the war goes on and conscription comes, our private world will not protect us. How the government will react to men who refuse to be compelled is uncertain but there must be a good chance that we shall be sent to prison. I love you for saying you will always stand by me as long as I am convinced that what I am doing is right but it would be against human nature if you did not have some doubts about whether our love could withstand that sort of separation as well as the public hostility towards anyone who defies the patriotic mood. So you can see why convincing you that I am sincere and not just a wont-fight-funk, especially now that you are tending the wounded, matters more to me than anything else.

I spent half Friday night wide awake worrying about this and came to the conclusion, which you may regard as wishful thinking, that after the war people will be glad some young men tried to prevent the conscriptionists removing one of our long-established liberties. If we can only defeat German militarism by becoming militarist ourselves, what sort of victory is that?

Thank goodness this recruiting business has its lighter side. There is a report in the paper this morning of a woman trying to give a white feather to the sentry on duty at the entrance to Horse Guards Parade. Presumably she though he should be in Flanders not in Whitehall. When he declined to accept it, she threatened him with her umbrella and had to be restrained by a policeman.

Saturday was a glorious English Spring day with a gentle breeze along the river and a clear blue sky from horizon to horizon. I walked alone to Grantchester and missed you badly because I felt certain that there would only be a few beautiful spring days while the war lasts that we can spend together.

On Sunday, my father persuaded me to go with him to matins where I had a pleasant surprise. You know what I think of those bellicose clergymen your father's church seems to specialise in producing, so you will understand my astonishment when the preacher at Great St. Mary's told the congregation that 'Christ bled and died for the men with whom we are at war'. Those words and the calm way in which they were received (despite what Adrian said about pacifist hunters, no one walked out) gave me hope that we may yet remain a tolerant and civilised nation.

On the way back to Grange Road, I had a less pleasant surprise. My father told me he had been asked to join the government's War

Propaganda Bureau and was thinking of accepting. He prefers, I have noticed, to raise difficult subjects when we are walking side by side not facing one another across the table. Given his views, he cannot possibly write anti-German propaganda but he has been approached by John Bury, one of his few close friends in Cambridge, and Bury has told him that all the country's academic stars, including my father's great rival, Gilbert Murray of Oxford, have agreed to join the Bureau, thus giving the impression that those who refuse are not in the first rank. Very shrewd. Vanity is the academic's Achilles Heal.

We spent the rest of the morning and over lunch trying to persuade one another to think again. He wants me to abandon the No Conscription Fellowship and I want him to reject the War Propaganda Bureau, the difference being that he is asking me to betray my convictions and I am asking him not to betray his. We settled nothing but as I was leaving for the station he tried one last argument. 'Think of Katherine,' he said. If only he knew how much I do.

Please write as soon as you can. I need your letters, which I shall keep in a safe place. Keep mine safe too so that 'when you are old and grey and full of sleep' you can take them down and wonder what it was you once saw in this scribbler.

With all my love,
Tom

No.10 General Hospital
Rouen
B,E,F,

30 April 1915

My darling Mummy,
I am sorry not to have written straightaway but we have been hard at it since the moment we arrived because the hospital is

ridiculously understaffed. There are two Nursing Sisters and two VADs responsible for 90 patients when we are told that in military hospitals in England they have three Sisters and three VADs for 30 patients. Matron says there is a big drive to recruit more VADs for hospitals in France but there is a limit to what these unqualified nurses can do.

We had a bit of trouble with the VADs when we arrived because they had been doing the dressings and giving injections and we had to tell them that was our job. The soldiers call them 'Sister' but we are too busy to fuss about that and even Matron chooses to ignore it. When the Assistant Matron met us at Rouen Station she warned us that Matron was something of a battleship and so she is as she steams full ahead through the wards every morning but she is not the terrifying figure that Eva was at the London and off duty I find her quite affable.

No.10 G.H. is a camp run on army lines and we are frequently reminded that we are on active service. Thank goodness we learnt the bugle calls in Aldershot. The call that really matters is to tell us another convoy of wounded has arrived and we are expected to respond to that wherever we are, even in the Land of Nod. As Nursing Sisters, we sleep two to a room in one of the wooden huts and I have had the good fortune to find someone nice to share with. She is Kitty Westmacott, a staff nurse from Harrogate who qualified the same year as I did but at St.Thomas's. We met on the train here and got on really well so it is ripping to have her as a friend and roommate.

Almost all the men in the wards that Kitty and I are responsible for are from Scottish regiments and they are wonderfully brave and cheery except when it comes to having their dressings changed. I was not prepared to find so many of them so young. In one ward there are five boys aged 17 – Kitty calls it 'the children's ward' – and although we are only a few years older, we find ourselves feeling quite maternal, which makes it difficult when it comes to bad news. The bad news they don't want to hear is that their wound is not 'a Blighty one' and I can see that having to tell them they are not going home will be one of the hardest parts of the job.

I am down to my last franc because we had to spend three days in Boulogne while they decided they didn't want us there after all and payday is not until the middle of next month. Darling Mummy, do you think you could put it to Daddy very tactfully that a few notes in a registered letter would be much appreciated? So would soap if you should be thinking of sending a parcel, as that is a luxury money can't buy.

I have had a long letter from Tom, so full of his love that I think I should have gone away sooner but I cannot help worrying about him because he is as uncompromising as ever in his attitude to conscription. I wish I believed it was a cause worth fighting for but the feeling out here is that the only thing that matters is winning the war as quickly as possible so that we can all go home and if that means conscription, then the sooner it is introduced the better. No one here thinks there is a great principle at stake. Perhaps I shouldn't but I pray every night that Tom will soften his attitude. Sticking to his principles, as he calls it, is a rival I don't know how to deal with.

I had my first compliment today from a sergeant major in the Gordon's who was leaving us to go back to the front. He said, 'Goodbye, I shall always think of you as Sister Sunshine'. Do you think it is conceited of me to tell you such things? I hope not but I think they will please you as they do me.

Do write soon and tell me what is happening at home and how Amy is getting on.

With heaps of love and to Daddy too.

From your loving daughter,
Katherine

We had crossed from Southampton to Le Havre under cover of darkness with a destroyer escort, arriving in the French port at dawn. Le Havre was full of troops: French soldiers wearing baggy scarlet trousers and blue overcoats who saluted us in the street and our own Tommies cheerfully giving away their cap badges to any French girl who asked. From Le Havre we travelled to Rouen third class on a French passenger train that was in no hurry to reach its destination and it was on this dawdling journey that I first made the acquaintance of Kitty Westmacott who was to be my best friend and constant companion in France and Belgium. We were both from the North of England, Kitty's father being the manager of the fashionable teashop in Harrogate.

At Rouen, we were packed into a general service wagon and driven to No 10 General Hospital, a vast military camp of tents and wooden huts spread over the race course outside the town. Kitty and I were based here for fourteen months, though for two of these we were seconded to a Red Cross Rest Station at Gournay-en-Bray.

As Nursing Sisters with civilian hospital experience, we were each put in charge of two twenty-eight bed wards. The VADs, partly trained nurses who had taken the place of male orderlies, were responsible for the non-medical tasks such as washing and feeding the patients and cleaning the wards but we took the blame if the medical officer and the matron on their rounds found anything amiss.

We were professionals and accepted criticism in silence but we both disliked the way the army doctors treated the patients. There was something callous about the haste with which wounded men were sent back to the front. Tom worried, and not always jokingly, that I might find the doctors attractive but at Rouen there was little love lost between the Nursing Sisters and the medical officers. The army rule was that any man who could not be 'rendered fit for duty' in a fortnight had to be sent to England, a sensible rule because beds were needed, but it encouraged some doctors to accuse any man who was not an amputee or at death's door of trying to work his passage home. I had to bite my tongue whenever doctors swore at an ordinary soldier on my wards and called him a 'scrimshanker' or a 'bloody malingerer', language they would never use to a wounded officer. Kitty told me to harden my heart. 'We're not angels of mercy any more,' she said. 'We're in the repair and reconditioning business.'

The wounded came to Rouen by train from the railhead near the Casualty Clearing Station. At the start of a major offensive the trains came several times a day and as we had to supervise the transfer of the wounded to ambulances as well as their reception on the wards. We were dead beat at the end of the shifts but in the quieter months we had an afternoon and an evening free each week and could walk in the countryside or have a lift into town. Rouen, unlike Le Havre, had not been taken over by the military but there was no shortage of convalescent officers on the lookout for female company and no shortage of occasions when they could meet the Nursing Sisters and the VADs.

It was a situation that Kitty was happy to exploit. She was a forward hussy who did not wait to be asked; men were fair game and her opinion of them was unromantic. When I asked her what she looked for in a man, she replied 'clean fingernails'. She told me it was our duty to make ourselves available but for several weeks I turned down invitations because I was engaged to Tom. 'What the eye doesn't see, the heart doesn't grieve over,' Kitty said.

The only photograph I have of Kitty was taken by the visiting chaplain at Gournay-en-Bray on Easter Sunday 1916. Kitty and I are standing outside the chateau in the spring sunshine. She is short and dark and I am tall and fair and, despite the fact that we are about to go on duty distributing chocolate eggs to the men on our wards, Kitty manages to strike an individual note. Instead of the regulation headdress I was wearing, she has on the back of her head one of those plaited straw hats the French peasants wore for working in the fields.

Kitty and I were inseparable. We shared a room at Rouen and Gournay-en-Bray and when in 1916 I transferred to a Casualty Clearing Station on the Somme, Kitty came with me. Some of the other Nursing Sisters were surprised we were such good friends because they thought a clergyman's daughter would be uncomfortable with Kitty's cynical outlook on life but I found Kitty's lack of sentimentality refreshing. I liked her forthrightness, her humour and her resilience and her ability to handle the pressure with a light touch. At the end of one all-night shift in the theatre tent at the Casualty Clearing Station, she was arranging the bare feet sticking up from the bucket as though they were a bunch of flowers and when I approached with the last amputated leg, she whispered, 'It's a great life if you don't weaken'. Even her catch phrases, which in someone else would have become tedious, sounded sharp because she used them sparingly and to the point.

Kitty was the one person I could talk to about Tom and the only person in the hospital who knew that my fiancé had refused to enlist and was campaigning against conscription. She was more sympathetic to Tom's position that I was because she took a cynical view of the motives of the men who had volunteered.

'They're all on the run from something or someone,' she told me as we lay awake in the darkness. 'Just as we are.'

When I said that I would always be in love with Tom, whatever I thought of his politics, she was silent for a while as though being in love was a concept she did not recognise. Then she said, 'Most men are boring after forty minutes; imagine waking up beside the same man for forty years.'

'Tom isn't boring,' I insisted.

'Then you're lucky, darling,' she said and I heard her turn over and punch her pillow.

Though I might have been reluctant to admit it, Kitty's unsentimental view of men helped me to live with the pain of being separated from Tom and eventually undermined my refusal to accept invitations though I always insisted that Kitty should come with me. We would make up a foursome for a fancy dress dance at the YMCA or a champagne dinner at the Hotel de la Poste and, on the way home in an ambulance or a duty truck, discuss the men who had paid the bill, usually in rather unflattering terms.

Sometimes I showed Kitty one of Tom's letters because I wanted to talk about my anxiety that he would push his opposition to conscription too far. Kitty thought a man of principle was bound to be a bad husband because he was only interested in himself and his cause; if Tom refused to compromise, I would know what sort of man I had fallen in love with. Yet from her reading of his letter she was sure Tom would abandon the cause sooner or later.

'It's the later that worries me,' I said.

Over the summer months Tom's letters did nothing to allay my fear. Far from fizzling out, the No Conscription Fellowship was gaining support and, after a long debate in which Tom and Fenner played a prominent part, it published a Statement of Principles that all members could sign up to.

'Who would have thought that men of peace could have such warlike disagreements?' Tom wrote. 'Most of us accepted Clifford Allen's argument that, as human life is sacred, whatever other powers the State may possess, it must not have the power to order men to kill. That accommodates the pacifist who says he will never use violence as well as those who, like Fenner and myself, are opposed to this war but might use violence in a good cause if there was no alternative. The trouble is that it also lets in the militant Marxists, to whom the sacredness of human life means precious little. We can't very well refuse them membership as they are opposed to conscription but you can imagine what the Northcliffe papers will say when they find out that Marxists are using the Fellowship as a flag of convenience.'

I was not really interested in the arguments that so preoccupied Tom and his friends but in the same letter he told me that the Fellowship was following the example of the suffragettes and setting up a shadow organisation, the first clear indication he had given that he was prepared to go to prison for his beliefs. His shadow, who would take over his role if he was arrested, was an elderly Quaker called Theodore Taylor.

'Tell him you don't want to marry a martyr,' Kitty advised but I could not do that. I knew Tom was not ready to compromise yet and I pinned my hope on being able to persuade him when I went home on leave in October.

Then one day in late September there was an article in one of the London papers mentioning Tom and Fenner by name as leaders of 'the stab-my-country-in-the-back campaign'. According to the paper, conscription was now inevitable and this had resulted in a dramatic increase in the membership of the No Conscription Fellowship from five hundred to five thousand.

In the wards of No 10 General Hospital, where the first trainloads of wounded were arriving from the British offensive at Loos, the news of this sudden increase in the number of men who said they would not be compelled to fight was greeted with derision. I wanted to be loyal to Tom but more than ever now I was convinced that he was allying himself with people whose motives were less honourable than his.

No.10 General Hospital
BEF

9 October 1915

My darling Mummy,

It was wonderful to receive your parcel, which cheered us a lot when we were feeling pretty low. Kitty and I and the two other Nursing Sisters in our hut share our parcels and I am glad to say your parcel was voted top hole by everyone. The meat roll and peppermint creams were much appreciated as they are such delicious luxuries here and the soda cake was unanimously pronounced A1.

Yes, we did have a few days warning that a big push was coming because the order went round to 'clear the hospitals' and lots of men who never thought they would be sent back to England were put on a train for Le Havre, singing and cheering like schoolboys given an unexpected holiday.

On the day our men went into action, we could hear the guns distinctly from early morning, then when the first train arrived we knew straight away that the casualties were heavy. Men were arriving with the same field dressings that had been put on when they were hit. The Casualty Clearing Stations couldn't cope with the numbers and sent on to us anyone who didn't need immediate surgery.

Practically all ours were surgicals too and we had to get them from the train to the ambulances without enough stretchers, so they helped one another along and seeing them do that almost brought tears to my eyes despite my training.

When we got them to the hospital, they were undressed by the orderlies and washed by the VADs. Many of the men were covered with lice, not unknown in Whitechapel but a shock to some of the girls. A few hours later, I was in the front of an ambulance on my way back to the station to meet the next train and so it has gone on day after day with no off duty time because even when you collapse onto your bed, you have to listen in your sleep for the bugle telling you to fall in as another convoy has arrived. I don't think I have ever been so tired in my life.

The hardest thing to deal with is still the young boys who are desperate to be sent home. They seem to think we have some influence with the medical officer and it is pathetic to hear them ask every time you go onto the ward, 'Is it a Blighty, Sister?' One boy begged me to speak to the MO on his behalf and said he would kill himself if he had to go up the line again but there was nothing I could do. He shouldn't be here at all at his age.

You are a darling to say that you will write to Tom on our anniversary. It is almost impossible to worry about him when I am so busy but sometimes when I am travelling in the ambulance or too tired to go to sleep, I do worry that he may be ruining a fine future by siding with the wrong people. I don't doubt for one moment that he is sincere, he doesn't have to prove that to me, but I am terribly afraid that he will end up in prison and that his whole life will be blighted for a lost cause. Conscription is coming isn't it? It's bound to now. I love him so much, though love isn't blind as they say and I have to think of our future.

If only I could talk to him but this is no time to put in for leave as you can imagine.

Ever so much love to you both.

From your loving daughter,
Katherine

5 Myddleton Square
Finsbury

12 October 1915

My darling,

Happy Anniversary of the day you said 'Yes' which together with the day we met (about which more in a moment), the day we are married, the day our first child is born, your birthday and mine, and the birthdays of our next five children, will give us more Holy Days than a religious calendar but of them all 15 October will always be my favourite. I didn't take your 'Yes' for granted and I never shall.

You know, don't you, that I fell in love with you when we first met but I don't think I have ever told you the precise moment. When I looked up and saw you standing by the door, I felt a shock, there is no other way to describe it. You thought I frowned to frighten you away but it was just to steady my nerves. So I was already falling when you delivered the coup de grace by saying with such relish that you had never heard of the newspaper I worked for. Your mother should have warned you that a look of triumph on such a beautiful face is asking for trouble because that was the moment when I knew I would never be able to live without you.

I understand about your leave but still hope it will be soon. I am not surprised your hospital is struggling to cope as the official communiqués cannot disguise the fact that this offensive is turning out to be a disaster. Sir John French told The Times that the New Divisions 'have done magnificently' but anyone reading between the lines knows that what he means is that they have done magnificently considering they are raw recruits, half trained and badly led. The rumour is that so many regular officers were killed earlier in the war, the only ones available at Loos were territorials whose experience of command consisted of peacetime manoeuvres on Salisbury Plain. The long casualty lists make it difficult for me to tell you that I must see my protest against conscription through to the end if I am to remain true to my beliefs.

Damn, that sounds self-righteous. If it does, it is my father's fault because he has decided after all to betray everything he once believed in. They are going to write anti-German propaganda to win over the Americans – my father, Gilbert Murray, John Bury and all the other leading academics. One day they passionately admire Germany and passionately despise Russia, the next day they sing Russia's praises and condemn the Germans as barbarians. How can these men who devote their lives to the pursuit of truth argue a case they know to be false? After the war they will continue their glittering academic careers and no one will be so impolite as to mention that when truth needed them most, they betrayed her. Thank goodness I am not and never will be an academic.

I envy you your distance from England because it is no longer the country we knew. It isn't just the academics who have sold their souls; the suffragettes are handing out white feathers and demanding conscription. I wish what you say about the men in your wards bearing no resentment against the German soldiers could be more widely known but I'm afraid it would be censored by the Press Bureau. This is an Alice in Wonderland war where the soldiers forgive their enemies and the civilians are consumed with hate.

And yet even here there are contradictions. Yesterday, Fenner and I went to a recruiting rally in Trafalgar Square, part of Lord Derby's last push to get volunteers. We were followed by a plain-clothes policeman who made no attempt to conceal his identity and, when we reached the Square, asked how long we intended to stay as he proposed to go to the Strand Corner House for a cup of tea. He has trailed Fenner several times before apparently and they are on friendly terms.

In that brief exchange was so much that I love about England; it couldn't have happened in Berlin or in Paris for that matter. How dare the papers accuse us of wanting to stab our country in the back. Fenner and I love our country, not the false England of the press barons and the bloodthirsty bishops but the real England where a Special Branch officer checks with his quarry before going off for a cup of tea.

That is our England, darling, and we are fighting for it in our different ways.

Remember me when the doctors are flirting with you over their surgical masks.

I am longing to see you soon.

With all my love,
Tom

When the Battle of Loos ended in early November, I put in for leave but my request was refused. Matron told me that I had to take my turn in the rota and that there were several Nursing Sisters ahead of me who had been in France for a year. So much for the War Office promise of leave every six months, I thought.

I don't know whether I would have been able to persuade Tom to abandon his cause for the sake of our future if we had met face to face; perhaps not, but I was bitterly disappointed at not being given the chance. I never doubted Tom's love for me but I was jealous of the power his cause had over him and tried to convince myself that his true motive, whether he was aware of it or not, was to show me that he had the courage of his convictions.

Tom hid his own disappointment in a flurry of letters in which his insecurity and excitement jostled for my attention. He wanted to be reassured that I had not met someone else – he was haunted by fantasies of handsome doctors and brave young officers sweeping me off my feet – but at the same time he could not disguise his excitement at the prospect of 'going into action against conscription' after all the waiting.

He wrote with pride that he had been the chief organiser of the No Conscription Fellowship's first national convention in London and that, thanks to his planning and Clifford Allen's oratory, it had been a triumph. To a man, the delegates had stood in silence to pledge themselves to 'resist conscription whatever the penalties may be'.

Just as I had feared he would, Tom had publicly pledged himself to break the law and to accept the consequences.

CHAPTER THREE

I was at Gournay-en-Bray when Tom was arrested on 24 March 1916. Kitty and I had been sent to this small town north of Rouen to help set up a Red Cross Rest Home for convalescent officers in the chateau belonging to the de Villars family, the descendents of one of Louis X1V's marshals.

Conscription in the form of the Military Service Act, under which all single men of military age were 'deemed to have been enlisted', had come into force on 10 February and had been enthusiastically welcomed by the army in France, our wounded men arguing that it was high time the single men who had stayed at home were 'fetched'.

We received the London papers only a day late so I had been able to follow the debates in the House of Commons. Asquith had easily outmanoeuvred the opponents of conscription by claiming that the new law was not a fundamental change in British life, as Tom had always argued that it would be, only a necessary step to ensure the married men were not called to the colours when so many single men were still available.

To Tom's bitter disappointment, the Prime Minister's political skill had also divided the members of the No Conscription Fellowship. The majority, despite their pledge only a few weeks before 'to resist conscription whatever the penalties may be', decided to compromise. The law allowed a man with a conscientious objection to military service to apply to a local tribunal for exemption; if the tribunal thought he was genuine, the man was sent to the army's Non Combatant Corps or allowed to do civilian work of national importance.

This concession to liberal opinion provoked an outcry in the popular newspapers and, even though I had always thought Tom was wrong about conscription, I was glad that he refused to take this easy way out. 'For us to accept any concession in the Act would be the same as accepting conscription', he wrote to me. 'We cannot now say that we do not mind being conscripted after all as long as there is no risk of being killed. How utterly hypocritical that would be.'

Whatever Kitty said about men of principle, I think I would have lost all respect for Tom if he had compromised at this stage. I did not want him to suffer the penalties for defying the law but as I lay awake, fearful of what was going to happen, I realised that his stubborn integrity was one of the things I loved most about him.

Tom and Fenner and the other 'absolutists' or 'hardliners' in the Fellowship decided that, in order to publicise their rejection of the new law, they would apply to the tribunals for absolute and unconditional exemption knowing that it would be refused and that they would be arrested and handed over to the army.

5 Myddleton Square,
Finsbury

24 March 1916

My darling,

I shall be arrested at ten o'clock this morning. A constable from the local station called the evening before last and asked when it would be convenient for him to arrest me. He thought I might wish to have some time to put my affairs in order so I suggested that he should come back at ten today. What an extraordinary country this is, though I don't expect to be treated with such consideration when I am handed over. Two days after the tribunal hearing, I received notice to report to Mill Hill Barracks, which of course I ignored, so I assume that is where I shall be taken. Don't attempt to write to me there. For the time being, send your letters to me c/o Theodore Taylor at the office and he will do his best to see that they reach me.

The enclosed cutting from the Islington Gazette gives a fair summary of the tribunal hearing. I am sorry to have dragged you into the proceedings but the chairman implied that I was an irresponsible young man who cared for no one but myself and I could not resist telling him that I was engaged to be married. Apart from the Military Representative, the tribunal members were not hostile, just uncomprehending. I think they were relieved that I had not brought my supporters, as the previous applicant was a Marxist who played to his friends in the gallery and they responded by jeering the tribunal members and singing the Red Flag.

These tribunal hearings are a meaningless farce. How can local worthies and unworthies sit in judgment on a man's conscience? At the office we have been receiving reports from all round the country of conscientious objectors being insulted and bullied by local tribunals and, although it is only these bad cases we hear about because no one writes to tell us when a tribunal has been scrupulously fair, we publicise them in the Fellowship's new journal, The Tribunal. Typical or not, the bad cases demonstrate that conscription cannot be made to work fairly in a country that values freedom of conscience.

My bag is packed. We have been advised to take only essentials and that we may not even be allowed to keep these. I have my shaving things, toothbrush, a spare pair of socks, Palgrave's Golden Treasury and Yeats and a packet of biscuits. Please don't worry about me, darling, I am in good spirits. This is the course I have chosen and I will see it through.

I have not told my father because he might be tempted to appear at the police court and I would rather it was not known that I am the son of a Cambridge professor who works for the War Propaganda Bureau. He will find out soon enough. I have written a short note to your mother.

I love you with all my heart and our love will keep us both strong in whatever trials lie ahead.

Tom.

ISLINGTON GAZETTE
17 March 1916
FINSBURY MAN REFUSED EXEMPTION
WOULD KILL 'TO PROTECT FAMILY'

A Finsbury man was refused exemption from military service by the Hampstead Local Tribunal yesterday because he said he was prepared to kill if that was the only way to protect his family. Mr Tom Kennedy of 5 Myddleton Square, Finsbury was told by the tribunal chairman, Councillor Sir Roland Harris, that even if his objection to conscription was sincerely held, it was not a conscientious objection in the meaning of the Act. Mr Kennedy claimed absolute exemption on the ground that the state had no right to compel a man to take human life. When asked by the Military Representative, Major McCarthy, whether he would kill if that was the only way to protect a female member of his family from being raped, Mr. Kennedy replied, 'If there really was no other way, yes.'

Major McCarthy: ' Then you can have no objection to killing German soldiers who raped the nuns in Belgium.'

Mr Kennedy: 'Using force to protect your loved ones is very different from killing strangers because the government tells you to do so.'

Major McCarthy: 'Who are you to question the government's orders?'

Mr Kennedy: 'Who are you to question my integrity?'

The chairman told the applicant that he would do his case no good by answering back.

Major McCarthy told the tribunal that in his view the applicant was one of those well educated young men who used clever arguments to save their own skin. He was a prominent member of the No Conscription Fellowship, an organisation dedicated to undermining conscription; to grant him any form of exemption would be to open the floodgates for every self-centred slacker in the country.

In answer to a question from the chairman, Mr Kennedy said he was engaged to be married to a nurse who was serving in the military hospital in France.

Major McCarthy: 'Are you not ashamed to be at home when your fiancée is at the front?'

Mr Kennedy: 'I am proud of what my fiancée is doing and I am proud of what I am doing.'

Exemption refused.

After hearing the tribunal's decision, Mr Kennedy said he would not 'waste everybody's time' by appealing. Told that he would be arrested and handed over to the military, Mr Kennedy replied, 'Good.'

Tom managed to send me a letter from Mill Hill Barracks, 'a military caravanserai in North London', describing in humorous terms the permanent staff's attempts to make him obey orders. How exactly do you refuse to undergo a medical examination? His battle of wits with the medical officer apparently reduced them both to mirth. His only serious clash with authority occurred when he explained to the officious young subaltern in charge of recruits that although he was willing to put on uniform that did not imply that he accepted military discipline.

From Mill Hill, Tom was sent to a Non Combatant Corps camp near Shoreham on the south coast where a number of absolutists were being held. He still preferred to treat the whole experience as something of a joke because that was his way of playing down for my sake the risk he was taking but in my last letter to him before he crossed the channel, I begged him to be careful. In France it was no secret how the army dealt with soldiers who refused to obey orders.

Happy Valley Camp
Shoreham-by-Sea
Sussex

19 April 1916

My darling,

The comic opera continues. We wear uniform but that is the extent of our co-operation. The colonel has decided that we shall not be given any orders as he is keen to avoid conflict so the question of whether to obey does not arise, at least not until the War Office finds out and the colonel is sacked. The regimental sergeant major is appalled by the colonel's decision and growls like a chained dog as we saunter pass.

There are about three hundred men from the Non Combatant Corp here awaiting passage to France and I have no doubt we shall be going with them. There are fifteen conscientious objectors, all absolutists and members of the Fellowship though none I have met before. Eight sleep in the guardroom, the rest of us on the floor of the detention hut.

For occupation we till the ground along the camp perimeter and aim to grow vegetable which the colonel has promised will go only to the civilian population though whether that will satisfy my more fanatical comrades I am not sure. One or two of the absolutists are hair-splitting types who go to extraordinary lengths to check that nothing we do is remotely connected with the war. There was a fierce argument in the hut last night because some of us had gone along to the open-air church parade and joined in the singing of 'Onward Christian Soldiers'. Most of us are reasonably sane however and have no wish to see our stand against conscription reduced to a theological quibble about whether growing Brussels sprouts constitutes a compromise with the military machine.

Because there is little to do, we speculate on what will happen to us in France. Some give the impression that they would welcome the chance, as they put it, 'to remain faithful even to the gates of death' but needless to say I have no such thoughts. In France, I shall politely refuse to kill any Germans and will probably be sentenced to a term of imprisonment which with any luck I shall serve in England.

My father has written asking me to reconsider because he fears for my safety but the last thing I want is for him to interfere. He says I should not be associating with conscientious objectors who are 'ex hypothesi cranks'. Well there are some cranks, there are bound to be, but I am not a crank and nor is Fenner.

Our hut is locked at sunset and I am sitting on the chalky ground outside writing this before the sun disappears behind the hill that separates us from the sea. You must be wondering what sort of marriage ours will be with you working long shifts on the wards while I spend idle, inconsequential days on the Sussex Downs but don't worry, ours will be a marriage of equals.

This enforced idleness is as alien to me as it would be to you. I long to do something but instead of chaining myself to the railings outside Number Ten or throwing myself in front of the General's horse, I have to wait to see what the military decide to do with me. I was not cut out for this role; I could be a Russian revolutionary or even an Irish rebel but I am not much good at passive resistance.

Please write as soon as you can. This is the time of day more than any other when separation hurts and I long for us to be together. If I cannot write again when we leave for France, remember that I love you very much and that my silence is only temporary. Look out for a familiar face next time you enter a French café.

Goodbye for now, darling, and with all my love.

Tom

Red Cross Rest Station
Gournay-en-Bray
BEF

23 April 1916

My darling Mummy,

It has been a perfectly heavenly day, very sunny and just right for Easter Sunday. We had a lovely Easter communion in the large ward this morning. A padre came from brigade, an enthusiastic young fellow who ate an enormous breakfast after the service. Cook provided him with kidneys and bacon and boiled eggs all of which he wolfed down, giving us the rather lame excuse that at headquarters he has to make do with a French breakfast but we absolved him of the sin of gluttony because he had brought enough chocolate eggs for us to give one to every patient.

This place is more or less straight. The scarlet blankets for the beds came last week and look very smart and today for the first time the men are wearing the bright blue pyjama suits when they are out of bed. The assistant director of medical services has been to inspect us and we have had an official visit from the Principal Commandant of VADs in France, a Miss Rachel Crowdy, both of whom said they were impressed by what we have achieved in a short time.

I have written to Tom's father today asking him to do all he can to see that Tom is not treated as a deserter if he refuses orders in France. There is some talk among officers here that the army intends to make an example of the first conscientious objectors who are sent over but I cannot believe that Mr Asquith would let any real harm come to them.

I honestly cannot tell whether Tom is alright because he is so good at describing everything in a light-hearted way. I have written to tell him that I have renewed my contract with the War Office for another year but I have not said anything about the reason I gave you. He thinks I have signed on again because there is little point in my coming home if he is in France or in prison but you know that I am hoping that my service over here will stand in his favour if it ever comes to a court martial. That is partly the reason I have put in for a transfer to a Casualty Clearing Station which will be near the front line. Kitty and I are not keen to go back to Rouen. We shall be in range of the German guns and we all know that the Germans have no respect whatsoever for the civilised rules of warfare but I am not afraid.

Darling Mummy, you mustn't worry about me. There are days when I am down in the dumps because the war looks like going on for years and I cannot believe Tom and I will ever be married but most of the time I am in good heart. I have Tom's letters and yours and Kitty's friendship, and thanks to you and Daddy, I have my faith which will never let me down. I pray each night that God will bring us all safely through.

It would be tremendous good luck if we were posted to the same Casualty Clearing Station as Theodore Hardy. In my application I mentioned that the Anglican chaplain at No.43 was a very good friend of the family.

With heaps of love to you both,
Your loving daughter,
Katherine.

Tom's letter of 19 April was the last I heard from him until the middle of October apart from a brief note to say that he loved me and that he was somewhere nearby. How that note reached me I will leave Tom to explain in his account of his time as a soldier refusing orders in France. He wrote this account when he was released from prison in December 1916 but I did not read it until the following spring so that the only knowledge I had of what was happening to him came from my mother who was able to glean a few details from Tom's shadow, the Quaker Theodore Taylor.

'Unwilling Soldier' by Tom Kennedy

On the afternoon of 30 April we were taken by lorry from Happy Valley Camp to Seaford Station with a draft of Non Combatant men destined for France. It was a fine spring day, our morale was high and as we came down the hill to the town we had our first sight of the sea. A train was waiting. We were ordered to remain on the platform until all the Non Combatant men had collected their kit and got on board, so there we stood, fifteen men who had no intention of becoming soldiers, guarded by one NCO who glanced frequently at the station clock as though he feared the train would leave without us. It crossed my mind that we might not be going after all and I remember feeling disappointed.

The military policemen marched onto the platform from the station entrance, about eight or ten of them accompanied by an officer who was smartly dressed in service dress and Sam Browne belt. When the squad came to a crashing halt beside us, we saw that each man was carrying two pairs of handcuffs. That was the moment when I realised that the comic opera version of army life was about to be overtaken by reality.

The officer said, 'Good afternoon'. He had only one arm and the end of his empty sleeve was tucked tidily into the front of his service dress. He told us we had a choice. We could accept military discipline now and go to France as free men with a clean conduct sheet or we could continue to disobey in which case we would be taken to France as military prisoners. His voice was quiet, his tone courteous – he might have been offering us a choice of China or Indian tea – and although we would soon learn to trust a sergeant's obscenities rather than the politeness of young men with pips on their shoulders, we were still green in army ways and inclined to believe that here at least was an officer who was prepared to treat conscientious objectors with respect. But there was never any doubt what our answer would be.

The officer stepped back as the military police came forward. In five minutes we had all been handcuffed with our hands behind our backs and bundled into the guards van. Those who refused to be bundled were carried. It was all done in a business-like manner with hardly a word spoken on either side, the officer watching with an air of professional interest like a hill farmer watching a sheep dog demonstration at a country fair. When he saw that we were all safely in the pen and our kit bags tossed in after us, he gave the order for the guards van to be closed and locked.

We did our best to make ourselves comfortable, despite the handcuffs, sitting on our kit bags with our backs to the wall. Three hours and many stops later we arrived at Southampton Quay where, when the guards van was opened, we were surprised to see the one-armed officer and his sheepdogs already on the platform. This was our last opportunity to reconsider he told us, as the military police removed our handcuffs. He felt it was his duty to remind us that this was a war for Christian civilization, but, as he was speaking he caught my eye and I will swear we exchanged a look of understanding. He did not believe what he was saying about Christian civilization and he knew that I did not either. Poor man. He could no longer persuade himself that the cause was just so he had no hope of persuading us.

We reaffirmed our intention to refuse to obey military orders. 'Then I advise you not to resist being taken on board,' the officer said. There were Australian and Canadian troops on the ship as well as British, all returning from leave and in no mood to be sympathetic to 'conchies'. As we walked up the gangplank with our kit bags on our shoulders, someone shouted 'Put them with the colonials,' and there was a great roar from the crowded decks that could have come from the terraces of the Coliseum. Yet as the military police forced a passage for us through the crush, I heard words of encouragement as well as jeers, 'Good luck, mate', 'Stick to it, mate', both these in Australian accents, so perhaps the colonials weren't so hostile after all.

We spent the night alone in the hold, wrapped in our greatcoats and using our kit bags as pillows. At dawn, the troopship, which had the curious name of the "St. Tudno", docked at Le Havre where all the other men were disembarked before we were allowed on deck. We had no idea where we were going or how long our journey would be but we had agreed after a long debate, in which Beamish, the most awkward of our group, kept finding a new reason to disagree, that we would not disobey orders until we reached our final destination. Our first stop was Cinder City Camp, a dreary assembly of huts half an hour's march from the docks where we spent the whole day hanging about with the men from the Non Combatant Corps waiting for news until as the light faded we were given five minutes notice of our departure for Rouen. I was too excited to be cautious and rushed up to one of the NCOs to ask whether Rouen was our final destination. The Lance Corporal shrugged his shoulders. How should he know? 'They'll crucify your lot before they're finished,' he added.

At Le Havre Goods Station we boarded a train made up of cattle wagons with a sliding door that was kept locked during the journey.

Each wagon had a notice on the outside, '40 hommes, 8 chevaux', but we had a wagon to ourselves with only two armed soldiers as our escorts, so we had room to stretch out and doze. I refused to abandon my extravagant hope of surprising Katherine and spent the journey imagining the various possibilities, such as walking on to her ward or into a café where she was sitting alone writing a letter to me or seeing her on the next platform when we arrived in Rouen and, ignoring the shouts of the NCOs, crossing the track to take her in my arms.

It was after midnight when we arrived and there was no adjacent platform, just a vast, open-sided shed where soldiers, most of whom were holding rifles and carrying their full kit on their backs, were standing in groups, talking, smoking or just staring into the darkness. We could not tell whether they were on their way to the front or home on leave and with the Non Combatant Corps flash on our shoulders we were disinclined to ask. The longer we waited in the shed, the more likely it seemed to me that Rouen was not going to be our final destination, so with the aid of Ian Sutherland's back, I wrote a note to Katherine, sending her my love and telling her that I was close by. I addressed the note to Gournay-en-Bray and asked one of the NCOs on duty to deliver it to the General Hospital in the hope that it would be sent on.

The note reached Katherine exactly three months later when she was in the Casualty Clearing Station, having been sent to her by the parents of a young subaltern who had been killed on the Somme. I cannot explain that. I gave the note to a corporal who looked older than the other NCOs and he pushed it under the clip on the board he was holding. 'I will if I can' was as far as he would go. I can only speculate that he was returned to his unit before he could deliver the note and killed earlier in that battle. The young subaltern, his platoon commander, found the note among the corporal's belongings and, rather than send it to the family, transferred it to his own wallet perhaps with the intention of making sure it reached its destination when he came out of the line. But he never did. When Katherine showed me the note it was not dog-eared or blood-stained, just a little worn along the creases.

We left Rouen at dawn in a train with so many box wagons it hardly ever managed more than a walking pace and, as this time the sliding doors were left open, men could jump down to pick wild flowers or green apples and still have time to clamber back again. When the train stopped, as it did frequently, several men got down and provoked a bellow from the NCOs, 'Get back on the train', so that each halt became a game of grandmother's footsteps, with the men trying their luck and the NCOs seeming to join in the spirit of the thing. Were some of these men heading for the Somme? I don't know but on that May morning they could have been on a school outing and whatever our feelings about the army and our secret anxiety about our own fate, we could not refrain from joining in the cheers that greeted every successful sally.

We reached Boulogne in the late afternoon. At the station, an incident occurred that made me wonder whether Beamish was unhinged. One of the soldier escorts who had travelled with us in the wagon asked Beamish to hold his rifle while he jumped down onto the platform. Beamish took the rifle without thinking but when he had handed it back, he started to wipe his hands obsessively on his uniform and then demanded to be allowed to go to the station latrines to wash the stain of the rifle from his fingers. When the NCOs told him not to be 'bloody stupid' and to fall in with the rest of us, Beamish lay on his back on the platform and refused to move. He was lucky not to be hurt because the platform was still crowded with men who were not bothered about what was underfoot. Eventually two of our NCOs dragged him clear and frog-marched him to the waiting transport. Watching this, I found myself irritated by Beamish's performance which made fools of us all.

Boulogne-sur-Mer may have been a pleasant seaside town before the war but it is now one huge British army camp. Henriville, where we were to spend the next three weeks, is a hillside covered with huts and tents just outside the town. On a fine day, we could make out the whiteness of the English cliffs and from time to time we could hear the dull boom of howitzers from the front, a reminder to us that Boulogne was technically 'in the field'.

It was soon obvious that the camp commander, a Colonel Wilberforce, did not know what to do with conscientious objectors who had been dumped on him without warning and who had declared their intention to refuse orders. We were told that he had telegraphed the War Office for instructions and that in the meantime we would be billeted with the Non Combatant Corps and allowed to use the camp facilities as 'prisoners on parole'. Boredom was the chief enemy, so much so that we looked forward eagerly to our three meals a day which always consisted of bully beef and biscuits and hot sweet tea. At night we slept twelve to a tent with our feet at the tent pole and our heads against the flaps.

On 18 May, at the end of our second week at Henriville, Colonel Wilberforce received his instructions. We should be put to work on the docks and if we refused, court martialed. The following morning, when the bugle call was sounded, we stayed in our tents but instead of being court martialed we were paraded for COs Orders and given 'three days cells with bread and water'. Thus began the army's at first deceptively mild attempt to break our resistance.

As a punishment, three days cells is no more than irksome and disagreeable. We were split into groups of five and put into the three available cells in the guardroom, a tight fit at night time but not during the day when we were allowed into a small enclosed yard where there were washbasins and latrines. Three times a day a guard brought us water and one biscuit each.

From this undemanding imprisonment we emerged rather pleased with ourselves for having passed the first test with ease, only to be told that we had all been committed for a Field General Court Martial and would be required to submit a written statement of our reasons for disobedience. The three days cells had just been a holding operation while the adjutant prepared the paperwork.

We were not unduly concerned. We knew that Boulogne was as much 'in the field' as a front line trench and that the ultimate penalty for disobedience in the field was death but we had convinced ourselves that our friends at home with their parliamentary allies would never allow the army to go that far. The court martial proceedings were perfunctory: four officers seated at a plain wooden table, the adjutant reading the charge and the RSM shouting us in and out of the hut one by one. Our statements were not referred to and may not even have been read. We pleaded guilty and were sentenced to twenty-eight days Field Punishment.

Boulogne Field Punishment Barracks, located in the former Fish Market near the docks, is so notorious for the brutality of its regime that men would rather face German bullets than risk being sent there. The Germans are accused of brutality but the British can be just as brutal when they put their minds to it. When the gates of the Barracks closed behind us, we were in a world where a soldier's protection under military law counted for nothing. We were entirely at the mercy of the guards, NCOs who seemed to have been selected for the pleasure they took in inspiring fear and inflicting pain, and against whose authority there was no appeal. We only saw an officer twice and never to speak to. The first occasion was on the day of our arrival when we had been standing to attention on the oval-shaped drill ground at the centre of the complex for nearly an hour. The officer said, 'Those men willing to work take one pace forward.' With his clipped voice, small stature and narrow, mean face, he reminded me of the young officer I had clashed with at Mill Hill. After a brief pause during which no one moved, he said, 'Put these men in irons, sergeant' and, turning smartly on his heal, walked off parade, his job done.

The violence of the onslaught left us frightened and bewildered as it was intended to do. Unlike the military police at Seaford, these guards set about the task of handcuffing us with obvious relish; punching and kicking anyone who showed the slightest slowness to react or inclination to resist. Andrew Huckstep was knocked to the floor and kicked several times, once on the side of the head, and we made no protest. The handcuffs were figures of eight which were screwed down so tightly to hold one wrist on top of the other that you felt the flow of blood to your fingers must be cut off. Powerless to defend ourselves, we were rushed to the punishment cells, the guards using their sticks freely to beat us on our way. Each man was pushed into a small cell about seven foot long and four foot wide, with a concrete floor and iron walls and here we were left for several hours wanting to call out to one another but afraid to do so.

It must have been towards evening when the cell doors were opened and we were ordered out. We looked like men whose spirit had already been broken: some had urinated in their trousers and it showed, others hung their heads and one or two had smudged cheeks as though they had been crying. Then to our astonishment, someone started to sing.

O God of Love, O King of Peace
Make wars throughout the world to cease...

And others who knew the hymn joined in, swelling the chorus as the guards yelled for silence.

The sinful wrath of man restrain
Give peace, O Lord, give peace again.

Later, I heard that it was Beamish who had started the singing and that he had been punished with one hour's shot drill but his defiance at that moment probably saved us from a complete collapse of morale.

As we marched onto the parade ground we saw that, all round the side, soldiers were standing with their backs to the wall and their arms outstretched. It took us a few moments to realise that they were tied in that position. Field punishment Number One, the sergeant thought we would be interested to know, had replaced flogging 'and more's the pity', but if we thought it was a humane alternative we would soon find out that we were wrong.

We took our places on the wall. Our hands were tied at the extremity of our reach to a rope that ran round the wall on rings and our knees and ankles were strapped together, and there we stood like scarecrows, feeling the humiliation as much as the discomfort, so that long before the end of the two hours we were praying for it to be over. We were tied up three evenings out of four throughout our sentence and it is an experience I never wish to have again. If only the people at home could witness these mass 'crucifixions' (as the punishment is inevitably called) they would be able to see exactly how discipline is maintained in the British army.

'Crucifixion' and shot drill – a back-breaking exercise that left men giddy with exhaustion and that was awarded for the slightest hint of insubordination such as looking a guard in the eye – were the official punishments prescribed in King's Regulations. Yet in the Fish Market, it was the unofficial, unrecorded punishments that terrorised the prisoners. Men were beaten up in their cells at night for no reason at all and if they cried out the guards forced into their mouths a bar of soap wrapped in a cloth. Does the Prime Minister know, as he settles down to his game of bridge with his lady friends, what happens in the Fish Market every night? We were not subjected to these unofficial punishments, I think because somewhere at the back of those brutal minds was the thought that, unlike the other prisoners, we might have influential friends. As we refused to work (the other prisoners worked on the docks alongside the Labour Battalion), we spent most of the day handcuffed and silent in our single cells. Our handcuffs were removed for one hour in the morning for 'ablutions' and for one hour in the evening after tying up when we ate our biscuits and drank our water. At night time, our hands were secured in front instead of behind our backs so that we could use the bucket.

I set myself the task of remembering the lines of all the poems I had at one time learned by heart and chose one poem each day to take with me to my 'crucifixion', just as other men took prayers or passages from the Gospels they had committed to memory. Poetry was an excellent antidote to Field Punishment Number One, especially Macaulay's 'Lays of Ancient Rome', all the more so because the guards who prowled along the line of men, mocking and laughing, could not have the slightest idea what was going through my mind.

The second time I saw an officer was on the last full day of our sentence. I had been selected with two others to meet a visiting

Member of Parliament. The mean-faced little officer described us as men who were due for release the following day. We had been ordered to stand at ease with our hands behind our backs so that the visitor could not see the red scars on our wrists.

The visitor said, 'I suppose you men will be glad to be getting back to your units.'

'Yes, sir.'

'Have you any cause to complain of your treatment here?'

'No, sir.' We were not stupid.

The visitor smiled, though at what it was difficult to tell, and as he was steered away by the officer, we were marched back to our cells where our figures of eight were screwed on again.

We were released from the Field Punishment Barracks on the morning of 17 June. Returning to Henriville was like coming home even though the tents and huts on the hillside were sodden after the night's rain but any happiness we dared to feel was abruptly dispelled by the news that only two days earlier four conscientious objectors in the camp had been sentenced to death. I did not believe it. I had been so certain that our country would never take that step. The condemned men were in the guardroom and we were allowed no contact with them but as 'prisoners on parole' we soon discovered that the death sentence had been commuted immediately to ten year's penal servitude and that the men were awaiting transfer to a civil prison in England. I am still amazed that senior officers risked alienating liberal opinion by insisting on this charade. Who was it intended to impress?

As far as we were concerned, any prison sentence seemed preferable to being sent back to the Fish Market so when Colonel Wilberforce told us that the War Office had instructed him to give us the choice of joining the Non Combatant Corps, 'which is doing a splendid job', or being sent back to England to serve an unspecified prison sentence, we were unanimous. A week later we arrived at Southampton early on a damp, sea-misted morning and, with our soldier escorts, boarded a train for Winchester.

The journey from Boulogne to Winchester was the last time we were all together and the last opportunity therefore to discuss, as we had so often done in the past, what the future held and where we stood, each of us, in relation to our original commitment to oppose conscription whatever the consequences. We all agreed that our experience in France had made us more than ever convinced of the evils of compelling men to be soldiers but we could not agree on how far we should continue to refuse to do any form of civilian alternative service. The prospect of imprisonment, if not for ten years, then certainly for as long as the war lasted, made a few of us question what the purpose of that would be. However, most of the men said they would not compromise and that witnessing to their beliefs by remaining in prison was the best way to convince the public of the rightness of their cause.

When we talked of forgiving those who had ill-treated us in the Fish Market, I confessed that I harboured thoughts of revenge. This confession appeared to disturb my fellow travellers who insisted that their absolute rejection of violence had been strengthened by their experience. I did not know whether to admire these men who were still prepared to turn the other cheek or to suspect that they were deceiving themselves. Beamish was one of their number. What a strange man: cranky, quarrelsome, obsessive and yet defiant when the rest of us had lost our nerve. I still can't make him out. He says he feels no hatred for his tormentors but he has a wild look in his eye and I should not like to meet him on a lonely path. Perhaps his pacifism is his peace of mind.

To the question, 'Are you still a CO, Tom?' I replied that I was but my objection had been to conscription and that battle seemed to have been lost. No one said anything but I think even those I knew best now regarded me as different, not as a traitor to their cause but as a stranger, so that although we all walked through the gates of Winchester prison together, for the first time I felt that I was on my own.

December 1916

On 25 June, two days after the gates of Winchester Prison closed behind Tom and the other conscientious objectors, Kitty and I arrived at No 43 Casualty Clearing Station, which was rapidly expanding its capacity in preparation for a major British offensive.

Chapter Four

The commanding officer, a lieutenant colonel in the RAMC, said he was not allowed to tell us when the offensive would begin, only that we had to make ourselves familiar with our duties as members of one of the surgical teams as quickly as possible but the four Nursing Sisters – two Red Cross and two QAs – with whom Kitty and I shared a tent assured us it was an open secret that our men would go over the top on Saturday morning. We were not surprised. From a long way off we had been listening to the artillery bombardment and when we got off the train at the railhead, the thunder of the guns was deafening.

No 43 Casualty Clearing Station was a mobile unit under canvas occupying a site near Beauquesne about ten miles behind the front line. The sense of urgency and the informality of the station suited us both. When the offensive started, no one stood on ceremony and people were willing to turn their hands to whatever needed to be done, none more so than the Anglican chaplain, the Reverend Theodore Hardy. He was a padre, assistant anaesthetist, stretcher-bearer, male nurse and an occasional waiter who brought refreshments to the surgeons and nurses in the marquee that acted as an operating theatre.

Theodore Hardy was the priest-in-charge of Hutton Roof, a scattered rural community close to Kirkby Lonsdale, and he had been a frequent visitor at the Rectory so I knew him well. His wife had died just before the war and, rather than brood in his remote vicarage, he had applied to the Chaplaincy Department in 1915 only to be turned down on account of his age. He was fifty-one. But he had persisted and in early 1916 he had arrived in France as a Temporary Chaplain, 4th Class.

Later in the war, this quiet and unassuming man was awarded the VC, DSO and MC for his outstanding bravery. At the Casualty Clearing Station, he was a friend to all regardless of rank and he helped to guide me through some of the most difficult months of my life. Even Kitty, who had little time for army chaplains, except the Romans who went over the top with the men, respected Hardy and he responded by asking her to help him write letters for the dying men when she came off duty in the theatre. He told us that he would prefer to serve in the front line and when I asked him why he replied simply that he was a widower, that both his children were grown up and that he had no fear of death.

On Saturday 1 July, our surgical team came on duty at 5am but there was little to do except check and check again that everything was ready in the operating theatre. When the theatre sister was satisfied, she said we could go outside for a breath of fresh air but Kitty stayed behind; she had her eye on one of the surgeons as a possible companion for a night out in Beauquesne when the fighting died down.

There was a faint haze over the cloudless sky that promised a glorious summer day and I could not help thinking of that other July morning and of my decision not to walk down to the river and all the happiness and heartache that had flowed from that moment. I did not know yet that Tom was safely in Winchester Prison. I had written him a short letter, not knowing whether it would reach him but wanting to put down on paper that I would always love him whatever happened. Having written it, I thought it sounded as if I was trying to reassure myself as well as him but I sent it all the same.

When Kitty came out to join me looking pleased with herself, the artillery bombardment started to build to a crescendo, a signal to the men waiting in the packed front line trenches that there was an hour to go.

'Poor sods, poor bloody sods,' Kitty said, though whether she meant the Germans or our own Tommies I could not tell.

The previous evening, our commanding officer had called the staff together for a final briefing. The medical service had learnt from the mistakes of 1915 and this time there was more than adequate provision for the number of casualties expected, he said. Advanced Dressing Stations were in position and mobile surgical teams were ready to deal with men so seriously wounded they would not survive the ambulance journey to the nearest Casualty Clearing Station. Nothing had been left to chance.

There was no precise moment when I knew that something had gone wrong, just a growing awareness during the first hour that far more casualties were being brought in than we had been told to expect. There was a rumour that in the confusion some ambulances had brought their wounded to No.43 instead of the other Casualty Clearing Station in the area but by 8.30am, when Hardy told me all eight surgical teams were now on duty, I realised something far more serious was happening though in the rush and frenzy of the operating theatre there was little time to speculate on what that might be.

By noon, our station was completely overwhelmed. All the beds were full and outside in the hot sun wounded men were lying on stretchers or waterproof sheets. I don't think any of us knew even then the extent of the terrible tragedy that was unfolding in No Man's Land but any orderly or stretcher-bearer could make the calculation that the number of casualties was at least ten times higher than we had planned for.

The memory of those days and nights in the first week of July stayed with me for many years and even now I sometimes have clear recollections of the faces of badly wounded men as though they were calling from the past 'Remember me'.

No 43 Casualty Clearing Station
BEF

12 July 1916

My darling Mummy,

I don't think anybody could describe truthfully what went on here when the battle started. On Saturday and Saturday night and Sunday, Kitty and I were on duty in the operating theatre with only a few hours rest snatched when we could.

We are both experienced nurses and know what shells and bullets can do to men's bodies but we have never seen such dreadful wounds. Some men looked as though they had been torn open by wild animals – we have been told that they walked shoulder to shoulder into the German machine gun fire – and many died on the operating table.

If men survived it was thanks to the surgeons who never stopped as long as another man was waiting. Our marquee had four operating tables and our two surgeons, their white smocks soon drenched with blood, moved from table to table, doing what only they could do – tying up the arteries after amputating a leg on one table and taking off a shattered arm at the shoulder on the next, leaving us to do the stitching up and dressing. They shouted instructions at us in colourful language which we didn't mind and one said to me, 'This isn't surgery, Sister, its butchery', but their butchery saved the lives of hundreds of men.

We were under such pressure on Saturday night that Theodore Hardy was recruited as an assistant anaesthetist. You should have seen him, trying to hold steady by the light of the acetylene flares the chloroform bottle over the gauze that covered the patient's face but he never lost a man. The surgeons told him he had chosen the wrong profession, to which he replied that he had once been the headmaster of a school and had learnt early on how to put people to sleep. The men call him 'the dear old padre' but he has more stamina than a much younger man. He has asked Kitty and I to help with writing letters for men who are dying and we do that whenever we have time.

I am not allowed to tell you the number of casualties but it will give you some idea if I say that when Kitty and I had a short break and went outside, we could hardly move in any direction for fear of treading on a wounded man. Some were dead already and others were only alive in their eyes. Do you remember when we were walking on the Old Coach Road and found a dog that had been crushed by a cart and had somehow managed to crawl into the ditch to die? Well, that's what some of the wounded men reminded me of. They are so brave and don't complain but I cannot help thinking they have paid a terrible price for our politicians' refusal even to consider a negotiated peace.

Darling Mummy, that is me speaking, not Tom. He is brave in his own way, isn't he, and I wish Daddy would recognise that as I do. And Tom is wrong in his own way, too, but I understand better now why he felt so strongly about the war and conscription. I have not heard from him since 19 April and cannot hide my anxiety from Kitty and the others in my tent. Please let me know at once as soon as you have any news.

Heaps of love to you both, darling Mummy and Daddy.

From your loving daughter
Katherine.

My mother's letter crossed with mine. Tom was safe. Better that he should be in prison, I thought, than running the risk of being court martialed as a deserter in France.

Tom's Quaker shadow, Theodore Taylor, had written to my mother to explain the situation. Tom and the other absolutists in Winchester Prison had been sentenced to two years with hard labour. For the first month, Tom would have to spend all but forty-five minutes of every twenty-four hours alone in his cell with no exercise, no books except the Bible, no communication with his fellow inmates and nothing to do except stitch canvas for mailbags. For the first two months, he could not receive a visit or send or receive a letter.

I could not imagine Tom tolerating that prison regime for long but if I had been able to visit him and he had asked me what I wanted him to do, I do not think I could have given him an unequivocal answer. During those first few weeks of the Battle of the Somme I found it almost impossible to think clearly about our future and this was not entirely the result of the extraordinary pressures of the operating theatre.

I wrote to Theodore Taylor straight away and received a prompt reply. The absolutists could secure an immediate release from prison if they abandoned their objection to military service and joined the army. Meanwhile, I would be glad to know that men like Tom and Fenner, who was in Walton Prison in Liverpool, were coping better than most with the loneliness and boredom of prison life. Tom had quickly devised a scheme for communicating with other prisoners by tapping a modified Morse code on the hot water pipes that ran from cell to cell and Fenner had even managed to publish an occasional newsletter written on toilet paper and called the Walton Leader.

They were at their old game of outwitting authority but that would not compensate for long for their loss of freedom and Tom in particular was bound to ask himself what value there was in continuing to resist. Knowing him, I guessed that he would also be prey to jealous fantasies that were all the more difficult to dismiss because we could not write to one another. Early in the war there had been newspaper stories about 'husband-seeking nurses' and I remembered now how often Tom had returned to the subject in jest.

I never doubted my love for Tom but in the highly charged atmosphere of the Casualty Clearing Station, it was not unusual for a Nursing Sister, despite her professionalism, to feel something more than compassion for a man who was dying and for whom she was, just for a short while, the only girl in the world. For a few days, I was attracted to another man and he to me but I did not think I was being disloyal to Tom; I was taking part in a play that had no meaning outside the theatre that the war had created.

There were strict rules in the base hospitals forbidding relationships between the staff and the patients and it had been one of my jobs to speak sharply to a VAD on my wards who confused pity for love and, if the girl insisted she was serious, to tell her that she would have to wait until the man went convalescent. In the Casualty

Clearing Station, where life was hectic and men were moved on so quickly to the railhead or the cemetery, rules hardly seemed necessary.

For the first ten days of July, the only wounded men I saw were on the operating table or waiting their turn on the stretchers but as the pressure eased a little, Kitty and I would spend half an hour here and there writing letters home for men who were dying or too badly wounded to write themselves. Most men wanted to disguise from their loved ones the seriousness of their wounds but Hardy insisted that it was kinder to tell the truth. He showed me the words he used if a man was not going to recover and I noted them down.

'He bids me make light of his wounds but I cannot honestly do so and I do not think it is any kindness to hide from you that unless God in his great mercy gives aid beyond any ordinary help can afford, he is unlikely to recover. Remember he is yours forever in God's sight.'

One of the first letters I wrote, sitting on the side of the bed and resting the pad on my knee, was for a sergeant who had lost both his hands. He told me that he had put his pistol to a German soldier's head but did not have the heart to pull the trigger so he brought the man in as a prisoner and was badly wounded by a bomb on the way. In the random manner of such explosions his prisoner was unhurt and carried the sergeant to the British lines. I was writing to the sergeant's mother and knew that I would have to tell her about his hands though he begged me not to.

Some men were so badly disfigured that they did not want a letter written and said they would rather die than go home. In some cases I thought it would be a mercy if they did. When Kitty asked Hardy what he had been praying for at the bedside of a man whose face had been taken off by shrapnel, Hardy replied, 'Lord now lettest thy servant depart in peace.'

It may seem strange that I should have been repelled by rats when I was dealing with so badly wounded and disfigured men but I was. When the orderlies brought tea to the wards, the rats invariably followed in the hope of picking up crumbs and they were tolerated because they helped to keep the wards clean. Kitty ignored the rats or gave them a casual kick if they came too close but they gave me the creeps so as soon as I had finished my letter I left that ward and moved to another. Which is why on this particular day I went to the officers' sick marquee on my own to ask the sister-in-charge if anyone might want a letter written. One side of the marquee was a moribund ward and the other a holding area for officers awaiting rail transport to a base hospital.

The sister-in-charge directed me to a bed in the moribund ward and a Captain Melrose of the 10th Worcesters who had been brought in the previous day with a gunshot wound in the chest and who, despite an operation, was not expected to live.

My first impression of Captain Melrose was that he had been placed in the moribund ward by mistake. He was wide awake and cheerful and when I asked whether he wanted me to write a letter for him, he replied that he did not want to worry his wife unnecessarily. There was more than a hint of bravado in his performance that Kitty and I had come across before in men who did not have long to live, especially officers who seemed to think they had to keep up the pretence until the last minute.

I said, 'It is no kindness, Captain, to hide the truth from your wife.'

For a few seconds, his pale blue eyes seemed to be studying my face, then he closed his eyes and I thought it possible that the effort to be brave had been his last and that his life was already slipping away. With his fair hair and freckled face he looked like a young boy who had fallen asleep after a long day in the sun. I waited a little longer and then left, telling the sister-in-charge that I would come back later to see how he was.

Absence makes the heart grow fonder – though Kitty was too cynical to have that as one of her phrases – 'out of sight, out of mind' suited her better – but absence also makes it difficult for the separated lovers, starved of one another, to resist the offer of a passing romance. That anyway is how I interpret my experience and the experience of other women separated from their loved ones during the war.

Kitty and I came off duty just after midnight in the middle of a thunderstorm. We should have waited for the storm to pass but I insisted that we make a dash for it so that we arrived at the officers' sick marquee soaking wet and earned a disapproving glance from the sister-in-charge. In the dim light, the Reverend Hardy was kneeling beside Captain Melrose's bed saying the Lord's Prayer and pausing as a priest does in the marriage service for the Captain to repeat each phrase. Kitty stood at the end of the bed but I sat on the side, waiting for them to finish. When they had said their Amens, Captain Melrose looked straight at me and said, 'I love you.'

Such sudden declarations were common enough and not taken seriously. I said, 'You love your wife, Captain, now try and get some rest.'

I told Hardy that I thought I would stay a while and he nodded and thanked me for coming back to see Harry Melrose. When I turned to look at Kitty, she was standing with her arms folded and had on her 'I hope you know what you're doing' face. She would have flirted with the Kaiser but although all men were fair game, wounded soldiers were not. A QA, her black eyes seemed to be saying, always keeps her distance from the patient.

Kitty left and I stayed with Captain Melrose for no more that ten minutes. Each day I looked in to see how he was and each day he was a little better so his cheeriness was justified after all. I made a point of keeping my visits businesslike so as not to encourage any tender feeling on his part but he just smiled at my briskness as if to say, 'I know perfectly well what you're trying to do but it's too late.' Then one night I went in and saw that his bed was occupied by another man.

'Captain Melrose will be on his way to Boulogne by now,' the sister-in-charge told me and I hated the note of satisfaction in her voice. Two weeks later I received a letter from Captain Melrose's wife, thanking me for helping to save 'my dear Harry's life'.

To Kitty's silent enquiry, I replied that there had not been the slightest chance that I had been in danger of falling for Harry Melrose but when I told her that I was thinking of applying for a transfer to a military hospital in England, she gave me a hug and said, 'The sooner you marry Tom the better.' Was I really thinking of going back to England? It had been an off-the-cuff remark but once the thought was out in the open, I recognised the emotions that were driving it – my hope that Tom would soon be free, unease about my feelings for Harry Melrose, anxiety that I was finding it more and more difficult to remain detached in the face of so much suffering and even a grumbling resentment against the army which had gone back on its promise of leave.

My contract did not run out until April 1917 but as I had already spent nearly eighteen months in France without leave, I hoped I might be allowed to transfer at the end of the year. I would write to tell Tom my decision and make sure my letter arrived on the first day he was allowed to receive one.

As the long drawn out offensive on the Somme continued through August and September, with the pressure on the Casualty Clearing Station rising and falling with each new attempt by the generals to prove that the tremendous losses of July had not been in vain, I sometimes found myself wondering whether Harry Melrose would write but he did not. Instead I received a letter from an unexpected source.

Trinity College
Cambridge

2 September 1916

Dear Katherine,
Your mother and I have been in correspondence about Tom's situation and this is what prompts me to ask your help. I believe that you and I share the same frustration at Tom's refusal to recognise that there would be no shame in coming out of prison now and agreeing to do something towards the winning of the war.

My colleague, Professor Gilbert Murray, has written an open letter to the so-called 'absolutists' urging them to accept civilian work of national importance under the Home Office because they have made their protest and vindicated their courage. If you, Katherine, could ask Tom to be content with what he has achieved, there is a good chance he will see sense. I'm afraid my intervention would only reinforce his stubbornness but he will listen to you.

The Home Office Scheme will come into operation next month so there is some urgency, especially as there is talk in Whitehall of sending those absolutists who refuse the Scheme back to the army and to the full rigour of military discipline. I am afraid that if that happens to Tom, he might defy the authorities once too often. I love my son dearly and have never doubted his sincerity but he can be so determined to do what he believes to be right that he does not think about the consequences.

Bless you for the fine work you are doing in France. I am afraid that you have discovered in the Casualty Clearing station something that most of us deny and that is that our veneer of civilisation is very thin. In bello veritas. But that is increasingly just as true of the home front as it is of the battlefields.

You know it is my fondest hope that you and Tom will soon be married. Your father's reservations, though entirely understandable when Tom was so publicly opposed to any form of service, should be modified if he accepts the Home Office Scheme.

With my kindest regards

Yours very sincerely,
Grant Kennedy

Despite the professor's request, I did not mention the Home Office Scheme in my letter to Tom. I hoped that if I told him I was coming home at the end of the year, he would decide to give up at last his opposition to the war. From his father's letter, it appeared that he would then have a choice either to abandon his opposition altogether and join the army or to compromise and accept compulsory civilian work under the Home Office. If he chose the former, he might be killed and if he chose the latter he would be discriminated against after the war, for the country would not easily forgive those who had refused to fight. In the ideal future of my dreams, Tom joined the army and survived, all stain of having opposed the war removed.

In mid-September the rains set in and serious fighting stopped for ten days. The lull in the fighting gave me a chance to talk with Theodore Hardy. We had seen each other every day for two months but seldom with time to talk alone. He shared a tent with two other chaplains, a Roman Catholic priest and a Presbyterian minister and they took it in turns to use the larger tent next door for their services.

Hardy and I talked in the chapel tent or as we walked in the autumn sunshine between the rains. He told me why he wanted to go to the front line and I told him everything about Tom though I said nothing about Harry Melrose. For a shy man, Hardy talked easily about his feelings and in a wonderfully inhibited way about his love for his wife, Florence. Unlike Kitty, he was a romantic. Men and women deceived themselves for all sorts of reasons, he said, of which lust and loneliness were the most common but there was such a thing as true love, he knew that for certain because he had experienced it himself. If Tom and I had found true love together, then we should not let anything stand in the way of our being married.

'I know your father well,' he said. 'However much he disapproves of Tom's activities, I shall be very surprised if he does not like and respect Tom as a man.'

He promised to write to my father but when I said that I hoped he would come to our wedding, he shook his head. He was expecting to hear any day that his transfer to a front-line battalion had been approved. Then he told me something that I have never forgotten. When he arrived in France he was given advice by a younger chaplain called Studdert-Kennedy who had been in the line and was known to the troops as 'Woodbine Willie'. According to Hardy, Suddert-Kennedy said that the more padres who were killed in battle doing Christ-like deeds, the better for the Church, adding, 'Most of us will be more use dead than alive.'

I did not for one moment believe that Hardy was seeking death but over the coming months, when I read accounts of his bravery and selflessness, I remembered Studdert-Kennedy's words.

With a few evenings free, Kitty and I accepted an invitation to the officers' club in Beauquesne where we had supper and played cards and danced to a gramophone. Despite my protestations that I could hardly remember what Harry Melrose looked like, Kitty diagnosed a slight case of fever and prescribed the company of other men. She was popular at the club because she flirted freely but treated her dancing partners in an off-hand manner so that the young subalterns straight out of school thought she was playing hard to get. Her surgeon had let her down but she had no difficulty finding others to pay our bill.

I danced with different men but they all seemed the same and the more I danced with these gauche schoolboys the more I realised how deeply in love with Tom I was and how much I wanted to go home to him.

No.1483 Kennedy
H.M. Prison
Winchester

20 September 1916

My darling Katherine,

There is something about writing on this blue lined paper that inhibits flights of fancy but plain words, earthbound, cannot describe my excitement when I was handed your letter and saw your handwriting for the first time in so long. I am a little daunted by your ability to ensure that your letter arrives like an arrow on the very day I am allowed to receive one but I love you for it.

Your news has given me so much joy that I am suddenly absurdly optimistic about the future so that my dreams are flying high and pulling me this way and that like a kite in a storm. I do realise the

War Office will take its time to approve your transfer but hurry home, darling, before the storm carries me off.

Sometime next month I shall be sent to Wormwood Scrubs to await a review of my case by the Central Tribunal. If they offer me worthwhile civilian work under the Home Office, I shall accept it without any agonized debate. Fenner is refusing and will stay in prison or be returned to the army. Of all my friends in the Fellowship, he is the one I respect most but, at the risk of sounding like Gilbert Murray, the Regius Professor of Hypocrisy at Oxford, while I admire Fenner's steadfastness, I do not think staying in prison serves any purpose.

Now that my two months are up, I am allowed to tell you what I have discovered in the Bible. It is called the Song of Solomon, not the Rector's bedtime reading I imagine, but full of beautiful poetry.

Rise up, my love, my fair one, and come away,
For, lo, the winter is past, the rain is over and gone.

Even in the blackest moments, I never lost hope, my fair one, that we should have our Springtime together. And these lines, too, I shall note down and carry with me wherever I go.

Set me a seal upon thine heart, as a seal upon
thine arm; for love is strong as death.
Many waters cannot quench love, neither can the
Floods drown it.

I am so proud of what you have been doing and a little envious, too, but that is just the primitive male instinct that feels it is contrary to the natural order of things that you should be part of the battle while I am safe at home. Do I gather Theodore Hardy is that rare bird, an Anglican padre who goes near the frontline? If he is, I salute him and look forward to meeting him one day on the fells. Please tell him that not all conscientious objectors are cranks and that a man who is labelled a wont-fight-funk respects a man who risks his life to bring comfort to others.

I don't know how long it will be before I am released or where I shall be sent so please still send letters via my Theodore at the Fellowship's office.

Goodbye for now, darling. It is wonderful to think that we may see one another again soon.

With all my impatient love,
Tom

CHAPTER FIVE

Home Office Work Centre,
Ballachulish,
Fort William,
Scotland

13 December 1916

My darling,

This time two weeks ago I was a prisoner in Wormwood Scrubs and today I am a navvy building a road between Ballachulish and Kinlochleven. Technically, I am in Army Reserve W but unless I abscond or refuse to work, I shall be treated as a civilian for the rest of the war, not something I say with pride, though, God knows, I am glad to be out of prison.

My transition from West London to the Western Highlands was remarkably easy. At the Central Tribunal hearing, the chairman, who introduced himself as 'Salisbury', conducted the proceedings with the gruff courtesy you might except from a grandee who has been asked to undertake a disagreeable public duty, while the tribunal members could hardly have been more friendly. The following day, I was told by the governor that I had been recommended for release to work on the Home Office Scheme.

On Monday morning I walked out of Wormwood Scrubs in the clothes I had been wearing when I was arrested; like a faithful hound, the brown paper parcel containing my personal belongings had somehow tracked my movements so that when I went into the room to put off my prison uniform, there it was with my clothes, my Golden Treasury, my Yeats and even the two biscuits I had left behind. With a railway warrant in my pocket and no escort at my shoulder, I walked to the nearest underground. My instructions were to meet the other men who were joining the Home Office Scheme at King's Cross to catch the night train to Glasgow, so I had the whole day to myself – an extraordinary luxury after the last six months.

Theodore Taylor was not in the office but Bertrand Russell was there as he is acting chairman while Clifford Allen is in prison. He does not look like a philosopher, certainly not of the absent-minded variety, more like a man-about-town, neat and dapper with well-cut, expensive clothes. When I introduced myself he said, 'You're Grant Kennedy's son', and invited me to go with him that very afternoon to Garsington where Philip Morrell, the Liberal MP, has a house and where I should find 'kindred spirits' but I explained that I was hoping to see my father before travelling to Scotland.

Russell was not critical of my decision to leave prison but he told me that some of the absolutists are demanding from their prison cells that those of us who accept civilian work should be thrown out of the Fellowship. What he did not tell me is that he has himself been thrown out of his lectureship at Trinity, Cambridge for advocating resistance to conscription. My father told me the story when I caught up with him later in the day at the Athenaeum.

I had had no chance to warn my father that I was coming so when he heard I was in the hall, he came hurrying down the grand staircase obviously pleased to see me but then, taking one look at my crumpled clothes and open neck, he suggested that we should walk up to Piccadilly to find a café. My dear father, I think I shall always be something of an embarrassment to him and I am sure one of his secret hopes is that you will reform me or at least encourage me to wear a necktie.

We talked freely in an empty café but not about his work at the War Propaganda Bureau. He said he was very glad I had accepted the Home Office Scheme though he could not imagine what work of national importance I was going to do in Scotland. He asked about my time in France and in prison but I found myself reluctant to talk much about either. I told him I had met Bertrand Russell that morning. 'I hardly know him,' my father said. 'He is very seldom in college.' Then he told me the full story of Russell's dismissal. The college council was within its rights but twenty-two of the college fellows, including Edgar Adrian and my father, have signed a letter of protest. Adrian I would have expected but I was surprised and glad that my father had signed. He came to King's Cross with me and shook my hand and said, 'Good luck, Tom', like a father seeing his son off to boarding school.

Do you love your father? I know you do but isn't it easier for girls? I don't know whether I love my father but I am happy that we are closer now. Sometimes when I went to Grange Road, we met like travellers who now and then find themselves waiting for the same train and pass the time of day before going to their separate compartments.

So here I am, one of a motley collection of bank clerks, artisans, journalists, schoolmasters, research scientists and civil servants inexpertly wielding pickaxes and shovels on a Scottish mountainside to finish a road that Irish navvies started before the war. It is not the sort of alternative service we hoped for but we are determined to keep our side of the bargain and to make the Scheme work. We have all been in prison and experienced the brutal side of army discipline and, without feeling sorry for ourselves, we have used this shared experience to build a bond between us. Mercifully, there has been no quibbling about whether the road might one day be used by the military, so I suppose you could say that our conscientious objections have grown up.

The spirit of goodwill in the group – there are twenty-nine of us with more to follow – is greatly helped by the character of the chief foreman, a Macdonald from Glencoe, the next village on Loch Leven, who has built roads all over the Empire. He never raises his voice or expresses an opinion about conscientious objectors. We respect him as a professional and he treats us as willing amateurs with a lot to learn. He can split a large boulder with a single blow from his sledgehammer and enjoys demonstrating exactly where to strike.

The war seems very far away but we talk about it often. In the popular press we are portrayed as lilywhites and shirkers whose only concern is to save our own skins but we are as appalled as anyone else by the terrible loss of life and although what happened on the Somme may seem to justify our opposition to this war, it also sows seeds of doubt about whether opposing the war is still a good enough reason to stand aside. Don't the men in the trenches long for peace as much as we do?

I wish with all my heart that you and I could talk about this together because your opinion means more to me than any other and I need to know what you really think, to look into your eyes and hear your voice when you say you do understand why I am on a Scottish mountainside and not at the front.

Have you heard about your transfer yet? No one here knows whether we shall be allowed any leave but when I think of you coming home, I have a great surge of energy and wield my pickaxe like a madman until Mr Macdonald shouts at me to slow down. Should I tell him the truth – that just the thought of being in the same country as the woman I love makes me dizzy with desire?

Thank God, we shall be together soon.

Until then, all my love darling, and all my hopes for the future. Tom

In late November 1916, at about the same time as Tom was released from prison to build a road between Ballachulish and Kinlochleven, the fighting ended on the Somme and the pace of life in the Casualty Clearing Station changed dramatically. Casualties were still brought in but there were days when we had time on our hands. The weather changed too. After weeks of rain, there were cold clear nights and a hard frost and Kitty and I slept with an army greatcoat on top of our blankets and two pairs of our socks on our feet.

I received my movement order in the same week as Theodore Hardy. To his joy, he was posted to the 8th Battalion of the Lincolnshire Regiment at the front but, in typical army fashion, the War Office told me that, although my transfer to a military hospital in England had been approved, I was to go no further than the base hospital at Boulogne until a definite posting had been found.

Kitty and I saw Hardy off at the railhead and wished him good luck. When it was time for me to go, Kitty came on the hospital train to say goodbye. We had been the best and closest of friends since the day we left England and we tried to cover our sadness at parting by exclaiming in amazement at the luxury of the officer's berth in which I would be travelling, all polished wood, clean sheets and plump pillows. We held out until I said I wanted her to be a bridesmaid. She laughed at the thought at first and then she burst into sobs and I took her in my arms and we wept on each other's shoulder. 'Goodbye, darling,' she said and kissed my cheek. 'Make sure you marry the right man.'

I was prejudiced against Boulogne from the start because I did not want to be there and although the matron of the base hospital, which was housed in a former casino, was glad to see me, I was too anxious to be going home to feel that I was a full member of the nursing team. Without Kitty to accompany me, I turned down invitations to dance and dine with officers passing through Boulogne on their way to the front. When Christmas came, I volunteered for duty. The VADs decorated the wards and on Christmas Eve we formed a choir to sing carols, going from ward to ward carrying lanterns as we used to do at the London. In my pocket was Tom's homemade Christmas card.

'Darling, I am sorry I have no card to send but the Ballachulish postie, despite her cheeks as red as holly berries, makes no concessions to Christmas. Nor would she approve of my Christmas message but I hope you will. I love your body, soul, mind and spirit, though not always in that order. I love the way you always smile when I am riding my hobbyhorses and the way you frown a little when you are reading. I love the way you look when you do not know I am looking at you. I love your stillness, your high cheekbones and your golden hair. I love the way you saw right through me on the first day and the way you will be a mystery to me until the last day. I love you for saying 'yes' when any well-brought-up lady would have said 'Perhaps.' Happy Christmas, darling.

All my love,
Tom

Tom wooed me with words and I needed his words of love in those winter months more than ever before because I felt an intense frustration at the delay and I believed we were being kept apart now not by his stubborn integrity but by the army's incompetence. If the War Office could not organise the transfer of one Nursing Sister, it was time for a lesson in German efficiency.

Every morning, I looked at my pigeonhole hoping there would be a letter. Tom wrote twice a week from Scotland, describing his life and thoughts, the football match against the locals, the long sermon in the kirk on the text 'For many are called but few are chosen' and then, in a letter late in January, he hinted for the first time that he was disenchanted with the way his stand against the war and against conscription had turned out. The Home Office was closing his Work Centre at Ballachulish and concentrating all the conscientious objectors in one large centre on Dartmoor, a formula for trouble he thought.

If Tom was preparing to end his protest and join the army, I wanted to be with him. Once he made his decision, the army would want to get their hands on him as quickly as possible but I was determined that we should be married before he was sent overseas.

At last, my orders came through. I was to sail from Boulogne on 28 February and to report to the Neurasthenic Centre at Lancaster Military Hospital with the rank of Assistant Matron on 14 March, which meant I would have two weeks leave at home. Overjoyed, I wrote to my mother and to Tom telling them that with any luck I would be arriving at Victoria Station on the early morning of 1 March.

The matron at the base hospital who had sympathised with my frustration suggested that, as I would soon be leaving, I should give Boulogne a chance and take time off to explore the town. One of the sights, she told me, was the arrival of a new draft of British soldiers marching up from the docks and running the gauntlet of the local urchins who ambushed the columns, begging chocolates and cigarettes and offering to fix up an appointment with their sister for five francs.

So, wrapped in my cloak against the raw February afternoon, I joined the spectators and was amused to see the urchins fly away like birds at the sergeant's shout only to reappear a few moments later, while the officer at the head of the column tried to maintain an expression of dignified unconcern. Which is why I noticed this particular officer who was not marching at the head of his men but walking alongside the regimental sergeant major and chatting to him. He must have sensed my interest because when he was still a few yards away from where I was standing, he looked directly at me as he had done in the moribund ward but he gave no sign of recognition unless it was in the abruptness with which he turned away.

I assumed, or rather I pretended to assume, that he did not want to renew the acquaintance but when I returned to the hospital I asked if there had been any messages. Later that evening, when an orderly knocked on my door and said that there was a Major Melrose in the hall, I could think of no good reason not to go down.

The fair hair, pale blue eyes and freckled face were the same but whatever had seemed boyish about him in the Casualty Clearing Station had gone. He looked world-weary. He was in Boulogne for one night and would be glad if I would join him for dinner. I told him I was going home to be married in a few days time. 'Then we both have something to celebrate,' he said. 'You are going to be married, Katherine, and I am going to rejoin my regiment at the front.'

I was happy to accept the invitation for the most mundane reason; I was bored with sitting alone in my room every evening. I was afraid, too, that he might misinterpret my refusal as an attempt to suppress an emotion I did not want to acknowledge. 'I'll get my cloak,' I said.

Boulogne at night was a rough frontier town where, despite the freezing temperature, the streets were swarming with soldiers and military police, so that Harry took my arm and drew me close to him as we made our way to a restaurant near the Gare Maritime that had been designated for officers only. As we walked as one, I planned my tactics so that I would remain in control. I was not in love with Harry but he had persuaded himself that he wanted to fall in love with me. So that evening, I played a game, the rules of which he seemed to understand. When he sought an opening to declare his imaginary feelings, I refused to give him the opportunity. When he ordered champagne I asked about his wife. When he advanced his hand, I withdrew mine. When he told me that I had saved his life by giving him a reason to live, I said I was glad to see he had been promoted – Major Melrose sounded very grand.

In the end, Harry accepted defeat with a wry smile and talked of military matters. He was taking his men to Poperinghe tomorrow to link up with the Worcesters again in the Ypres Salient. His battalion had lost half its strength on the Somme and he doubted whether the conscripts he had brought over from England were good enough to fill the gap.

'And you,' I asked him. 'Have you fully recovered?' He knocked on his chest twice with his knuckles as though he expected to hear a reassuring answer. 'I'm as fit as a fiddle,' he replied. After being discharged from hospital, he had been given a dull job at the regimental depot but as soon as the medical board had moved him from C3 to A1 he had asked to be returned to his battalion. He said he was looking forward to seeing old friends, those who were left.

There was a midnight curfew in Boulogne and, although it did not apply to officers, it was generally observed by them. Harry said, 'I hope you will be very happy, Katherine,' and, raising his glass, he drank the last of the champagne.

I thanked him, relieved that he did not appear to be interested in the man I was going to marry, confirmation that the evening had no significance for either of us beyond the pleasure of each other's company. I would write a note for Kitty saying that she would be pleased to hear that the patient thought to be suffering from a fever had been wrongly diagnosed.

Two days before I sailed, I received a letter from Tom.

Princetown,
Dartmoor
Princetown Work Centre,
Devon

23 February 1917

My darling,

I would love to be at Victoria to meet you but there is no chance I'm afraid. They will give me a forty-eight hour pass for the weekend after next and I can be at Kirkby Lonsdale at nine-fifty on the Friday night. Forty-eight hours or what is left of it is far too short but we will be together at last. I can't wait or concentrate and am prey to all sorts of fantasies about things going wrong.

Every day I am more disillusioned with the way our stand against conscription has turned out and I do not think I can continue with this pretence that I am doing work of national importance. This place seems to have been designed to bring out the worst in every-body. About 300 of us are housed in the cells of the former prison and the work we are required to do has the lunatic logic of a penal settlement. Today, I have been one of a team of eight men har-nessed to a roller engaged in rolling a field. There are plenty of horses and one man and a horse could have done the job in a third of the time but there are not enough jobs to go round so to keep our critics in parliament and the press happy we must act our parts in a pantomime horse.

The stupidity of this plays into the hands of those who are intent on making trouble. The lazy, the 'fed-ups' and the cranks make common cause with the Marxists and anarchists who are here in large numbers. It took only three days for the Northcliffe press to find us and the Home Office agents made no attempt to prevent them taking photographs and interviewing the men, with the result that the papers this week have carried headlines such as 'Princetown's Pampered Pets' accompanied by pictures of smiling men who appear to have nothing to do but pose for the cameras. You can imagine what that does for the public's opinion of conscientious objectors.

There are men here who despite everything are still willing to make the Scheme work but they are rapidly losing heart because men who have used the conscience clause to get out of army service and don't give a damn what the public thinks of them are running rings round the Home Office agents. We never thought all the men who claimed to be conscientious objectors would be genuine but we thought the majority would be and now I am not so sure.

The irony is that I was offered a chance to work at Garsington and turned it down. We were given a three-day pass to travel from Ballachulish so I spent two nights with my uncle in London.

When I called at the office, Theodore Taylor suggested that while I was in London I should go round to the Morrell's house in Bloomsbury to see about a job at Garsington. Russell had evidently recommended me. The Morrells have a number of conscientious objectors working on their farm and in the gardens at Garsington and have asked the Home Office for more. Having nothing better to do, I went round` to Bedford Square that evening and found a party in full swing. I never thought I was such a puritan but when I saw the room full of people holding glasses of champagne and prancing about to gramophone music in clothes that looked as though they had been borrowed from a children's dressing-up box, I felt a Cromwellian revulsion. Perhaps the thought of your Casualty Clearing Station was too much in the forefront of my mind.

Our hostess, Philip Morrell's wife, Otteline, was weaving an exotic dance in the centre of the floor surrounded by swaying and bobbing admirers including Russell. I turned to go and saw a man in a dark suit standing by the wall watching me and clearly as ill at ease in these surroundings as I was. When I joined him, he told me that the scene we were witnessing made him think of the rich and powerful who barricaded themselves in their town houses during the Great Plague and partied while people were dying in the streets. 'Are you on leave?' I asked. 'I should be in the army,' he replied, 'but my wife would not let me go. I wangled a medical certificate from a friendly doctor.' His name is Toynbee and it turns out he is married to Gilbert Murray's daughter though he evidently does not share his father-in-law's lust for killing Germans.

The dance ended with shrieks of laughter and our hostess came over to us leading Russell by the hand. I must have sounded priggish to Russell when I turned down her offer of the job at Garsington but the prospect of becoming a pet monkey in her circus disgusted me.

An hour in Bloomsbury and two weeks on Dartmoor have convinced me of something that I have known for some time but not admitted to myself and that is there are only two courses open to a man of military age who has any trace of integrity left – to go to prison for his beliefs or to go to the front. I have considered asking for a transfer from the Army Reserve to active duty and the senior Home Office agent says it can be quickly arranged but after all this time I am still reluctant to betray the cause. I hate the thought of going back to prison even more but if you are to have any respect for me after the war and I am to have any respect for myself, I must do one thing or the other, doing neither is as dishonest as greasing the palm of a friendly doctor.

Don't read despair into my disenchantment; I shall be glad to escape from this shabby compromise. And when I realize that in only a few days time I shall see you and hold you again, everything else in my life is out of focus. Despair? I am the happiest man in the world.

All my love and much more.
Tom

It was just as well that matron at the base hospital had warned me that on the train to Victoria the subalterns would behave like hooligans and grab all the seats in the officers' carriages, leaving the Nursing Sisters to stand in the corridor. As soon as our ship docked at Folkestone, I hurried to the platform and, even so, had to use my elbows to secure a seat in one of the first class compartments. I was dead tired yet wide awake with the excitement of coming home and as the train pulled out of the station my poor opinion of subalterns was changed by a romantic gesture. A lieutenant took out his silver hip-flask and offered it to me. When I smiled and shook my head, he proposed a toast to 'England, home and beauty', which was taken up by the other officers in the compartment who turned to me and raised imaginary glasses as though I represented everything they had been fighting for.

At Victoria, the mass of soldiers going on leave pressed towards the exit and I let them go, so that by the time I reached the barrier much of the crowd had dispersed and it was easy to spot my mother, smiling and waving. Darling Mummy, I thought, she is always there when I need her most.

On the long journey to Kirkby Lonsdale we talked about the family – Amy had given up her job teaching at the Clergy Daughters School and was now a VAD at Wilton House near Salisbury which the Countess of Pembroke had converted into a private hospital for wounded officers – but it was not until the train left Crewe that we had the compartment to ourselves and I felt free to talk about Tom. I wanted my mother to understand that whatever Tom decided to do, I was determined to marry him as soon as possible.

'Your father and I both understand,' my mother said. 'The war has changed your father. I don't think he will ever believe that Tom was right but he admires Tom's moral courage. He still worries about you marrying a man who will be shunned after the war but he will not stand in your way.'

'I want more than that,' I said. 'I want his blessing and I want him to marry us.'

'You shall have his blessing and of course he will marry you. You have always been the apple of his eye.'

My father's change of heart, which was of such great importance to me, had not been a sudden conversion. During the two years I had been away, his certainty that England was in the right and Germany in the wrong had not wavered but the terrible loss of life over the last twelve months on the Somme and at Verdun had made him question in private what the purpose of prolonging the war might be. He had read my letters from the Casualty Clearing Station many times and on some mornings last summer, he had sat at the breakfast table running his eye down the casualty lists in disbelief. He had never said to my mother or to anyone else that he was in favour of a negotiated peace but when a group of parishioners had asked him at Christmas to hold a service of prayer for peace, he had readily agreed and was surprised and moved that so many people came.

My father's doubts about the conduct of the war had given my mother opportunities to talk about Tom and gradually she had seen his hostility replaced by a recognition that the man I wanted to marry was a patriot in his own way.

My mother asked me what I thought Tom would decide to do and I replied that I was almost certain he would join the army.

'And go on active service?'

'Yes.'

'Then we must tell your father that the wedding will have to be soon, before Tom is sent overseas.'

We changed trains in Carnforth and had to wait an hour for the local service so that it was dark when we reached Kirby Lonsdale. My father, who had been watching for our arrival, had fallen asleep in his chair and was wakened by the sound of the front door closing. In the warmth of his welcome any lingering anxiety I had about his attitude to Tom and to our marriage disappeared.

Princetown Work Centre
Princetown
Dartmoor
Devon

3 March 1917

My darling,

In one week exactly I shall hold you in my arms and kiss you. Just to be able to write that after so long is wonderfully exciting.

I have made my decision. Former absolutists are barred from joining the Friends' Ambulance Unit and the Red Cross so I have asked to be returned to the army and as I will not serve in the Non Combatant Corps, which I regard as just another dishonest evasion, I am bound to be treated as available for active service. If I am given a choice, I shall express a preference for the infantry. The Home Office agent says that I should receive orders to report to a training battalion when I come back from my weekend leave.

If that makes the decision sound easy, well so it was because, after thinking about it for so long, the pieces of the argument fell into place. I have done all I can to prevent conscription and there is nothing to be gained by returning to prison. I am not a pacifist and I have no time for the ruses people like Toynbee use to stay out of the trenches. I am not at all ashamed of my conscientious objection but once conscription was introduced the justification for it was no longer there. Although it has taken me several months to accept that, I am not sorry to have suffered a little for the cause I believed in.

As if to reassure me that I had made the right decision, one of our more flamboyant anarchists plucked a white feather from a chicken and presented it to me as we were assembling for work this morning. I am a traitor and a coward in their eyes. How curious the world is.

The agent thinks I shall be told to report to the depot of the Royal Fusiliers at Hounslow, the City of London regiment I would have joined last year if I had not applied for exemption. After six weeks training, I should have a week's embarkation leave before going overseas. Let's hope he's right. By my reckoning, that means we can be married in the first week in May.

I would have liked to ask Fenner to be my best man but he is still in prison. Theodore Taylor is rather old to be a best man though I am sure he would do it if I asked. What do you think? It is not as if I had a wide choice.

Goodnight darling. I love you with all my being.
Tom

CHAPTER SIX

Tom's visit to the Rectory on the weekend before he joined the army was so full of hope and the joy of our being together again that I shall always think of it as one of the happiest times of my life. Tom arrived late on Friday evening and I went to the station to meet his train. We had not seen one another for two years and I had forgotten that my future husband had a taste for the dramatic entrance. Just like a scene in the films, he emerged from the engine's smoke, an incomplete dark shape to begin with and then the man himself, bare-headed and carrying a small case.

He put down the case and, coming towards me, held out both his hands. When I placed my hands on his, I felt the roughness of his skin. We stood like that without saying a word, gazing into each other's eyes, savouring the moment of rediscovery, until we could resist no longer and our first kiss came as a wonderful release.

On our way back to the Rectory, I told him of my father's change of heart and he said that he, too, had been changed by his experience and bore no resentment against my father for opposing our marriage. 'The war has made us both doubt what we believed so strongly two years ago,' he said.

There was no light in the churchyard except from the windows of the Rectory and we lingered in the shadows, reluctant to share our reunion with anyone else. I raised Tom's right hand to my lips and kissed the rough skin on his palm. Wielding a pickaxe on a Scottish hillside would make it easier for him to pass himself off as a navvy, I said, knowing how easily my teasing provoked him but I was unprepared for the fierceness of his response. Kitty was right. The sooner we were married the better.

My mother and father did everything they could to make Tom welcome. My mother's strategy was to prevent at all costs a repeat of the bitter argument Tom had had with my father on his last visit. I noticed, not without a stab of jealousy, that she and Tom seemed to have established an understanding, exchanging glances if the conversation seemed to be drifting into a dangerous area.

Though it was late, my father insisted that we should all sit round the fire in his study. He had given up alcohol for the duration of the war, following the example of the king, so he offered Tom a glass of home made dandelion and burdock which Tom accepted cheerfully though I was sure he would have preferred a whisky.

Their conversation stuttered at first but once they moved on from polite exchanges to politics, they began to disagree like old friends. My father thought Asquith had been shabbily treated and that Lloyd George was as slippery as an eel but Tom argued that Lloyd George, whatever his faults, was the only politician strong enough to stand up to the generals and stop them launching another bloody offensive like the Somme.

For once, I was content to let the men think politics was their preserve because I could tell that by finding a subject on which they could disagree without ill feeling, they were wiping out the memory of their earlier quarrel but I could not help reflecting that I was the only person in the room who knew what the war was really like. When they discussed the prospects for peace in 1917, my father prophesied that we should have peace before the year was out. Tom glanced at my mother before saying, 'I hope you're right. I have no wish to be a hero.' And then he added, 'But it depends on what happens in Russia and what the Americans decide to do.'

There was a brief silence. Then my father stood up and put the guard in front of the dying fire. He shook Tom's hand and said, 'Goodnight Tom. I'm very glad to know you better.'

I have been told that bigamy was the one crime that increased during the Great War and it is true that some women rushed into marriages with soldiers they hardly knew so it is not surprising that my father, before he published the banns, should have asked Tom whether he was aware of any impediment to our being married. The four of us were sitting in the drawing room after breakfast on Saturday morning and had agreed that the best date for the wedding was 2 May, on the assumption that Tom's embarkation leave would start the day before.

Tom shook his head. He knew of no impediment unless it was his poor prospects of finding a job after the war. There was already talk in the newspapers of banning absolutists from all sorts of jobs because they had failed to serve their country.

'But you're joining the army Tom,' I said. 'That will make all the difference.'

I had spoken too emphatically and regretted it at once. It must have sounded to Tom and to my parents as though persuading Tom to join the army had been my goal all along. My father came to my rescue. 'Your fiancé is a man of unusual honesty and moral courage, Katherine, and no country worth our loyalty would discriminate against that.'

In the afternoon, Tom and I escaped. It was a wild March day and, buffeted by the wind, we had no hope of climbing to Fox's Pulpit as we had done on Christmas Eve in 1914, so we made a wide circuit following the beautiful river valley towards Barbon and then cut across the fields to Carsterton where I had been at school.

Coming back into the town, we stopped on the Devil's Bridge and leaned against the parapet to watch the river sweeping the broken branches downstream. It was our last full day together before we were married and we wanted to spend as much time as possible on our own without upsetting my mother and father. Tom was fascinated by the power of the water as it rushed under the bridge and I was looking at his profile and wondering whether our first child would have his dark complexion, when he said, 'If I am blinded or badly disabled, I don't want you to spend the rest of your life looking after me.'

Men in the Casualty Clearing Station had asked me to write almost exactly those words but I was shocked to hear Tom use them.

I said to him, 'I love you and I will look after you for ever Tom, even if you come back in one piece.' Making light of dark possibilities was his speciality but I was learning from him.

He had to leave on Sunday morning because by 1917 civilian trains could no longer be relied on. I went with him to the station and we walked up and down the deserted platform talking about what we should wear for our wedding, until the station master emerged from his hideaway to call, 'Carnforth, train for Carnforth'. Tom released the strap and let the window of his compartment fall. 'If we both wear uniform, do I have to salute you?' He asked as the train pulled away.

I laughed and replied, 'Yes, of course.'

The following day I reported to the Neurasthenic Centre at Lancaster Military Hospital. When I joined, the centre had eighty-three shell shock cases or, as the centre preferred to call them, psychiatric casualties, in a total hospital population of about five hundred. As an assistant matron, I was put in charge of the five shell shock wards even though I had had no training in psychological medicine and at first had little sympathy for some of the men. You have to remember that the idea that a soldier could be a casualty as a result of some form of mental breakdown was new and was not accepted even by some of the doctors at Lancaster. One of the doctors, who had worked in medical insurance fraud before the war, told me when I arrived that in his view treatment was a poor substitute for what he called 'firing squad therapy'.

I tried to keep an open mind but it was difficult when I recalled the boys in the 'children's ward' at Rouen and the men in the Casualty Clearing Station. The patently genuine cases were men whose symptoms ranged from total paralysis and deaf-mutism to curvature of the spine and other men whose shattered nerves made them incontinent so that they were painfully embarrassed to tell a nurse they had wet their bed.

All my patients were other ranks – officers had their own shell shock hospital at Craiglockhart in Scotland – and gradually, as I got to know them better, I developed a professional interest in their condition though I continued to suspect that one or two of them were exceptionally clever actors.

Tom and I wrote regularly to one another and to my great relief he seemed to be adapting easily to army life. I had been afraid that his past might be held against him or that he would refuse to conform to some of the sillier demands of military discipline but he was a good soldier who was content to serve in the ranks and to observe the curiosities of army life with a journalist's eye.

Private T. Kennedy
501784
Regimental Depot
The Royal Fusiliers
Hounslow
Middx

28 March 1917

My darling,

Our training ends on 30 April and, although as you know nothing is certain in the army, 2 May still looks all right and that will give us as many days as possible for our honeymoon. I asked our platoon sergeant about embarkation leave and after the ritual expressions of outrage that I should have dared to ask so soon, he told me that embarkation leave was not an entitlement, that some drafts were given six days and others none and that it was entirely at the discretion of the War Office.

Time passes quickly despite the boring, repetitive nature of our training. For the last ten days, I have been doing willingly what I did under protest before and Sergeant Baxendale, mistaking my familiarity with army life for keenness, holds me up as an example to the other men who have come straight from their city offices and have great difficulty learning how to put their puttees on correctly. The secret of my success will, I hope, remain a secret but I am already regarded as something of an authority on military matters by my platoon. They are Londoners, mostly married men whose call up was deferred and who probably prayed the war would be over before their group came up, so I don't think they will hold my past against me if they discover the truth. I have no idea whether the officers and NCOs know that I was a conscientious objector but I fancy not because they would have made a comment by now.

At least half our days are spent on the square. Today we took two hours to learn how to salute at the pay table and every mistake we made was greeted with insult and obscenity. The idea, I am sure, is to destroy our individuality and rebuild us as a single unit that will obey orders without question but swearing at us from dawn till dusk will never achieve that. These are intelligent men who want to know why they are being told to do apparently pointless tasks such as polishing the nails on the bottom of their boots, yet the army treats them as dumb animals whose only role is to respond unhesitatingly to words of command. There must be a better way to instil discipline and esprit de corps. Yesterday, I learnt, but only by chance, that the Royal Fusiliers had won the first two VCs in this war and even I felt something akin to regimental pride. Why doesn't the army try that for a change instead of this endless drill? Saluting at the pay table! How the Germans must be quaking in their leather boots. Don't worry; our letters are not censored until we go overseas.

What is happening in Russia is very exciting but it is typical of the army's mentality that we have been told not to discuss the events in Petrograd, presumably because they fear we might shoot our officers and take over the depot. My father and Gilbert Murray will have been delighted to hear that the Tsar has abdicated as they will no longer have to portray him as a champion of liberty but, for my part, I shall be content if the Provisional Government demands that the Allies make peace.

Write soon to tell me the doctors at Lancaster are all old and grey and that you have refused promotion to matron.

With all my love, darling.
Tom

Royal Fusiliers
Hounslow

Sunday 8 April 1917

My darling Katherine,

I have the honour to invite you to a wedding at the Church of St. Mary the Virgin in Kirkby Lonsdale on Wednesday 2 May at 12 noon or any other hour that is convenient for you, remembering that the last train from Carnforth to London leaves at five minutes passed five. I don't know whether to thank God or Lloyd George or Sergeant Baxendale but our embarkation leave is fixed for 1 to 6 May. I must catch the troop train from Victoria at the crack of dawn on 7 May. My father will book rooms for himself, Theodore Taylor and myself at the Royal Hotel on Tuesday night and I am writing to Brown's Hotel in Mayfair to make sure that, wherever else our honeymoon takes us, we can spend the last night there.

You can imagine how Sergeant Baxendale broke the news. He cannot understand the War Office's decision. We are the worst intake it has been his misfortune to train and he dreads to think what will happen to us in the Bull Ring at Etaples, which he calls 'Eat Apples', where the training is ten times harder than here. It goes without saying that we are a disgrace to the regiment and that the Royal Fusilier battalions in France would rather go into action under strength than have us as replacements.

I am beginning to like Sergeant Baxendale. Not only does he bring good tidings and stubbornly clings to the idea that I am a born soldier who should sign on after the war but increasingly he allows us to hear the note of self-mockery in his outbursts. Rumour has it that he will be coming with us to France which I hope is true because he is a regular who went out in 1914 and was wounded whereas our platoon officer is an eighteen year-old straight from public school who wears white gloves to inspect our barrack room so that he can detect any speck of dust.

We still spend too much time learning useless drill movements but bayonet practice and visits to the butts break the monotony and it would be churlish of me not to admit that when we start singing over the last mile or so of our weekly route march, we feel good about being soldiers. After each march, we have a foot inspection when it is drummed into us that care of the feet is a soldier's second most important duty, the first being of course to obey orders instantly and without thinking.

Only three more weeks. As the day approaches, the married men are giving all sorts of advice, some of it contradictory and almost all of it unprintable but there is wide agreement that I am especially fortunate to be marrying a nurse and then I smile to myself because these men will never know just how fortunate I am.

You shouldn't worry too much whether all your shell shock men are genuine. At least they have been to the front. My madness is of a different kind and happily there is no cure.

With much love, darling,
Tom

Royal Fusiliers
Hounslow

25 April 1917

My darling,

Do you remember when you asked me why I wanted to marry you and I replied 'Because I want you all to myself' and you said that was the wrong answer? Well, the right answer is because I am in love with you and want to spend the rest of my life with you and want you to be the mother of our children but wanting you all to myself hasn't gone away and probably never will.

Don't be surprised if I appear at the Rectory looking like a travelling man with all his worldly goods on his back because the army insists that we go on leave in full marching order. I shall have to drop my kit at the Royal Hotel before the rehearsal. I don't think I shall fluff my lines on the day though my heart will be pounding when I turn round to see you coming up the aisle so if I sound breathless when I make my vows you will know why.

Our training continues until Monday when some high-up is coming to inspect us and no doubt to tell us how lucky we are that the war has lasted long enough for us to make our contribution, while we stand at ease and dream of leave and love and speculate on how long it will be before the Americans can arrive in sufficient numbers to make the Kaiser see sense. I don't want to kill anyone and I cannot work up any feeling of hostility towards the ordinary German soldiers who must be longing for the war to end as much as we are. I don't think my views about the war have changed. I take part in it reluctantly and only because my hopes of preventing conscription have collapsed so I am intrigued that Sergeant Baxendale thinks I am a born soldier. Perhaps he sees in me something that I do not want to see in myself. He hinted the other day that when our training in France is completed, I should put in for promotion to lance corporal. More pay of course but he clearly does not know that my past would disqualify me.

Darling, this is the last letter I shall write to you as your fiancé and it may be the last letter that will not have to be censored though one of the married men has been told that he will be able to send uncensored letters from the front if he certifies the contents are only private and family matters.

Until Tuesday with all my love, darling.
Tom.

Tom and I were married by my father in his church of St. Mary the Virgin on a perfect English day in early summer. Tom had suggested that as our two families would barely fill the first pew on either side of the aisle, my father should issue an open invitation to his parishioners and on the day so many came with their families that our wedding had something of the atmosphere of a church fete. Tom and I were delighted to see them all but Mrs Bickersteth might have been overwhelmed if the parishioners had not brought their own contributions to the reception. From mid-morning they started arriving, the men in their Sunday best and all the women, young and old, wearing hats. They placed their cakes, scones, savouries and plates of sandwiches on the trestle tables Mrs Bickersteth had hurriedly provided. It seemed as though the people of Kirkby Lonsdale, who had once put white feathers in the collection bag, had conspired to use the occasion of our wedding not just to forget the past but to defy the shortages and hardships of the present. Where the sugar and butter came from my mother could not imagine and thought it better not to ask.

Even Mrs Bickersteth's gloomy philosophy – she had already vetoed poppies in my bouquet because they would bring bad luck – could not check the festive spirit. When the cake-bearers greeted her by saying, 'It's a lovely day for a wedding, Mrs Bickersteth,' and she replied, 'So it is but we shall pay for it later,' they just laughed. What did they care about later when there was so much to enjoy today?

I wore my mother's wedding dress of creamy raw silk and the veil of Bruges lace my great-grandmother had worn when she married the young ensign who had fought at Waterloo. The dress had been kept in a black tin trunk in the attic and although we had hung it out in the breeze for several hours, it still had a faint smell of camphor, which I thought Tom might notice.

My godfather, John Garth, a sheep farmer from Kingsdale, gave me away and my only bridesmaid was my younger sister Amy. It would have been wonderful if Kitty had been able to come over but she did send a postcard with a picture of the town of Ypres on one side and on the other: *Good luck, dearest Katherine, it's a great life, remember. We have moved to Poperinghe and the war has started up again. Miss you. Love Kitty.*

I was not at all nervous until I stood in the South porch with my godfather waiting for a signal from the churchwarden that the congregation had settled. Then I confess that for a moment I had second thoughts, not about marrying Tom but about marrying at all. The churchwarden soon reappeared and held open the door for us and as we entered the church the organist played the opening bars of the bridal march.

My mother and Mrs Bickersteth had decorated the church without a penny spent. At each end of the altar step was a large flower pot filled with sweet cicely, columbine and bluebells backed by fresh beech and chestnut leaves. Mrs Bickersteth had picked the bluebells at the last minute in the wood beyond the Rectory garden.

John Garth was in no hurry and I was glad because I wanted my wedding dress to take everyone, but especially Tom, by surprise. At the rehearsal the evening before I had told him a white lie. He had walked over from the Royal Hotel with his father and his best man, Theodore Taylor. When I saw him for the first time in the uniform of the Royal Fusiliers, I thought that his Sergeant Baxendale was probably right, for Tom looked every inch a born soldier.

I would have loved to have been close enough to see the expression on his face when he saw me in my wedding dress and veil. According to Mrs Bickersteth, who was not even there but guarding the wedding cake in the Rectory garden, Tom's expression was the subject of debate and diagnosis during the signing of the register, some people saying that he frowned to hide his lust while others argued that he was seeing his bride's true beauty for the first time and was frowning to hold back his tears. When he stepped out to stand beside me, the highly polished nails on the soles of his boots clattered briefly on the tiled floor.

I wrote to Kitty soon after Tom had left for France, complaining that the marriage service was far too short – one moment you were standing with your fiancé facing the altar and the next it was all over. When Tom lifted my veil and kissed me, I still thought of him as my fiancé and when we walked forward hand in hand to kneel at the altar for my father's blessing, I had to tell myself that Tom was now my husband and I was his wife. 'His hand holding mine was hot and rough,' I wrote to Kitty. 'It reminded me that he had said he was marrying me because he wanted me all to himself. Well, for a few days he had his heart's desire but I shall have to wean him from his possessiveness.'

We walked down the aisle arm in arm, Tom cheerfully acknowledging the smiles of strangers, and out into the sunshine, breaking the daisy chain that Mrs Bickersteth had hung across the porch.

The reception in the Rectory garden was a crowded, happy, informal affair with children running hither and thither and some of the parishioners walking round the tables to ensure their cakes were well displayed. The only beverage served was my father's favourite dandelion and burdock but no one seemed to mind and all the toasts were drunk with the customary enthusiasm.

One of the joys for me that afternoon was to see my father and Tom's father together. Tom's father was a fellow of Trinity and Kirkby Lonsdale was a Trinity living. Yet I did not think they were just affirming the freemasonry of Cambridge men because each time I passed them in my weaving through the crowd they seemed to be more and more enjoying each other's company. When I found my mother, she said that she, too, had noticed how well the two fathers were getting on. 'They're probably congratulating each other,' she said with a smile. 'Men usually do.'

My father made a speech and so did Tom but the star turn was Tom's best man, the Quaker Theodore Taylor, who surprised everyone with a charming and eloquent speech to propose the health of the solitary bridesmaid and to wish Tom and I the chance to bring up our children in a world of peace. 'O God of Love, O King of Peace,' he concluded, in words that Tom would have recognised. 'Make wars throughout the world to cease.' At any other time, this sentiment might have made his listeners question his patriotism but not today.

I had always thought that the bride and groom should make a wish together when they cut the wedding cake but when Tom said we should both make our own wish, Mrs Bickersteth nodded approvingly though God knows which of her superstitious lay behind that. My silent wish was that Tom should come home safely.

He had arranged with the Royal Hotel for a Brougham to pick us up at 4 o'clock so that we should be in good time to catch the London train at Carnforth. I would have to wear my QA uniform to go away because on the morning of Tom's departure for France I was due to return direct to Lancaster but couples wearing uniform on their honeymoon were not at all unusual and neither Tom nor I gave it a second thought. While I changed, my mother hung the wedding dress outside the wardrobe to air for a few days before she put it back in the tin trunk with its camphor balls and sheets of tissue paper. I owed my mother so much and wanted to tell her before I left but when she put her arms round me all I managed to say was 'Darling Mummy' because I was afraid that if I said any more we would both burst into tears.

The parishioners lined the path from the Rectory to the South Gates where the Brougham was waiting. I kissed my father and Tom's father though Tom rather formally shook hands. The parishioners waved and smiled as we passed and some shouted 'Good luck'. Although Tom said it was amazing what a difference a uniform made, I think he was wrong and that the people of Kirkby Lonsdale did not have the war on their minds but were just wishing us well as a young married couple starting out on our life together.

For the first four nights of our honeymoon we stayed in a small hotel in Bloomsbury but on our last night we moved to Brown's Hotel in Mayfair. This was a favourite with officers on leave which made me think that Tom had chosen it to show me that despite the uniform of an ordinary soldier, he was as good as any of them.

Tom and I spent only five days and nights together as man and wife and we were both inexperienced but we were so much in love and so ready to cast off all restraint that we were not denied the ecstasy for which we had waited so long. Tom was a fiercely passionate lover and I opened my heart to him and I was sure we would have a wonderfull full life together if we were given the chance.

On the day of Tom's departure, the early morning sun poured in at our window, which was high up over Albermarle Street facing east towards Piccadilly. As Tom had said he hated the idea of saying goodbye to me at Victoria Station with all the men in his battalion crowding round, we had decided to say goodbye in the privacy of our room but I quickly realised that this was a mistake. In the small room that was all we could afford, Tom became impatient with the equipment he had to put on and our last kiss was rushed. Yet I knew he loved me and that what he would be remembering on his journey was not one snatched kiss but all the moments of intense happiness we had shared.

He left me a letter with instructions not to open it until he had gone.

Brown's Hotel
Albermarle Street,
London W1

An unearthly hour, 7 May 1917

My darling,
It is just 4 o'clock and the sky outside is already lighter. You are fast asleep, your face almost hidden by your golden hair and your breathing so soft I can hardly hear it. I am sitting by the window watching over you and thinking that if ever a man had a powerful motive for surviving this war and returning to his land of heart's desire, I am that man. I would never have believed that it was possible to be more deeply in love with you but I am because for these last few days and nights I have been in paradise. I hate being thrown out of paradise, particularly at this hour in the morning, but, unlike Adam, I plan to return.

We both know what could happen and we agreed not to dwell on that but I want to write down for you what I told you last night. I am not sure about life after death but I am sure that if I should be killed, my love for you will not die with me and that wherever you are, my love will be with you always.

I shall have to leave in two hours time but I wish I could slip out now while you are still sleeping and slip back one day soon when the war is over. I shall come back. I am far too unheroic to take foolish risks.

Goodbye for now, my dearest, darling Katherine.

With all my love for ever,
Tom

CHAPTER SEVEN

Tom wrote as often as he could or sent a field postcard to let me know he was all right. My letters from France had not been censored because QAs were treated as officers but a private soldier's letters were read by his platoon commander, in theory to prevent military secrets falling into German hands but everybody knew the real purpose was to hide signs of disaffection and low morale from the people at home. Once a month, a soldier was allowed to send an uncensored letter in an envelope with green borders as long as he signed the undertaking on the outside that the contents were 'nothing but private and family matters'. If Tom learnt nothing else in prison, he learnt how to cheat the system and I received two or even three green envelopes each month.

As long as he was not in the front line, I did not worry about him. He had seen enough of army discipline one way or another to stay out of trouble and the fact that he had been a conscientious objector does not appear to have been known to his superiors. Remembering how much I had appreciated parcels from home, I sent Tom some of the luxuries I had enjoyed as well as more practical things such as shaving soap and health salts.

With Tom overseas, I chose to work extra shifts at Lancaster and, spending more time on the wards, I increasingly identified with the patients and with those doctors who were sympathetic to them and not with the army's Top Brass who were very suspicious of our failure to return more men to active service. I had the impression that what these senior military men really objected to was seeing ordinary soldiers being treated as individuals and with the sort of consideration normally reserved for wounded officers. There may have been malingerers among our psychiatric casualties at Lancaster but, as Tom pointed out, they had all been at the front, in some cases for two or three years.

We divided the cases into slight, borderline and acute according to their symptoms not the length of their probable stay in the hospital for it was a curious aspect of shell shock that a man with acute symptoms could recover overnight but a man suffering from nothing more than chronic fatigue might not be discharged for several months. It was tempting to think of the slight cases as possible malingerers and the acute cases as genuine but the latter's sudden recovery sometimes made me think the reverse was true. I kept medical notes on all the men and two cases in particular have stuck in my mind. They were friends in the same regiment; one was very neurotic and could not stop shaking and the other suffered from complete loss of speech. One morning their symptoms disappeared and they asked to be returned to their regiment at the front. Were they hysterics or malingers? I did not know and neither did the doctors.

I shared my thoughts on such cases with Tom but he seldom commented and I was slow to realise why this was. Like other men in the trenches, he wanted to hear about ordinary, everyday things. His letters to me were a marvellous antidote to the twilight world of real and imagined shell shock. I could tell that he was in good spirits most of the time and that he had not lost his ability to see the funny side of army life. I tried to respond in the same cheerful manner but when rumours of a new offensive appeared in his letters and in the newspapers, I found it hard to hide my anxiety from him. We had both been so certain that Lloyd George would not allow the generals to risk the sort of casualties we had suffered the previous summer but once again there was talk of a 'decisive battle' and a 'final breakthrough' and I knew better than Tom what these fine phrases meant.

Every night I prayed for his safe return. From our earliest childhood, Amy and I had knelt at the bed side to say our prayers – 'Let your light so shine before men' our father had taught us – and even as a probationer at the London Hospital and sharing a room with Kitty in France, I had continued to do so. For all her cynicism, Kitty never mocked my religion though occasionally she asked me to put in a good word for her. The God I worshipped would have time for Kitty just as he would for my Doubting Thomas. Tom said that his doubts were the only evidence he had that his faith existed and I asked God to help him overcome his doubts because I had seen the look of terror on the face of men who were dying without hope. Many people lost their Christian faith during the war but I was lucky. My faith was so firmly secured in the love and teaching I had received from my father and mother that I was confident it would ride at anchor even when the worst storms blew.

Private T. Kennedy
N0: 501784
12th Royal Fusiliers
BEF

18 May 1917

My darling,

I never thought I would welcome being driven to the point of exhaustion every day but our training has this virtue that it helps me to forget if only for a short while how much I am missing you. But then the pain of being separated comes rushing back and even the most foul-mouthed canary – as the instructors here are called on account of their yellow armbands – shouting in my ear cannot make it go away again.

The Bull Ring outside Etaples is as bad as Sergeant Baxendale warned us it would be. The atmosphere is as bleak and bitter as the location. We have another four weeks to go and if one of our number does not lose his head before the end and stick a bayonet in one of the canaries I shall be surprised. Men are punished harshly for the slightest offence. 'Hesitating to obey an order' will earn a man

five days Field Punishment No 1 and just in case we were thinking
of running away, Daily Orders publish the details of men who have
been brought here to be shot for desertion. And we thought the
Germans were a militaristic people.

To put your mind at rest, there is no risk of this letter being
opened but we are only allowed one of these green envelopes a
month and all other letters have to be read by our platoon officer.
If he was a man I respected that would not be so bad but Second
Lieutenant the Hon Rupert Grice (he of the 'White Gloves') is not
fit to be in charge of a Boys' Brigade. I cannot stomach the thought
of his reading what I really want to say to you; so I shall either save
up two or three private letters to put in my monthly uncensored or
find a way to get more of these much sought after green envelopes.
They exchange hands for a high price and some enterprising men
make a handsome profit buying and selling.

We had a fine journey over, calm sea, blue sky, and we reached
Boulogne with our destroyer escort in under an hour and a half.
Then on the march to the station we were accompanied by women
and girls who wanted to swap their apples for our cigarettes and
White Gloves made a fool of himself trying to drive them off with
his stick. Thank goodness Sergeant Baxendale is still with us. Seeing
him quickly take control of the situation, I am sure I was not alone
in thinking that the sooner White Gloves is promoted or wounded
the better.

There are said to be 100,000 men here, raw recruits such as ourselves and men who have been at the front but who are thought to
have lost 'the offensive spirit'. In our first week, we have had three
lectures on the importance of this offensive spirit, in between ses-
sions of bayonet fighting, rapid loading and firing, learning how to
recognise tear gas and lots of drill. It is a 45-minute march from the
camp to the Bull Ring and by the time we are back to our tents in
the evening, we are dead tired. If the aim is to develop our stamina,
the intensive training works but if the aim is to make us keen to kill
the enemy, it doesn't. The canaries make it abundantly clear that
the offensive spirit means a lust for killing Germans, even German

prisoners. 'Remember boys', one instructor told us, 'every German prisoner means a day's rations gone.' But the general view over our hot evening meal in the Church Army's 'Tipperary Hut' is that if we had a choice, we would rather kill our canaries than German prisoners.

The intense dislike of these Base Wallahs – instructors, drill sergeants, military police – who have a safe job for the duration is so widespread it must be exactly what the Top Brass wants. Somehow or other the army has to engender the offensive spirit in men who wouldn't give a damn for the country's war aims if they knew what they were. There is no talk of patriotism here and certainly no hatred of the Germans so the only way the army can make us fight is to bully us until we are ready to bayonet anybody

Is it really only eleven days since we said goodbye? Time always dragged its feet when we were apart but now more than ever because I have tasted the fruits of paradise and know what I am missing. Write as soon as you can. I want to know everything you are doing and whether you have been home and how your mother and father are and whether Mrs. Bickersteth has found any signs of approaching peace in the entrails of a chicken.

Darling, please send another photograph – either the one you had taken in Cambridge or one in your wedding dress or both – because the photo I have is already badly creased. And a stick of indelible pencil, too, if possible.

Though I am very unhappy to have been taken away from you, I am not unhappy to have abandoned my conscientious objection. While I shall never be the born soldier of Sergeant Baxendale's imagination, I enjoy the comradeship and get on well with the other men in the platoon. Some are curious to know what I am doing in the ranks but they do not press me and my murky past remains a secret.

I love you so much.
Goodnight darling,
Tom.

501784 Private T. Kennedy
D Coy, 12ᵗʰ Royal Fusiliers,
BEF

13 June 1917

My darling,
I have sent you a field PC to say 'I am quite well' so that I can save this letter for my next green envelope.

I am quite well. The weather is glorious and we have survived our baptism of fire. There is a war going on but all the talk is of D Company's chances in the brigade football competition that starts when we go back for a period of rest.

We left Etaples in high spirits but had to endure a monumental military box-up before we started. We paraded in pitch darkness at 1.30 am to march to the station but then we were kept waiting in our cattle trucks for 12 hours, the train eventually leaving at 2pm. The transport officers who refused to accept any responsibility for the delay were lucky not to be lynched. No one told us where we were going but we arrived there after dark at about 10pm and marched to our camp where we heard the guns clearly for the first time.

The nearby town is called Poperinghe but it was not our final destination; 'Pop' is just the last outpost of civilization in these parts. Belgian people are still living there and it is the jumping-off point for all troops coming into this sector. Didn't you say that Kitty's Casualty Clearing Station was at Poperinghe? In the morning we were allocated to companies and, to our great relief, almost all of us are in D Company with Bob Baxendale as our platoon sergeant. However our prayers that White Gloves would be allocated to a different platoon or given leave and washed overboard in the Channel have not been answered.

From Poperinghe, we travelled by train to somewhere in Belgium where we marched through the ruined town and out to the canal bank to join the 12ᵗʰ battalion. It is a far cry from Brown's Hotel. We bed down fifteen to a dug-out with a couple of blankets each and duckboards on the damp earth. You feel the rats running over you all through the night but after the first few nights you don't bother with them. Most nights are spent on fatigues anyway, which for us means carrying a 60-pound trench mortar on the end of an iron rod for a mile and a half to the front line along a road that is swept by German machine guns. We were all pretty windy at first but Sergeant Baxendale kept us moving and seemed to know instinctively when to get off the road. 'Fritz is a methodical fellow' was all he would say by way of explanation when we returned safely.

19 June

We have just done five days in the front line and are back at the canal convinced that we are proper soldiers at last though we were in no real danger unless it was from the rats that were larger from feeding on the bodies in No Man's Land and provoked a correspondingly more aggressive response from us. Can the rats, too, be part of the army's master plan to develop the offensive spirit?

I left my pack in the dug-out the first time I was on sentry and found a big hole in it when I returned as the rats had been after my biscuits. Sentry duty is tedious because nothing happens but I have time to think about you and about the German soldier on sentry duty two hundred yards away who is thinking about his wife or girlfriend and who has no more interest in killing me than I have in killing him. We do two hours on and four hours off, the latter spent trying to sleep in the dug-out in full equipment and hoping that our fat rodent friends know the difference between the living and the dead. I do sentry duty with Jim Bellringer, my mucking-in partner – we brew tea together. He is typical of the married men who joined with me: older and better educated than the average conscript, fed up that the war has interrupted his career in the bank and worried that his family may not be able to manage on his separation allowance. Jim is not a bad soldier but he is no more inclined to take unnecessary risks than I am. He showed me a picture of his wife and two young daughters and I showed him my pictures of you and in this way we have sealed an unspoken pact to help one another survive.

We will have to do one more stint in the line before we have ten days rest back at Poperinghe. There are the usual rumours about a decisive battle on our front this summer that will win the war and see us home for Christmas and although publicly we dismiss the rumours as rubbish, privately we nurse them because we hope they contain a germ of truth. Shall we spend Christmas in Kirkby Lonsdale? I think we should but next year we must start looking for a place of our own.

I will write again as soon as we reach the rest camp.

Until then, all my love, darling.
Tom

501784 Private T. Kennedy
D coy, 12th Royal Fusiliers
BEF

28/30 June 1917

My darling,

It was wonderful to receive your two letters when we came out of the line. Thank God for normal, everyday things – never think I will find them boring. I remember your saying that you did not feel the war was real despite the terrible wounds and I have the same sense of unreality. Of course, we have had it easy so far but whether we are in the line or back here at rest camp, I find myself longing to know what you are doing in the real world where people are sane so please don't stop telling me.

Here we must at least pretend to be mad because sanity is a serious offence. Live and let live is our attitude to our German friends; the night patrols ignore one another even though they pass close by because no one wants to kill or be killed unnecessarily but if the

Top Brass discovered our troops were behaving in such a rational manner there would be hell to pay. No one, however, could accuse Jim and I of lacking the offensive spirit; our bag so far is five certain and three probable rats killed. But when it comes to German soldiers, to the Huns or as Sergeant Baxendale likes to call them 'the square-headed swabs', I don't think Jim and I will pull the trigger unless it is their life or ours.

I am sorry to be a few days late with this letter – the rest camp proved to be nothing of the sort. But today we have a pass to Poperinghe. On Sergeant Baxendale's recommendations, Jim and I and one or two others have come to Talbot House, a club run by two CofE chaplains where there is no distinction between officers and other ranks or between religious faiths. That sounded too good to be true but when I sat down in this battered armchair I found myself next to a Roman Catholic chaplain who has the rank of Captain but introduced himself simply as Peter Quinn. He was a monk at Downside Abbey before the war and when I expressed surprise he told me that several Benedictine monks had volunteered to serve as chaplains. He is much the same age as I am and is the Catholic chaplain attached to our brigade so I rather hope our paths will cross again.

Our second five-day spell in the front line was not much more eventful than the first. The only danger was from snipers and the occasional perfunctory burst of machine-gun fire. Sergeant Baxendale kept warning us against the stray bullets as though, like stray dogs, they were seeking a home. Our only casualty was a man in our section who twisted his ankle so badly jumping into the trench that he has been sent down to the hospital in Rouen and can't believe his luck. From time to time we were entertained by the skill and bravery of German pilots. On our last evening, a German plane came over with three of our chaps in pursuit. He machine-gunned one of our gas-bags and set it on fire and then, swooping low and up again to evade his pursuers, he did the same to a second before giving a cheeky wave in our direction and flying back to his own lines. It was a circus performance that won him a spontaneous cheer from our trenches though we should not have been so sporting if we had not seen the occupants of the two gas-bags parachuting to safety.

Despite the lack of activity, our confidence in White Gloves shrank by the hour. This time he chose to sleep in a billet behind the front line, reappearing in his Burberry each morning to check we were all on the firestep for Dawn-Stand-To. According to Sergeant Baxendale, it is not unknown for subalterns to slip away like this though it is frowned on by Company commanders and earns the contempt of the men. German snipers have picked off one or two of these young officers returning after a good night's sleep though I am sure the official record will show that they died splendidly at the head of their men.

After Stand-Down, White Gloves makes a tour of inspection of our sector of the trench. He thinks he knows how to talk to the men and put them at their ease but he hasn't yet grasped that many of the men in his platoon are more intelligent than he is and find his air of patronizing superiority insulting, especially as they know he would be a private soldier like the rest of us if he wasn't the Honourable Rupert Grice and hadn't been to the right school. There are good officers in the battalion and it is just our bad luck to be landed with a platoon commander who has all the failings and none of the virtues of someone from his background. It doesn't worry us too much because when we finally go into action we shall put our trust in Sergeant Baxendale.

Tomorrow the football competition gets under way. It is extraordinary how seriously the high-ups are taking it. After that, we start 'special training'. This must mean the battalion is going to be part of the offensive which nobody knows anything about officially but is certain to start soon and, despite our jokes about the offensive spirit, we are excited at the prospect of having a role in what may be the final act of this drama. I hardly dare hope that if all goes well we shall be together again in case I am tempting fate. You see, I am becoming as superstitious as the other men but it is very hard not to and I really do feel safer with three pictures of my beloved wife in my top left hand pocket.

Pray for our future, darling, because I find it difficult to do so – I am missing you so very badly in the present. If only it would end tomorrow. I can't say 'Don't worry' because you've been here and you know but try not to worry. We are the lucky ones – we have arrived late and missed the worst battles of the war – so our chances of coming home must be good.

With all my love, darling Katherine, darling wife,
Tom

501784 Private T. Kennedy
D coy, 12th Royal Fusiliers
BEF

14 July 1917

My darling,
Thank you very much for both your letters, I read them again and again.

Don't let the critics of your hospital get you down. If the army has taught me nothing else, it has taught me never to respect a man because of his rank. Deference is our national disease. There are so many things I love about England but not the way it is divided into officers and other ranks so that second rate men, like White Gloves, are in positions of authority for no better reason than that they were born into the right class.

On the question of highly-strung men (as distinct from the rest of us who are just scared out of our wits), Sergeant Baxendale told me a harsh truth. When he was out here earlier in the war, shell-shock hadn't been heard of so highly-strung men who could not be relied on were shot by their comrades at the start of the battle.

I have asked about Kitty's Casualty Clearing Station but it is five miles outside Poperinghe so we are unlikely to bump into one another. I have met Peter Quinn, the Downside monk, once again and the second meeting confirmed my good opinion of him. He was watching one of the football matches that take place every afternoon. When he saw Jim and I on the touchline, he came over to talk to us. These matches are fiercely competitive because the honour of the regiment is at stake but for us it is an opportunity to shout encouragement or abuse at the officers who are playing. White Gloves does not put his popularity to the test by appearing on the pitch but we have fun mocking the efforts of other officers, most of whom are clearly anxious to be considered 'good sports' by their men. It is straight out of the Boys Own Paper and quite different I would think from the behaviour of French or German officers. The senior NCOs never take part because their authority is just too important for them to risk being figures of fun.

Father Peter says he will be coming into the line with us. I am not sure whether all Roman Catholic chaplains do that or whether, like your Theodore Hardy, he is the exception. Doubting Thomas is not about to go over to Rome; I am just registering my respect for a man who refuses to kill the enemy but will risk his life to be there where he is needed without apparently having any qualms about being in the military. How petty and dishonest some of our conscientious quibbles now seem.

I have had a less welcome encounter. Do you remember the officer I clashed with at Mill Hill? Well, he is here as a Captain in the Military Police and I am pretty certain he recognised me though I doubt whether he can remember where he has seen me before. If he does remember, he may start asking questions about what a conscientious objector is doing on active service. I am not ashamed of my past but I would prefer my comrades (and White Gloves especially) not to know about it. After what Sergeant Baxendale told me, I don't want anyone to think I might let them down when we go back into the line.

That can't be long now as our training is finished. For two weeks we have been attacking replicas of the German trenches so we will recognise exactly where we are when the time comes. However, we have trampled over fields of hay, corn, broad beans and potatoes which are nothing like the shell-holes we shall probably have to advance over and we have made enemies of the Belgian farmers in the process.

17 July

An extraordinary experience early yesterday morning. We were still asleep when the ground underneath us started to vibrate and someone shouted out like a man having a bad dream, 'It's started!' We stumbled outside and then stood still in the grey dawn listening to the thunder of the guns.

So this is the overture to the great offensive that with any luck will end the war. I can't pretend I feel sorry for the German soldiers now because I have a beautiful wife to come home to and the more Germans our gunners kill the safer it will be for us. As usual we are being told nothing but we expect to be going up the line tomorrow or the next day which will mean a long march in full kit and that will be hell in this heat. I don't know how long it will be before I can write again but wherever we end up I will write or send a field PC as soon as I can.

All my love darling,
Tom

Private T. Kennedy
In the line

30 July 1917

My darling,

Sergeant Baxendale has told us to 'get your letters written' so Jim and I are sitting at the mouth of the dug-out, steel helmets on, each of us trying to shut out the roar of the guns. The noise is so overwhelming that I sometimes have to think hard to remember my own name.

The colonel briefed the battalion this morning and made a good job of calming our fears – action is imminent, remember the great fighting tradition of the Royal Fusiliers, expect only light resistance as the artillery has done a splendid job, walking pace, dress by the centre, don't take prisoners, disarm them and send them back to our lines. 'Walking pace' raised a few murmurs but he assured us that conditions in the German trenches were appalling and that small groups of German soldiers are even now hiding in shell holes in No Man's Land waiting for a chance to surrender. I hope he is right.

Unfortunately, the colonel was followed by the adjutant who reminded us that the severest military law would apply. So much for patriotism and regimental pride. The army has an extraordinary gift for saying the wrong thing at the wrong moment.

Our chief anxiety now is the weather. We pray that it will hold but there are rumours of a change coming and some men swear they can feel rain on the wind. After all these weeks of fine weather with only a few showers, I can't help remembering Mrs. Bickersteth's warning that 'we'll pay for it later'.

Well darling, we go over the top tomorrow morning. I am nervous, we all are, but I shall be all right once we get going. Whatever happens, remember that I will always love you and that I have the best of reasons to come through this unscathed.

With all my love now and forever, darling.
Tom

CHAPTER EIGHT

I had known there was a chance I would conceive on our honeymoon but had thought it unlikely. Tom and I had fixed our hopes on having a large family after the war. When I missed my period in July, I thought I might just be late but by the beginning of August I was as sure as I could be that I was pregnant. I had mixed feelings. I was very happy but also rather daunted by the prospect of my body and my life being taken over by the pregnancy.

As a nurse, I should have waited another month or so before telling Tom but I wrote straightaway because I was afraid he might be killed without knowing that he was going to be a father. Yet, even as I wrote the letter, I was feeling detached from him, not by war or distance, certainly not by any lessening of my love, but by the nature of the journey I would now have to make on my own.

On 1 August, the papers carried reports of the start of the British offensive in the Ypres Salient. I had not received Tom's letter written on the eve of the battle and the Royal Fusiliers were not mentioned in the reports but all his previous letters had suggested that his battalion would be involved. The first reports in The Times were optimistic and I read them aloud to my wards for the benefit of those men whose blurred vision or trembling hands made it impossible for them to read for themselves.

There was a cheer when I read out that the first day's objectives had been achieved. 'So far the omens are of the best', I read on. 'We have broken the German line on the whole front and our casualties seem almost universally to be remarkably light.' Yet the next day the paper reported torrential rain and by the end of the week I was omitting details such as 'our troops had to advance over liquid mud'.

Within a few days, the nation's hopes that this battle would produce the long-awaited breakthrough had been replace by a mood of resignation. I longed to hear that Tom was safe and that he had received my news but I knew better than other wives that it might be two or three weeks before he was able to write. I knew, too, that information about casualties usually arrived first so that no news was good news but even to think on those lines would have been tempting fate.

Monday 6 August was a Bank Holiday and, with the senior medical officer's approval, I had hired a charabanc to take ten up-patients to Blackpool for the day. After the week of heavy rain, the sun shone and the beach was crowded so we had difficulty finding a space to spread our waterproof sheets on the sand. The men, who were wearing their blue hospital uniform, took off their boots and socks and walked down to the sea and I sent my two nursing colleagues to keep an eye on them.

I sat down and, leaning back with my arms stretched out behind me, looked round at the other people. There were a few men in khaki, soldiers on leave or convalescent, but for the most part the crowd was made up of mothers with young children whose fathers were presumably away at the war. My attention was drawn to a young mother who was wearing a black armband on the sleeve of her summer dress and to her daughter, a curly-headed child of about two who was patting down the sand in her bucket with a wooden spade. If that child remembered her father at all, the memory would soon die and then the only way she would be able to think of him and to imagine what he would have meant to her if he had lived was if her mother created a new memory for her.

We had brought sandwiches for the men and when they had had an early lunch some stripped to the waist to sunbathe while others wandered off to inspect the stalls and sideshows. I was congratulating myself on the success of the outing when one of the nurses called to me to come quickly – Cox was in a fight.

I found him squaring up to the owner of a coconut shy that advertised 'three shies at the Kaiser' and being egged on by a group of rough looking lads who were laughing at his stammer and goading him to use his fists.

'Shell shock is it?' The owner of the coconut shy asked when I had sent Cox back to base and the boys had walked off jeering and whistling and kicking the sand.

'We call them psychiatric casualties,' I replied.

'Whatever you call them, dear, they don't belong here with normal people.' He was wearing a straw hat and looked shiny and well-fed.

As I walked away, I recalled that Tom had once said the war should be fought exclusively by men and women over military age. 'Put them in the trenches up to their fat bellies in freezing mud and we shall hear no more talk of a fight to the finish.'

Cox was sitting disconsolately on the sand, a little apart from the others as though he thought he had let them down. I went over to him and put my hand on his shoulder. 'Don't worry Cox, we'll be going home soon.'

That night I checked his medical notes. He had volunteered in the first week of the war and had joined the Hull Commercials. He had come through the Somme without a scratch but when the greatest danger was past and the battalion was at rest, he told his platoon sergeant he would refuse to go back into the line. He could have been shot but a humane regimental medical officer labelled him 'shell shock' and put him on a hospital train to Boulogne. A puzzling detail in his notes was that his chronic stammer started after he had been labelled 'shell shock' and not before.

One week after the Bank Holiday, I had a letter from Tom and the following day, one from Kitty. I don't think I realised how anxious I had been about Tom until I knew that he was all right.

501784 Private T. Kennedy
BEF
8 August 1917

My darling, wonderful K,

That is the best letter I have ever received and the best news a man could ask for. Are you sure? Yes of course you are. You are the most amazing woman and I love you so very much.

I was so excited last night when I read your letter that even though I was dead tired after coming out of the line, I couldn't sleep for long but kept waking up and remembering why I was so happy. Then all sorts of questions came rushing in – whether it is better for our first child to be a boy or a girl (I don't think it matters), whether you should go on working with your shell-shocked patients (not for too long) and whether I should tell my father (later, I think). But I could not resist telling Jim so the whole section knows and are insisting that at the first opportunity we go to the estaminet to drink our baby's health in vin rouge. When Sergeant Baxendale got wind of this, he said he would like to come too. The drinks will be on me but I can't think of a toast I shall ever be happier to pay for.

We were relieved two days ago and are in reserve. We go back into the line the day after tomorrow. Our colonel was killed and we lost eleven men from our company but the Royal Fusiliers did not suffer as badly as the Worcesters on our right who have been practically wiped out. The conditions when we went over the top were quite unlike anything we had prepared for. The German machine gunners hadn't been silenced by our bombardment and they took a terrible toll. Even so, we started well but by mid-afternoon the rain was streaming down and we were slowed down by the mud.

I can't write more now but there is a lot to tell and with any luck we shall be withdrawn to rest billets well away from the front in about two weeks time. Until then, try not to worry about me – the important person is inside you.

Goodbye for now, darling, and all my love to you both from a prematurely proud father.

Tom.

Nursing Sister K. Westmacott,
No.10 Casualty Clearing Station,
Poperinghe

10 August 1917

Dearest Katherine,

I am so happy for you and so envious. You will be a wonderful mother. My maternal instinct, as you know, has been on leave for some time but I'm sure it would return if I met a man who tickled my fancy.

Darling, I am glad you have told Tom because if he knows he is going to be a father, that will give him another good reason to keep his head down and leave the heroics to the single men.

The CCS is not the same without you, not for me anyway because there is no one who shares our sense of humour. I was tempted to put in for a transfer but when the chance to move came, I turned it down. The senior MO offered me promotion if I would go to No 61 CCS at Mendingham which is a special hospital for men with self-inflicted wounds. No one wants to work there because the men are nursed under guard and are moved out as soon as they are fit to face a court martial. I said 'No thank you' that wasn't the sort of nursing I came out here to do. I've nursed German prisoners without giving it a second thought just as you have but men who shoot off their trigger finger can look after themselves as far as I am concerned.

I met a major friend of yours in Poperinghe three weeks ago and, as I knew you were safely married, I went out to dinner with him at La Poupee. As men go, he was good company though he would insist on asking about you. When he had drunk a bottle of wine he tried to put his hands on me as they all do, so I said if he wanted a girl before going over the top there was a brothel for officers in the town. He laughed at that. It has a blue light outside instead of a red one, he told me, so that the other ranks don't go in there by mistake. 'Oh yes,' says I, 'and do the girls have to salute?' 'Only majors and above,' he replied. We had a good laugh together but he is not my type. I wish I knew who was.

Talking of officers, you should tell Tom not to write about how awful his platoon commander is. Those green envelopes must sometimes be opened by the censor at base and, even if Tom is right, it will mean trouble for him. You know how officers cover for one another and will deny anything that shows the regiment in a bad light.

I know you worry about Tom and there's nothing I can say to change that except that the mood here is more optimistic than I can remember. Harry Melrose was certain we were going to break through this time. Although you and I have heard that before, the feeling that this offensive in the Salient will be the beginning of the end is still widespread despite the rain. Part of me wants that to be true so we can all go home but there are things I shall miss about the life out here and I'm not sure I could face going back to a civilian hospital. I suppose I can always swallow my pride and get married but if I can't find a man worth bothering with when I'm spoilt for choice, what chance will I have in Harrogate?

Look after yourself, dearest Katherine, and write again soon. I loved your description of the wedding but you haven't told me enough about married life and it's time I knew.

Love and kisses,
Kitty

I had calculated that Tom's battalion would be withdrawn from the line on about 22 August so when I received a field postcard that day to say he was all right, I assumed they had been withdrawn a day or two early. That night I lay awake for a long time, imagining Tom ordering vin rouge for himself and his friends in the first estaminet they could find and raising his glass to propose a toast to our child-to-be; and then someone, Sergeant Baxendale probably, starts to sing 'For he's a jolly good fellow' and all the soldiers from different regiments join in.

Happiness for men at the front and for those of us waiting at home for news of them was always on loan – we knew it could be taken away at any time. Because Tom was out of danger for ten days, I was able to put my anxiety on one side. I still read the newspaper reports of attack and counter-attack and I thought I saw signs that the offensive could not go on much longer; surely the generals would not make the mistake they made on the Somme and continue fighting like compulsive gamblers who are convinced they can make good their losses. When The Times published the names of the officers in the Worcesters who had been killed or wounded, I looked down the list to see if Harry Melrose's name was there but it was not. I took this to be a good omen though there was no logic in that. I used to laugh at Mrs Bickersteth's old wives' tales but the war made us all, even Tom, open to offers of help from chance, luck and superstition.

501784 Private T. Kennedy
BEF

25 August 1917

My darling,
I hope my field PC reached you safely.

I can hardly believe our luck. We are on ten days rest and have been given what Sergeant Baxendale rightly calls a 'champion billet'. A barn floor with a few wisps of straw is usually good enough for the poor bloody infantry but Jim and I have a furnished room with a feather bed and a spring mattress. The old woman whose house this is calls us in the morning at 7.30 and brings us hot water for washing and shaving. It is just as well we had a hot bath and were given clean shirts and underclothes before coming here or she would have slammed the door in our face – though 'clean' is a relative description because we think we may only have exchanged our lice for someone else's.

I am writing this in the kitchen in front of a good fire as it is like autumn outside and still raining – it hasn't stopped for more than a few hours since 31 July. Who else but a British General could plan a major offensive to start on the very day the weather breaks? The staff has no idea what conditions we have been fighting in. When we were being withdrawn three days ago, we had to step off the duckboards to let the 32nd pass through and we sank so deep in the mud we had great difficulty getting out again; when we did our greatcoats were twice their normal weight.

The weather doesn't worry us here; on the contrary it means we only have light duties. Our one parade yesterday was a pay parade. Saluting at the pay table! For no reason other than the army's genius for getting it wrong, our pay comes in five franc notes which the owners of the two local estaminets say they can't change so there is not much danger of our drowning our sorrows in drink. Anyway, the real luxury here is not vin-rouging but being able to think about tomorrow and the day after tomorrow and the day after that and to know we shall still be alive.

There is something I must tell you and that has had to wait for this green envelope because it concerns our platoon commander, 2nd Lieutenant, the Hon Rupert Grice (after what happened 'White Gloves' is far too playful a name for him). When we went over the top on that first morning it was still dark and the noise of the guns meant we couldn't hear any orders. I am sure Sergeant Baxendale was shouting 'Keep your distance!' as he always did in training but the darkness and the drizzle that had made the surface slippery meant we were soon tripping on the barbed wire and falling all over the place. Jim and I kept in touch, literally for a time by holding hands, and we tried to keep our eye on Corporal Tyler but 'walking pace' and 'dressing by the centre' were meaningless in the chaos. Our objective was supposed to be the first two lines of German trenches but when we got there we found they had been abandoned so a group of us including Baxendale and Tyler huddled down and lit cigarettes. There was no sign of 2nd Lieutenant Grice and no one asked after him. Then he came round the corner of the trench with his revolver out of its holster pushing two German soldiers in front of him. We threw away our cigarettes and got to our feet. Sergeant Baxendale suggested that Corporal Tyler should send the prisoners back to our lines. 'No time for that,' said Grice and raising his revolver shot each prisoner once in the temple.

German prisoners are killed and they kill our men who surrender but that is in the heat of the moment. This was a cold-blooded execution. The CO said German prisoners should be disarmed and sent back but there is nothing we can do about it and Sergeant Baxendale has quickly stamped on any attempt to discuss what happened because he knows it will only lead to trouble for the whole platoon. It would be madness for us to make a complaint against Grice or to let him see how much we despise him so we shall cheer him to the echo when he appears in drag with the other officers at the battalion concert party tomorrow – but he has committed murder under the cloak of war.

Even when we are alone together, Jim and I don't talk about this nor do we talk about the men who have been killed. We are told that Death, like the Ancient Mariner, 'stoppeth one in three' so I can't help believing that every man's death increases my chances of surviving and that is something I would be rather ashamed to talk about. Our nerves are a bit on edge and we jump at unexpected sounds but it is amazing how quickly we have become normal human beings again. As for going back into the line, why think about that when we have seven more days of safety and soft beds?

I have news of Theodore Hardy. Captain Quinn, the Benedictine monk I have spoken of, visited our billet today and when I asked if he had come across Hardy, he told me that Hardy had been recommended for a DSO. Hardy went over the top on the first day with the 8th Lincolns and insisted on staying with the wounded in No

Man's Land when night came. Quinn went over the top on the first day, too, with the Worcesters and is lucky to be alive.

We are promised post tomorrow. I pray there will be a letter from you because I want to hear all your news, especially whether the next generation is making his or her presence felt. Could it be twins? I rather like the idea (but then I don't have to carry them around) and I shall spend some of my idle hours adding to our list of possible names just in case. Grace for a girl and Brodie for a boy are still my favourites. Take great care of yourself, darling. I am sure you should stop working very soon now and live at home until our baby is born.

I am so proud of you and I love you with all my heart.

Goodbye for now, darling.
Tom

The first three weeks in September were warm and sunny and I gave instructions for the windows in the wards to be opened wide. My mood was optimistic. Tom's battalion would probably be back in the line but he had come safely through the worst of the battle and I had persuaded myself that the offensive would soon be called off. I wrote to tell him that I had felt our baby move for the first time but that I did not want to stop working until the end of the month. In a civilian hospital in peace time, a pregnant nurse would not have been allowed to work but I was under contract to the War Office and the matron at Lancaster raised no objections.

There was no letter from Tom in the first half of the month and no field postcard either. I was not worried as there had been similar gaps between his letters before but by the last week in September, nearly five weeks since his letter of 25 August, I was searching anxiously for explanations. Tom wrote to me at the hospital but I had not asked him what address he had put for me as his next of kin in his pay book. If he had put the Rectory, then any notification that he had been wounded would have been sent there. But if it had, why hadn't my mother sent it on to me or telegrammed for me to come home? I decided to go home even though I told myself I was making a mistake because as soon as I left the hospital a letter from Tom was sure to arrive.

It is not far as the crow flies from Lancaster to Kirkby Lonsdale but the cross country journey by train in wartime took nearly two hours. I spent the time continuing to search for explanations for Tom's silence, alternately fearing the worst and finding a reason not to do so.

If Tom had been killed, I would have heard by now; the longer the silence, the more likely it was that there was some other explanation. It was possible that Tom had been reported missing or even that he was a prisoner in German hands; in either case, I believed the army would be slow to notify the next of kin. The most likely explanation was that Tom had been wounded. If he had been and was in a Casualty Clearing Station, would I receive a letter similar to those I had written for other men. 'He bids me make light of his wound but I cannot honestly do so.' Tom would make light of anything and I felt sorry for the nurse who tried to persuade him that his wound was serious. And what if he was so badly disfigured that he would rather die than come back to me? On the Devil's Bridge, he had said he would not want me to look after him yet the only thing that would matter to me was that he was alive. But – I reminded myself – very few wounds were disfiguring and it was remarkable how men recovered from wounds that were thought to be fatal. Of one thing I was certain – Tom had a powerful will to live.

We were approaching Kirkby Lonsdale when I thought of another possibility and was astounded that I had not thought of it before. If Tom had gone back to prison either of his own free will or because his record as a conscientious objector had in some way been used against him, he would not be able to write a letter for the first two months.

I suppose these explanations must have kept me from giving in to despair but as I entered the churchyard by the South Gates, I knew I must be prepared for news that Tom had been killed. I wasn't thinking of other possibilities now, I was hoping against hope.

When I was still some way off, the front door of the Rectory opened and I saw my mother and father standing together. My mother came forward alone.

'There is a letter, darling', she said. 'It arrived this morning.'

We went inside and my mother took the letter from the hall table and handed it to me. No, I did not wish to open it alone in my room. The envelope was marked 'Infantry Records Office'. I opened it and read the first words, 'Madam, it is my painful duty to inform you …. ' and, without looking up, I said quietly, 'Tom is dead.'

Though I read the details twice, they did not change. 'Private T. Kennedy … on the 23 September … the cause of death was Died on Service … and I am to express to you the sympathy and regret of the Army Council at your loss.' There was something at the bottom about the disposal of personal effects that made me think of Tom's copy of Yeats' poems and wonder whether the army would return it.

'Remember your baby, darling, it is Tom's baby too,' my mother said.

I gave her the letter to read. I had been expecting that if anything happened to Tom I would receive a personal letter from the chaplain – the sort of letter Reverend Theodore Hardy would have written, not this army form filled in by a clerk and signed by an officer who described himself as 'Major for Colonel'. Was this form all Tom was worth – we have taken your husband's life and here is the receipt?

I can only explain the emotional numbness with which I reacted to the news of Tom's death by recalling that wounded soldiers often insisted that although they had felt the bullet's impact, they had felt no pain. My pain, too, would come later and my tears. Until the evening, that is to say for two or three hours after I arrived home, I showed my parents no outward sign of grief, assuring them that I had prepared myself for bad news and that Tom and I had talked openly about the possibility that he would not come back. I was in a dream, one of those rare dreams in which part of your mind seems to be conscious and capable of thinking, 'I know this is only a dream and that I should soon wake up.'

I was lying on my bed in the darkness, one hand on the side of the swell where our baby was kicking, and fully dressed because I was reluctant to take off the clothes I had put on at the start of a different day, in a different life, when my father knocked on the door and called out 'Goodnight', as he had always done when I was at home. This touch of normality broke the spell and broke my heart. I just managed to reply 'Goodnight Daddy' before I choked on my tears.

I cried and cried for Tom and for the years we would not spend together long into the night until, exhausted by the outpouring of emotion, I arrived at a truce with my grief. I got up to draw the curtains and undress. In the moonlight, I could see clearly the Maids Memorial in the churchyard, a stone monument to five maids who were 'Hurried to Eternity' in a fire that destroyed the Rose and Crown Hotel. That phrase, which I must have read a hundred times, now came to my aid as a way of thinking about my loss. Tom had been 'hurried to eternity' but he would be mine forever in God's sight.

I knelt at my bedside and asked God in his mercy to take care of Tom and to forgive the doubts of an honest man. Then I prayed for all those who had been killed in the battle, drawing some comfort from the knowledge that Tom would not be alone but with a great crowd of young men from both sides who were beginning a new life together, a life that was beyond my understanding.

I slept but not deeply or for long. When I came downstairs in the morning, my father had gone across to the church and my mother suggested we should join him but before we could leave the house, the postman called with another letter for me, this time marked 'War Office'. For a cruelly deceptive moment, I thought there could be no reason for the War Office to write so promptly unless there had been a mistake, so I opened the envelope at once and read the short letter it contained.

War Office
Whitehall
S.W.

30 September 1917

Dear Mrs Kennedy,

In confirmation of the Infantry Record Office letter that was sent to you on the 29th instant, notifying the death of your late husband, Private T Kennedy, as having taken place on the 23rd of September, it is with profound regret that I now communicate to you the circumstances of his death.

Your late husband was found guilty of murder by Field General Court Martial and was sentenced to suffer death by being shot. The sentence was duly carried out.

I am, dear Madam,
Your obedient servant.
J K L Hamilton
Colonel

CHAPTER NINE

My unborn child saved me from breaking down under this terrible blow. My disbelief and horror at the bald statement of Tom's execution were quickly overwhelmed by a powerful urge to protect my child from the consequences of whatever Tom had done. In my shock and anguish, this was the only light I could see to guide me. Where it would lead and how difficult it would be to hide the truth, I did not even consider, my only concern being to ward off the immediate danger. At any moment my father might return to see what had delayed us and he would never be party to a deliberate deception.

I took the letter from my mother's hand, folded it and put it back in the envelope. 'No one else must ever know,' I said. My mother, on whose wisdom and strength I had so often relied, now took her lead from me, though I was certain she would have made the same decision. Her conscience was clear, she said, God would forgive the lies we would have to tell for the sake of the child.

From that moment we were committed to a conspiracy of silence and denial that, for all we knew, might have to last a lifetime; without any discussion, we had agreed to deceive those closest to us in a way that would be entirely alien to the Christian values of our family. Whether instinct or calculation drove me to that decision, I do not know, nor do I know whether I would have made a different decision if I had been able to foresee the difficulties and tensions of living a double life. To my father and Tom's father, to my sister Amy and to the people of Kirkby Lonsdale, I was a war widow whose husband had been killed in the Ypres Salient but all the time I was a spy behind enemy lines in constant fear of being exposed.

I wrote straightaway to Colonel Hamilton at the War Office asking him to confirm that Tom's execution would not be made public and he replied: 'I need hardly assure you that no indication of the nature of your late husband's death will appear in the Casualty Lists and that no information as to the circumstances will be released to the public by the War Office.'

It proved so easy to deceive people about Tom's death that I was ashamed, though I was always vigilant. When I wrote to tell Tom's father that Tom had 'died on service', because I did not know whether he would have been given the news, and received by return a touching and understanding letter of sadness and sympathy, inviting me to stay with him in Cambridge as soon as I felt able to do so, my first reaction was to search for clues in his choice of words that he might already know the truth.

When Tom's name appeared in the Casualty Lists under 'Died of Wounds' I hated myself for being so relieved to see it there. In the days that followed, all the letters of condolence had a double edge: they eased my pain and fuelled my sense of guilt. Reverend Hardy wrote and so did Tom's best man, Theodore Taylor, and I was surprised and moved to hear from Fenner Brockway who was still in prison. 'Tom was a good friend,' Fenner wrote, 'who had the moral courage to change his mind about the war and, although I did not agree with him, I admired his integrity. Now his spirit is free and united with the Life Universal in which Englishman and German, Austrian and Russian are one.'

I waited for the one letter that would make my double life easier to endure but if Tom had been allowed to write a last letter, it must have been delayed or suppressed by the army's obsession with censorship. Without a word from him, I found it hard to grieve; it was as if I refused to believe what I had been told until I heard it from Tom himself. I would gladly have escaped to Lancaster where the shell-shocked men would ask no questions and be told no lies but my midwife, Mrs Aysgarth, whose opinion I trusted, advised against it, and the senior medical officer, in his letter of condolence, had made it clear that he did not expect me to return.

Stuck in Kirkby Lonsdale with nothing to do, I found the whole business of public mourning almost unbearable. I attended the Requiem Eucharist my father had arranged but with reluctance and I offended his parishioners by not wearing black. After that I avoided the town as much as possible, preferring to walk on my own where Tom and I had walked before but when I was spotted, unfavourable comments were passed through Mrs Bickersteth to my mother. There were still some people in Kirkby Lonsdale apparently who thought that a woman who was five and a half months pregnant should confine herself to the home.

Lunesdale in autumn was as fresh and beautiful as the town of Kirkby Lonsdale seemed to me oppressive. Far away from other people and keeping an eye on Barbon Fell in case the weather changed, I walked with Tom and talked to him about our child and whether we were going to have a boy or a girl. Sometimes I would say to myself the lines of Yeats' verse that he had been reading when we first met and that had taken on a new significance for me:

'I had this thought a while ago,
My darling cannot understand
What I have done, or what would do
In this blind bitter land.'

I needed to understand what it was that Tom had done to deserve such a death. My mind was full of angry fantasies in which he was the victim of injustice, a scapegoat picked on because he had been a conscientious objector. If only I could have talked to Kitty, she was the one other person with whom I would have dared to share my secret. She had reacted to Tom's death in a typically Kittyish way. 'I hope you cried your heart out,' she wrote, 'as I am sure that is the best way but how should I know? I have never loved anyone enough to cry for them except you of course. Don't despair, darling, the grieving will end. When it does, Tom would have wanted you to have a full life and if you don't know what that means, I'll explain it all to you when we meet.'

I wrote back, asking her to be a godmother to our child and telling her she was the one person in the world I wanted to talk to; if she applied for leave early in the New Year, she would be in time to be introduced to her godchild.

Then on 22 October, three weeks after I received the news of Tom's death, the postman delivered an envelope addressed to me at the Rectory but not in Tom's hand. When I opened it in the privacy of my room, I found it contained two letters.

General Army Headquarters
BEF

14 October 1917

Dear Mrs Kennedy,

I am the Roman Catholic Chaplain Tom mentioned in his letters to you and I write to you as his friend to offer my deepest sympathy for your bereavement and for the tragic nature of Tom's death. I promised Tom I would ensure that his last letter reached you safely. I am very sorry that I am not able to deliver it in person. Although I am not allowed to give you any details of Tom's offence and trial, I have sought and obtained permission to tell you this much.

Tom's offence was one of the most serious a soldier can commit but he was convinced that his motive was neither selfish nor malicious and, though he bitterly regretted the consequences, he never wavered in his belief that he had had no choice except to act as he did.

Tom asked me to attend his court martial as 'prisoner's friend'. We had only met on three occasions but he was in our brigade and after talking with him when he was in custody, I formed the firm opinion that he was an honourable man who had made a terrible mistake. The 'prisoner's friend' is not strictly speaking a defending counsel but I did my best to see the court heard everything that could and should have been said on Tom's behalf.

At his request, I remained with him to the end. He faced his ordeal with great courage. His thoughts were of you and of your unborn child and of the future in which he would have no part. In the last hour, when we said the Lord's Prayer together, his voice, though quiet, was strong and sure.

It is with great sadness that I am obliged to stop there. Tom was a casualty of the war and I have expressed the hope to the authorities that he will be buried with his fallen comrades.

May God bless you and give you peace and fortitude at this very sad time. I shall remember you, as I shall remember Tom, in my prayers. If you would like me to visit you when I am next on leave, I will gladly do so. This address will find me.

Yours very sincerely in Christ.
Peter Quinn
Dom Peter Quinn
Captain, Royal Army Chaplain's Department.

Private T Kennedy
BEF

23 September 1917

My darling,

Please try to forgive me for the pain I have caused you and for the shadow that my death will cast over your life. If it is at all possible, I beg you never to let our child know how I died. Father Peter, who has been as good a friend as I have known, says I shall be listed as having died of wounds but that the War Office is required to inform you as my next of kin of the true circumstances. I wish with all my heart you did not have to know.

I cannot tell you what happened. If I do the censor will stop my last letter. I am only allowed to say that although I have been found guilty, I do not believe I have done anything of which you or our child need ever be ashamed. I go to my death with a clear conscience. I bear no grudge against the members of the court martial or against the men who will be ordered to carry out the sentence.

Now the time has come to say goodbye to you, my darling Katherine. I cannot say 'goodbye for now' as I have in the past because you know I do not share your firm belief in another life but that will not stop me hoping until my last breath that somehow, somewhere we shall meet again. Though I fear death, it is the loss of you and of the years we would have spent together that make it so very hard to say goodbye. Yet I know how lucky I have been; if life is measured in intensity of happiness not in years, I have already lived longer than other men.

Darling Katherine, I have loved you more than I have ever been able to express and surely that love will not die with me. When you hold our child in your arms and remember that no child was ever more truly conceived in love, you will know that my love for you has survived.

I don't know how to end and yet I must. The army insists on doing everything early in the morning and Father Peter is glancing at the clock – poor man, he is more exhausted by this business than I am but in a little while it will all be over.

Goodbye, my darling, dearest Katherine. It has to be. Take good care of yourself and of our child. Thank you for making me the happiest man in the world. Wherever I am going, I shall miss you terribly.

With all my love now and forever.
Tom

Tom's last letter is my most precious possession. When I remember the letters I wrote for dying men and think of all those other men who never had a chance to say goodbye, I count myself lucky that the man I loved was able to say goodbye in his own words, in his own hand. Just as at the very beginning, it was with words that Tom tried to win me, so too at the end he left me with words of love that I shall always be able to read as though they were written yesterday.

Tom's letter brought me joy in sadness. It also liberated me from any feeling of guilt at keeping the nature of his death a secret. It was what he wanted. But the letter did not tell me anything about the murder he was alleged to have committed. On the contrary, both Tom's letter and the Roman Catholic chaplain's seemed to be saying that what the army called murder had not been murder at all. Tom was an honourable man who had made a tragic mistake, he had done nothing of which his wife and child need ever be ashamed and he had gone to his death with a clear conscience. I did not need to read between the lines to be convinced that my fantasies had been well founded. Tom had indeed been the victim of a miscarriage of justice.

Thinking it strange that I should be asking a Benedictine monk for the truth about my husband's death, I wrote to Father Peter Quinn and told him that unless I understood why Tom had been executed, I would never be able to come to terms with his death or to protect our child if news of the execution was made public. He replied that he had sworn an oath of secrecy he could not break. All the officers of the court martial had sworn a similar oath that was designed to protect the family of the accused who would not want publicity and the family of the victim who had been told that he had died in battle. He sympathised with my wish to be told more but that would not be possible, certainly not while the war lasted and probably not for many years after.

The more I studied his reply, the more I believed that it did not rule out my discovering at some point in the future what had led to Tom's court martial and execution and that possibility, however remote, changed the way I grieved for Tom. Nothing, I had thought, not even the birth of our child, could ease the pain of loss and the bitter regret that we had so little time together but believing now that one day I should have the opportunity to prove Tom innocent provided me with a cause, a way of grieving that looked to the future and not the past. I had no idea what proving Tom innocent might involve or how I would reconcile this with my determination to keep the nature of his death a secret but from this time on, finding the evidence to overturn the verdict of the court martial was a dream I intended to turn into reality.

My baby was due on 22 January. Mrs Aysgarth, the midwife, lived nearby with her two children in a house just off Swinemarket. Her husband had volunteered in 1914 and was the galloper for a general in one of the cavalry brigades. As the family were regular churchgoers, I saw Mrs Aysgarth often when I was at home and, although we were not on Christian name terms, we had established a professional friendship. She was one of the modern midwives who had trained at the Midwives School in Manchester and she liked to talk with me about nursing and midwifery and how much more up to date we both were in our respective fields than the two elderly doctors who practised in the town.

She would not normally have visited a pregnant woman much before the baby was due but she dropped in to see me every few weeks, more for a chat than to check anything and I was always glad to see her. My mother and I talked openly about my pregnancy, which would have been unthinkable in many families, but Mrs Aysgarth was much nearer my age and, while she always called me Mrs Kennedy and expected me to call he Mrs Aysgarth, I thought of her as an older sister.

Her pride in being up to date in every aspect of her job was a helpful corrective to Mrs Bickersteth's superstitions that, as far as childbirth was concerned, dwelt exclusively on what could go wrong. Not that I took Mrs Bickersteth's pronouncements seriously but this was my first child and the only child Tom and I would ever have, so I welcomed Mrs Aysgarth's confirmation that avoiding men with a squint and not looking at the moon was the nonsense I had always supposed it to be. I had no reason whatsoever to think that anything would go wrong, though I did find it difficult to dismiss altogether a fear that my baby would not live. I attribute this irrational fear not to Mrs Bickersteth's superstitions but to one of the midwives in the East End telling me that in some large families, a stillborn child was regarded as a blessing in disguise because it meant one less mouth to feed. That had shocked me at the time and in recent weeks anxiety that my child would be stillborn or die soon after birth had preyed on my mind.

My father warmed to Mrs Aysgarth, partly because, like me, he saw her as an ally in the constant battle to keep Mrs Bickersteth's dark forces at bay. And he had another reason to be grateful to her. On one of Mrs Aysgarth's visits in late November he consulted her, as the wife of a soldier at the front, on whether to ring the church bells to celebrate what appeared to be a great victory. The papers that morning were full of a successful British attack with tanks at Cambrai which led people to believe that the decisive breakthrough had been achieved and rumours were reaching Kirkby Lonsdale that in every other parish the church bells were being rung. 'I wouldn't if I were you,' Mrs Aysgarth advised. 'If you ring the bells you'll raise women's hopes, then what will you do when their hopes are dashed?' A few days later, the German counter-attack drove our soldiers back where they had started and the decisive breakthrough that would end the war seemed as far away as ever.

My father gained credit for not celebrating a victory that never was but the mood in the town that winter was sour and angry, as it was in the country as a whole – a blind bitter land indeed. There were food riots in the big cities in early December and even in Kirkby Lonsdale women smashed the window of the grocer's in Main Street because somebody said he was selling margarine above the permitted price. Hostility to shirkers and 'rabbits' was felt everywhere; not far away in Kendal, a widow was attacked by a mob because the police found her only son, a deserter, hiding in the attic.

I was very proud of my father when he used his pulpit to condemn this mob role, something he would never have done earlier in the war, and I was sad to think how much he and Tom would have found they had in common if Tom had lived. But criticising what some people thought of as patriotic vigilance was not popular and in my father's seesaw relationship with his parish, Christmas 1917 was a low point. There was a heavy snowfall on Christmas Eve and on Christmas morning my father was out early clearing a path from the South Gates to the South Porch. Despite his efforts, the congregation at the eleven o'clock service with carols was much smaller than usual.

I felt my first faint tightenings on the morning of New Year's Eve, three weeks earlier than I had expected. Although there was no urgency, my mother sent for Mrs Aysgarth. 'Go for a walk, keep yourself busy,' Mrs Aysgarth said when she arrived. 'Call me again when the contractions are coming every five minutes or so.' When she returned, she would prepare the room and assign the tasks to my mother and Mrs Bickersteth but until then she had another woman to look after who had already been in labour for twelve hours.

I took Mrs Aysgarth's advice and, wrapping up warm against the winter day, I set off with my mother along the Old Coach Road to Kendal. Outside the smithy, the boys' sledges had made the surface so treacherous we decided to turn back and walk along Church Brow towards Underly Park. A strange, muffled silence hung over the valley that was white with snow as though nature itself was waiting for my child to be born.

'I'm still afraid that one day a stranger will come to the door and tell your father the truth,' my mother said. We seldom spoke about it. There was no need. Everyone had accepted so unquestioningly that Tom had died of wounds; the deception had acquired the status of fact. I took my mother's arm. 'Don't worry,' I replied. 'When the war is over and the men come home but not now, not today.'

When I went into the second stage of labour it was approaching midnight and I thought Mrs Aysgarth was beginning to sound more and more like a bullying sergeant major. 'Take a big breath and push, Mrs Kennedy,' she ordered and I could have sworn at her as I was doing just that. Two years in the army had enriched my vocabulary. 'I can see the head coming,' Mrs Aysgarth said a little later. 'Only a little more now, the baby is nearly here.'

Our baby son was born five minutes after midnight on New Year's Day. Mrs Aysgarth washed his face, wrapped him in a warm blanket and gave him to me and I wept with joy to hold Tom's child in my arms. Although he was born three weeks early, he was a fine healthy baby and weighed six and a half pounds.

CHAPTER TEN

At the beginning of February, our baby son was baptised by my father and given the names Brodie Thomas. Outside, the temperature had barely risen above freezing all day and our small party gathered in the Baptistery wore our overcoats and scarves. My sister, Amy, was the only godparent who could be there; Mrs Aysgarth stood in for Kitty and Tom's father for the Reverend Theodore Hardy.

Brodie cried lustily from start to finish but when we returned to the Rectory and I asked Mrs Aysgarth to hold him, he stopped crying abruptly as though his objection had only been to the religious service. Over tea in the drawing room, he was the centre of attention. He had Tom's determination to make himself heard, my father said, and Tom's father drew attention to the fair complexion and sea-blue eyes that were clear evidence of his Viking blood. Soon everyone was joining in the game of identifying Brodie's links with generations of Lovegroves and Kennedys, while I was thinking that the saddest thing of all was that Tom and Brodie and I would never be together as a family.

When it was time for Tom's father to leave, he asked me to bring Brodie to Cambridge when the weather was warmer, perhaps in late April or May, and I promised to do so. Did he know the truth? I had asked myself that question many times over the past four months and had come to the conclusion that as he worked for the government's War Propaganda Bureau there was a chance he had been told; and if he had, he would think that I did not know and that it was his responsibility to keep the secret from me.

I used this possibility to persuade Father Peter that we should meet as soon as he returned to England; if Professor Kennedy knew how his son had died, he may have been told the circumstances that led to the court martial, in which case I should be told as well. Father Peter replied briefly that he had been given a date for his return, 'which by happy coincidence is 21st of March, the Feast of St. Benedict.'

I looked at the map. Downside Abbey was a long way from Kirkby Lonsdale and I was breast-feeding Brodie but I saw no reason why Father Peter should not come to the Rectory in the role of an army chaplain who had met Tom on three occasions and wanted to express his condolences in person. I assumed that he would have no objection to being part of the deception for a day.

My assumption was not put to the test. On the Feast of St. Benedict, the German army launched an attack on the British lines with such overwhelming superiority in men and guns that our armies were forced to retreat. The decisive breakthrough for which we had all been praying had been made at last but by the wrong side.

I did not expect Father Peter to leave the men in his brigade until the crisis was over and I resigned myself to a long wait before I could question him about Tom's court martial. In Kirkby Lonsdale, people now spoke openly about the possibility of defeat. When I took Brodie for a walk in his pram each morning, strangers stopped me in the street to ask what was going to happen if we lost the war. Although I answered that England would never surrender, their questions made me fear for the future and what defeat might mean for the wife and child of a soldier who had been executed for murder.

At home, we followed the news with more anxiety than at any other time in the war. I thought of Kitty whose Casualty Clearing Station, if it had moved back to where we were in 1916, would be in the direct line of the German advance, and of Reverend Theodore Hardy because the Lincolns were mentioned in reports of the heaviest fighting. Sometimes I felt the pull to go back, to be with Kitty and to play my part in the great battle to defend all we held dear.

When the German advance slowed down, we were too worn out and too suspicious of better news to believe the worst was over but by the last week in April, fear of defeat began to fade and I decided to take up Tom's father's invitation. Brodie and I spent a week in Cambridge at the house in Grange Road where Tom was born and spent all his early years. We arrived on 2 May, our wedding anniversary, and Tom's father had bought flowers for me at a stall in Market Square.

'I have borrowed a pram from the wife of one of my colleagues,' he said proudly, as Mrs Danby, his housekeeper, carried off the flowers to trim the stems and find a suitable vase.

That evening, when Brodie was asleep, we walked in the garden and he told me he had never seen Tom so happy as on our wedding day. Then, after a pause, he added, 'It was strange to see him in uniform after all that had happened.' I said I sometimes blamed myself for Tom's decision to join the army but Tom's father shook his head. 'We both tried to persuade him to compromise, Katherine, but Tom made his own decisions. No one else is to blame for his death.'

But someone else was to blame, someone who falsely accused him, the court that wrongly condemned him, the senior officers who turned a blind eye to injustice; and if Tom's father knew the truth he would be a powerful ally against all these people.

Cambridge in the early summer sunshine, we walked with Brodie along quiet streets and through quiet colleges where all but a handful of undergraduates had gone to the war. Tom's father walked alongside the pram, obviously pleased to be seen out with his grandson except when Brodie was disturbing the peace.

'Shall we go down to the river?' he asked one afternoon when we were on King's Parade and Brodie, propped up with pillows so he could see over the side of the pram, was making strange cries that Tom's father thought were cries of delight but I recognised as impatience. We crossed the river by Queen's and I suggested that, instead of going along the Backs, we should walk some of the way to Grantchester. Beyond the last houses, the path swings away from the river and goes round the back of the bathing sheds where dons and undergraduates swim without costumes. Tom's father said he used to swim here when the water was warmer but that Tom preferred to swim on his own at Byron's Pool. I saw Tom naked leaping into the river. As a man, Tom's body was lean and muscular but when I imagined him as a boy he looked frail like someone who would feel the cold when he came out so I wrapped him in a towel to keep him warm.

'What will you tell Brodie about his father?' Tom's father asked. I should have answered 'the truth' or in some other way that gave him an opportunity to confess he knew how Tom had died but I was taken by surprise and lost my nerve. 'I shall tell him his father was a fine man,' I said. 'A brave man who had the courage to go his own way.' He nodded and we kept silent for a while. Perhaps my father-in-law was thinking, as I was, that we had both let slip an opportunity to be honest with one another.

Back in Kirkby Lonsdale, I waited for news of Father Peter Quinn. In France, the battle was neither lost nor won but during the summer months we were convinced that our armies were gathering their strength for a knock out blow. According to a letter I received from Kitty in July, the Germans had lost so many men, they were recruiting schoolboys.

Nursing Sister Westmacott,
No 10 C.C.S.
'On the Move'

15 July 1918

Dearest Katherine,
I expect you saw about Hardy's VC. I can't think what has come over the army that it gives the VC to someone who actually deserves it, especially as he wouldn't kill a German soldier for love or money.

The rumour is that he refused to accept the medal but the Division Commander told him he had to whether he liked it or not.

We have had a hectic time since March. The CCS was nearly overrun at one point and we were ordered to leave some of the most seriously wounded men behind when we withdrew. As you can imagine, that was hard and I hope to God the Germans treated them properly. The last few weeks have been quieter and I expect we shall be moving forward again soon.

But not me! I shall be coming home. I am escorting (a good word don't you think?) British and German wounded on a hospital train to Le Havre and then across to Southampton. They are going to hospitals in London District so once I have handed them over to the ambulance column at Charing Cross I am taking some long overdue leave to see my parents in Harrogate and then over the hills to see you.

It will be wonderful to be with you again and to meet my god-son. We can have such talks as we used to do.

Do you remember the 17 year olds in the children's war at Rouen? Well some of the German wounded they bring in here are just rosy-cheeked schoolboys, which makes me think they must be scraping the barrel and can't possibly last much longer.

We can't help feeling sorry for these schoolboys. A few weeks ago they thought they were winning the war and now they just want to go home to their mothers. The top-Sergeant, Karl Diering, is only 18. He had an infected shrapnel wound in his left thigh and we had to do a mid-thigh amputation. He is still in a lot of pain and I'm afraid the knocks and bumps of the journey to England will be hard to bear, which is one reason I am going along.

His schoolboys worship him and I am not surprised. They say their officers are rubbish, particularly the Prussian ones with names as long as the Western Front, and that it is men like top-Sergeant Diering who are holding the German army together.

No, I am not falling for Karl Diering. I'm just anxious to get him and his kindergarten safely to London. But it wouldn't be so bad, would it, marrying a German? He is charming and always very correct and even when he recovers, he'll still need me.

I'll send a telegram from Harrogate. I can't wait.

Lots and lots of love and kisses.
From Kitty

On 4 August, before going down to breakfast, I noted in my diary that for the first time Brodie had slept through the night. When I reported this news to my mother and placed Brodie in his high chair, my father looked up from his paper to say that a German submarine had torpedoed an ambulance transport ship in the Channel. Fearing for Kitty, I looked over his shoulder but there was no mention of a Nursing Sister or German wounded being among those who were lost. The 'Warilda' had taken two hours to sink so that despite the painfully slow task of transferring the wounded to the boats in pitch darkness, the majority of the six hundred wounded men and medical staff had been saved. Two day later, there was a further report headed 'Heroism of Nursing Sister' and I read it with an aching heart. When it was clear the ship was sinking, 'Nursing Sister Westmacott, QAIMNS, insisted on staying below with the cot cases who had not been rescued. A medical officer reported hearing someone shout, "You go up, Missy, we'll be alright", but Sister Westmacott refused to leave the English and German wounded for whom she was responsible.' Kitty and top-Sergeant Diering and his kindergarten of schoolboy soldiers were among the hundred and twenty-three who were drowned when the ship went down.

Dear, brave Kitty – her death, so cruelly unnecessary, almost made me doubt the existence of a loving God. My father tried to comfort me by saying that God would use Kitty's example to inspire others to love their enemies but I was beyond persuading and thought he sounded like a clever lawyer trying to defend the indefensible. Tom's death had drawn me closer to the God of my childhood and I had cast my cares on Him but after the loss of my friend I experienced only despair and although I still said my prayers, I had to will myself to believe that someone was listening.

Then, as if to confirm my pessimism, when the war showed signs of ending at last, an influenza epidemic swept across Europe killing hundreds of thousands. There were no cases in Kirkby Lonsdale but schools were closed and church services suspended and I refused to let anyone other than the family come near my son. The nursery became an isolation ward from which Brodie emerged only once a day for a walk in the wood behind the Rectory where I could be sure of not meeting anyone from the town.

Yet my faith never failed entirely and by one of those strange twists of circumstance, it was the death of another friend that helped to restore my belief in a loving God. Three weeks before the Armistice, I heard that the Reverend Hardy had died of wounds in the military hospital in Rouen where Kitty and I had worked when we first went to France. He had been shot by a sniper who had spotted him moving between the wounded men in No Man's Land.

This sad news prompted me to take out the pocket New Testament that Hardy had used at the front and had sent to Brodie as a christening present. In it, he had marked certain passages and made his own notes. Turning the pages, I felt certain that this brave and humble man, who had lived with the horror of war every day, had never doubted God's love or blamed God for man's murderous fall from grace. In St. John's Gospel, he had marked a verse I knew well. 'For God sent not his Son into the world to condemn the world but that the world through him might be saved.' I never returned to the unquestioning faith of my childhood but, thanks to Theodore Hardy, I rediscovered hope that through Christ's example, the world might be saved.

In Kirkby Lonsdale, 11 November was a dark, muggy day with steady rain and mist on the fells. A group of young boys went round the streets banging empty biscuit tins to celebrate victory but the rain soon drove them indoors. When the rain stopped in the late afternoon, I stood at the window of my room, ready to hold Brodie up in case the beacon on Barbon Fell was lit but there was no flicker in the gloom so I closed the curtains.

That evening when Brodie had gone to sleep, I took out my diary and wrote: *'The war between civilized nations ended at 11 o'clock this morning. No celebrations, just rain and weariness. In a few years, the war and the men who died in it will be forgotten. I must find a way of keeping Tom's memory alive for Brodie so that one day he will be able to know what a fine and honourable man his father was.'*

CHAPTER ELEVEN

'I shall wear my uniform for the last time, so don't look out for a Benedictine monk,' Father Peter Quinn wrote. 'It will be good to meet you at last and your family too. Don't worry, I am aware of all the sensitivities.' He was still in the army but had returned to Downside Abbey on indefinite leave while his demobilisation papers were being processed.

It had been my father's idea to hold a memorial service for Theodore Hardy, either at Kirkby Lonsdale or in his own small church at Hutton Roof, but fear of influenza had caused the service to be postponed until now, the early spring of 1919. 'If you were able to come,' I had written to Father Peter, 'it would be perfectly natural for me to want to talk to you alone. My father knows that Tom met you in Poperinghe.'

So many people said they wanted to attend, including officers and men of the Lincolns and the Somerset Light Infantry, the two regiments in Hardy's brigade, that the service had to be held at Kirkby Lonsdale and even then latecomers were standing at the back of the nave. From my place in the Rector's pew inside the sanctuary, I could see most of the congregation but I knew of no way to distinguish Captain Quinn from the other army chaplains. Tom had written, 'He is much the same age as I am' but that was the only clue I had so I relied on Peter Quinn finding me after the service.

My father gave the address and he had asked the Colonel of the 8th Lincolns to speak after him. The Colonel spoke movingly about Hardy's courage and devotion to duty and concluded by referring to what he called 'two incidents'. The spirit that Hardy encouraged among the men in the battalion, he said, was best illustrated by a sergeant who stopped a private soldier bayoneting a German prisoner by saying, 'Stop Jim, he's some mother's son.' That same private soldier a few months later was one of the stretcher bearers when Hardy received his fatal wound and remembered Hardy saying to him, 'I've been hit. I'm sorry to be a nuisance.'

That was all. The Colonel stepped down from the pulpit and resumed his seat opposite me in the sanctuary. He looked unhappy as though he feared he had not said enough but I caught his eye and smiled at him because I wanted him to know that in a few sentences he had captured the true nature of the man I remembered killed in battle doing Christ-like deeds.

The large congregation took a long time to leave the church and my mother and I waited until the end as we always did. As the nave cleared, I saw a chaplain in uniform standing at the west end talking to one of the churchwardens but looking in my direction. Was this the man who had been with Tom at the end and on whom I had pinned my hopes of one day proving that Tom had not been guilty of murder? My first impression as I walked towards him, while the organist was still playing and other churchwardens were moving along the pews collecting service sheets, was of a tall young man with Tom's dark hair who looked too much at ease in his officer's tunic and polished riding boots to be a monk.

He held out his hand. 'I'm Peter Quinn,' he said.

When he had accepted my mother's invitation to stay for lunch and had paid his respects to Hardy's family, I managed to draw him away from the crowd and suggest that if we wished to talk alone for a while, we could walk along Church Brow or down the Radical Steps to the river. As I had expected he would, he reminded me that he could not break his oath and, as I had planned to do, I said I only wanted to hear as much about his meetings with Tom as he was at liberty to tell me.

We spent less than an hour alone together on this first occasion, walking to the Devil's Bridge and back, pausing from time to time to watch the river and to think our own thoughts about what was not being said.

They had first met at Talbot House in Poperinghe. Tom had come in with a group of men and had sat down next to Father Peter to write a letter. He had not had much time for small talk, Father Peter remembered. 'When he discovered I was from Downside Abbey, he asked me whether I believed that God had foreknowledge of what was going to happen. A lot of men were interested in whether their fate had already been decided but they talked in terms of luck and superstition, the bullet with your number on it, that sort of thing. Tom wanted to have a serious theological discussion.'

I asked whether Tom was popular with the other men and he replied that he thought he was. At the divisional football matches it was obvious the other men looked up to Tom, as though they thought he could have been an officer but had chosen to serve in the ranks. They had met again briefly when the Fusiliers came out of the line and it was on that occasion that Tom had told Father Peter I was expecting a baby. 'He was very proud and very excited,' Father Peter said.

We had reached the Devil's Bridge which rose high above us, and, I chose this moment to say to Father Peter that I refused to believe Tom had been guilty of murder.

'Tom is with God and has received God's mercy,' he said. 'I can understand why you think so, Katherine, but Tom was not a victim of injustice. He was a casualty of the war just as much as if he had been killed in battle. I honestly believe it would be best for you and for your child if you can think of Tom's death in that way.'

But I would never be able to do that while I remained in ignorance of what Tom was supposed to have done and I told him so. I wanted him to know that, however binding the oath he had taken, I would not give up until I had discovered the truth.

When we returned to the Rectory, I introduced him to my father. Brodie, who had only just learnt to walk and seemed to have a permanent bruise on his forehead as a result of his bumps and falls, demanded attention. Father Peter bent down and lifted him in his arms. 'Heavens, what a weight,' he exclaimed and Brodie hit him on the nose. Out of the corner of my eye, I saw Mrs

Bickersteth watching this scene with her customary expression of disapproval. Although there was a Catholic church in the town, it occurred to me that Father Peter might be the first Roman Catholic priest to cross the threshold of the Rectory and that Mrs Bickersteth was thinking the previous rector would never have allowed such a thing.

My father at least had a reason to be guarded in his dealings with a Roman Catholic priest – the Pope did not even recognise Anglican orders – but Father Peter's pleasant and open manner and the fact that he was wearing the King's uniform must have disarmed any suspicion on my father's part because the two men were soon in discussion over lunch about the problems of returning to the monastic life. 'It is a lesson in humility,' Father Peter was saying. 'For nearly four years I have been my own master and now I am a junior monk again. Last week I was reprimanded for excessive laughter in the refectory.'

Tom had written in his last letter that Father Peter was 'as good a friend as I have known' and I was beginning to understand what Tom had liked about this Benedictine monk who could see the funny side of monastic obedience and had risked his life regularly to bring comfort to the dying. The fact that they did not share the same religious conviction would not have mattered to Tom at all.

Father Peter left for the station after lunch, having promised my mother and father that he would come back one day if the Abbot gave him permission. Brodie and I walked with him across the churchyard that was filled with daffodils. As Brodie refused to hold my hand and ran off unsteadily among the tombstones, tripping on the long grass and picking himself up again, I asked Father Peter how long the War Office could be trusted to keep its promise not to reveal the details of Tom's court martial. He did not know but thought it would be at least for fifty years. If he could find out he would write to tell me.

'I hope you will visit Downside when Brodie is older,' he said. 'There is a Benedictine convent in the village where you can stay.

Until then, please write to me from time to time about Brodie. He is going to be a handful.'

'He already is,' I said.

'Goodbye Katherine, God bless you both.'

I continued to live at the Rectory throughout Brodie's childhood. Two or three times a year, my father said he thought he should retire but neither the bishop nor the family took him seriously and he did not press the point. So Brodie grew up in Kirkby Lonsdale and played with the local boys and learnt to love the fells and the Lune Valley as much as I did. He had my fair complexion and my sea-blue eyes – he was a Viking, I told him, whose ancestors had settled here hundreds of years ago – but I was sure he had inherited his father's restless and enquiring mind because almost as soon as he could put a sentence together, he pestered adults with questions and was seldom satisfied with the answer he was given. No one suffered more from his tenacity than Mrs Bickersteth whose old wives' tales, which had been tolerated in the family for years, were now subjected to analysis and criticism. 'How do poppies bring bad luck?' Brodie demanded to know.

'I am sure all mothers see such flashes of future brilliance in the questions their children ask,' I wrote to Father Peter. He replied that as the youngest of thirteen children he had never been in a position to hear the brilliant questions his older siblings asked but he doubted whether they would have been clever enough to undermine Mrs Bickersteth's universe as effectively as Brodie.

I was proud of Brodie but I feared his enquiring mind. How long would he just accept that his father had died of wounds without asking further questions? As soon as he was old enough to understand, I explained to him that his daddy was not here because he had been killed in the war and that Tom was with God and was waiting for us in Heaven. When the town's war memorial in the churchyard was consecrated by my father at an open-air service with a bugler from the Yeomanry sounding the Last Post, I told Brodie that his father's name was not on the memorial because he had not been a Kirkby Lonsdale man.

'Where is his name?' Brodie asked and I told him it was on his father's grave in Belgium near the battlefields where he had fought. The War Office had told me that Tom's grave had not been registered but later I received an army form which said he was buried in the British Cemetery in Poperinghe and that his grave was 'marked by a durable wooden cross with the inscription bearing his name, rank and regiment and the date of his death.' At first, Brodie said he wanted to see his father's grave and I identified a travel company that offered a package deal including cross-channel steamer and hotel accommodation but that autumn, when he was five and a half and had started at St Mary's Church School, his interest in the trip and in talking about his father faded. I put this down to the fact that no other child in his class had lost a father in the war and Brodie did not want to be different.

I suppose I should have been thankful that Brodie did not want to know more about his father but I was sad that when I read to him Tom's letters from the front, I could tell he was not listening. He had no memory of his father and the mood of the times did not encourage children to look back at a war they had never known. Despite the war memorials and the two minutes silence on Armistice Day, so scrupulously observed in our part of the world that the train on the branch line stopped and the driver and his fireman climbed down from the cab to stand beside the track, most adults seemed eager to forget the war as new fads and fancies took over. But my fear that the war would come back to harm Brodie was never far beneath the surface.

In the late summer of 1926 when I was thirty-five and Brodie was a young man of eight, Amy married a regular officer she had nursed during the war at Wilton House and once again a soldier waited at the altar steps and Mrs Bickersteth stood guard over a wedding cake in the Rectory garden. There were uniformed officers in the congregation and at the reception they asked questions about which regiment my husband had been in and where he had been killed. Their expressions of sympathy and of fellow feeling for a man who had been at Third Ypres should have reassured me but I feared that any one of them might by chance have known about Tom's execution.

Not long after Amy's wedding, I received a letter from Harry Melrose. He was home on leave from India and wanted even at this late date to send me his deepest sympathy. He had learnt of my husband's death and discovered my married name when he had asked after me at the QA's London Headquarters. It would probably have done me the world of good to see Harry Melrose again and listen to him trying to convince himself that he was in love with me and I could hear Kitty telling me not to be a fool but I tore up the letter and threw the pieces on the fire. Harry's regiment had been in the same brigade as Tom's Royal Fusiliers and I could not risk the possibility that he had heard about the execution of a Private Kennedy.

These alarms made me determined to persuade Father Peter to break his oath. Brodie was approaching that part of his young life when he would be most vulnerable to the shock of being told that his father was not one of the glorious dead but a convicted murderer. Now more than ever, I needed to have the evidence, which I was sure Father Peter could give me, that what the army called murder had not been murder at all.

As an only child living with his widowed mother and his grandparents, Brodie grew up so quickly I was afraid of losing him too soon but as the child turned into a boy, he remained a loving and devoted son who seemed to be as happy curling up with me on the sofa in front of the fire as he was climbing on the fells or going out at dusk with his friends from school to watch one of the local men who trained owls and flew them over the meadows at voles and rats. Twice a year I took him to stay with Tom's father in Cambridge and a strong bond developed between grandfather and grandson, a bond of which I was sometimes jealous because I felt excluded. The Professor was trying to make up for his failure to create a bond with his own son, I thought, by lavishing attention on Brodie.

At school, Brodie's teachers complained that he asked too many questions and when I met the headmistress in the town, she always frowned before telling me that Brodie was doing very well. I do not think any of them understood Brodie. In some ways he was just like Tom. He was popular and enjoyed the company of other boys but he did not appear to need close friends. He was bright and independent, impatient and stubborn. He joined in the rough and tumble of a rural boyhood but his favourite occupation was writing poetry. While I loved to catch these glimpses of Tom in his son, I did not tell Brodie too often how like his father he was.

I wrote regularly to Father Peter to let him know how 'the Handful' was getting on and he sometimes gave me advice, usually along the lines of 'I shouldn't worry too much about that if I were you' and I wondered whether he took the same approach to the behaviour of the boys he was teaching at Downside School. In these letters about Brodie I argued for my being in a position to tell him exactly what his father had done in case the fact of Tom's execution was made public. Although Father Peter assured me several times that the War Office could be trusted, I pointed out to him that Parliament or public opinion might force the War Office's hand. Since the war ended, there had been an almost continuous discussion in the newspapers about shell shock and the execution of soldiers who had lost their nerve. I followed the reports of the Shell Shock Committee with a professional interest but I became increasingly anxious that the campaign to abolish the death penalty for soldiers might provoke a demand for the court martial records to be opened.

The leading campaigner was a Labour Member of Parliament called Ernest Thurtle and, after much hesitation, I wrote to him. I did not reveal that I had a personal interest but said the worst thing for the widow of a man who had been executed must be not being told any details of his offence and suggested that, while the court martial records should remain closed, relatives should have the right to know the whole truth.

From: Ernest Thurtle MP (Labour)

House of Commons
London SW

20 April 1929

Dear Mrs Kennedy,

Thank you for your letter and for your thoughtful suggestion that relatives should be given all the facts.

I regret that on this point I am unable to help. Records of all cases, as viewed by the military authorities, are in the possession of the War Office and access to these records is not permitted even to members of parliament or relatives of the deceased. The Judge Advocate General has ruled that the records of Field General Courts Martial should remain closed for seventy-five years.

The priority now is to persuade parliament to abolish the death penalty for the specifically military offences of cowardice, desertion and quitting post. We shall have a majority in the Commons but plenty of opposition in the Lords, so our campaign still needs support. If you have any evidence you think might be useful, please forward it to me.

Meanwhile, I am sending you my leaflet, Shootings at Dawn, which I published a few years ago to alert the public to what had been done in their name. I served in the army during the war and was severely wounded at Cambrai but I have nothing but sympathy for the men who were executed and for their families.

Yours sincerely,
Ernest Thurtle

Thurtle's letter gave me no hope that he would help me find out what Tom had done but at least it confirmed that the court martial records would be closed during my lifetime and far beyond. I turned to the descriptions of the executions of soldiers during the war. In the weeks immediately after the news of Tom's death, I had found it almost impossible to drive from my mind the horror of what had happened to Tom on that September dawn in 1917 but in the years that followed, I had gradually brought the nightmare under control so that I had no hesitation in starting to read.

'Two men came and led him out of the hut where he had been guarded all night. As he left the hut, his legs gave way then one could see the fear entering his heart. Rather than marched to the firing spot, he was dragged along. When he got there, he had his hands tied behind his back, he was put up against a wall, his eyes were bandaged and the firing squad was given the order to fire. I wondered at the time, "What on earth will happen if they don't kill him completely?" and I was anxious about that but when they fired he fell to the ground writhing as all people do – even if they have been killed they have this reflex action of writhing about which goes on for some minutes. I didn't know whether he was dead or not but at that moment the sergeant in charge stepped forward, put a revolver to the man's head and blew his brains out.'

I was profoundly disturbed by this and the other equally harrowing accounts of executions. The nightmare I thought I had long ago brought under control now raged unchecked. Did they put a revolver to Tom's head and blow his brains out? Did they have to drag him to his execution? No, that at least could not have happened. Tom would have walked bravely, proudly, a better man than any of them.

I sent the leaflet to Father Peter, making an impassioned plea to be told what Tom had done to deserve that death. 'It is not just for Brodie's sake that I need to know,' I wrote, 'but for my own too. If you cannot help me now, I do not think I shall ever have peace of mind.

Downside Abbey,
Stratton on the Fosse
Near Bath
Somerset

5 May 1929
Dear Katherine,

I am very sorry these accounts of executions in the war have been sent to you. In view of Mr Thurtle's campaign, there must be some doubt as to whether they are reliable but I understand very well your distress.

I have spoken with the Abbot Ramsay. He is a dear friend whose opinion I value greatly. He advises me against breaking the undertaking I gave during the war but he made it clear that if I decided not to follow his advice, he would not consider that as a formal act of disobedience against my vow.

I have thought and prayed about your request and I have decided to go against the Abbot's advice. I cannot believe it is right that you should be kept so completely in the dark long after the war has ended, so I have been trying to find a way to reconcile my undertaking never to speak about Tom's court martial with my wish to help you. I cannot guarantee, Katherine, that knowing the truth will give you peace of mind. That is a risk we both must take.

What I propose is this. I am prepared to let you read a full written account of Tom's court martial on the condition that you promise not to share this information with anyone else while the details of the court martial remain closed to the public. I agree that if Brodie should hear of his father's execution from any other source, you have a right to tell him the whole story or to bring him here to read the account for himself.

If you are prepared to accept this condition, I suggest that we meet here as soon as you are able to make the journey. Let me know the date and I will see that the nuns are expecting you.

I did not reply to your last letter so let me take this opportunity to send my congratulations to Brodie on his scholarship to Queen Elizabeth the First Grammar School. I don't see why you should say he has his father's brains when it has been evident to me since we first met at Hardy's Memorial Service that his mother is a woman of high intelligence and strong will, not to mention powers of persuasion.

I send you both my blessing and my prayers.

Yours very sincerely in Christ,
Peter

I accepted Father Peter's condition and at the first opportunity, when Brodie was spending the weekend on my godfather's farm near Sedbergh, I travelled to Downside.

The window of the parlour looked out over the school fields where boys in white flannels were playing cricket, while on the boundary two monks in black were walking together and other boys were lounging on the grass in the late afternoon sun. Father Peter had met me at Chilcompton Station and driven me in the monastery car to St. Benedict's, the Victorian house in Stratton on the Fosse that served as a convent for the small community of nuns. He suggested he should come back after Vespers when I would have had time to read his account of Tom's court martial. He could not miss Compline which was as 8 o'clock but there would be plenty of time to talk again in the morning.

In contrast to the sunlit scene outside the window, the parlour was rather gloomy with heavy, uncomfortable looking furniture and a musty smell as though the room was very seldom used. But I was not interested in my surroundings.

CHAPTER TWELVE

An account of the Court Martial and Death of Private Tom Kennedy in 1917, by Dom Peter Quinn, sometime Captain in the Royal Army Chaplains Department.

I am writing this account for Katherine Kennedy, Tom Kennedy's widow. I was Tom Kennedy's defending officer or prisoner's friend and my account is based on notes I made at the time or shortly after Tom's death.

The officers who are members of the court are sworn to secrecy on oath but the defending officer is not normally required to give an undertaking that he will not write or talk about the court's proceedings. In Tom Kennedy's case, however, the Divisional Commander, who convened the court martial, asked me to give such an undertaking because he feared the discipline of the army would be adversely affected at a critical time if the details of Tom's offence were widely known. I accepted this argument but I am now – May 1929 – breaking that solemn undertaking because Katherine Kennedy has a right to know the full story and because the argument about the discipline of the army no longer applies.

Tom Kennedy was charged with murder. When I received his request to be his defending officer, I went to see him in Poperinghe where he was being held in custody. We had met three times before and although these meetings had been brief, we had got on well and a degree of trust already existed between us. I asked him whether he was guilty and he replied that he had killed a man but had not intended to do so and considered himself not guilty of murder.

Then I asked him to recall in as much detail as possible exactly what had happened and to give me any background information that might help his case.

He chose to give the background first because that would explain why he acted as he did.

Together with other young members of the Independent Labour Party, he had opposed the war and, when it started, had devoted his energies to the campaign to prevent compulsory military service being introduced. He was not a pacifist because he believed there could be circumstances in which it was morally justified to use violence, even to kill, in order to prevent a greater evil. But that was the individual's choice. The government should not have the power to compel its citizens to kill.

When conscription was introduced in 1916, he applied for exemption as a conscientious objector. His application was refused and he was arrested and handed over to the military. For eight months, he was a soldier refusing orders and then a prisoner at Winchester Prison. When the government offered him a chance to do work of national importance out of prison he decided to accept but he became increasingly disillusioned by the type of work he was required to do and by the attitude of some of his fellow conscientious objectors whose sincerity he questioned. The contrast between the life he was leading and the work Katherine was doing as a nurse close to the front line in France helped to convince him that he could not in all honesty continue to claim to be a conscientious objector. He had tried to prevent conscription and had failed. It was time to accept that failure and join the army.

He married Katherine Lovegrove in May 1917 and a week later sailed for France with a draft of the Royal Fusiliers to join the 12th Battalion, then stationed in the Ypres Salient. He had no trouble adapting to army life, he got on well enough with the other men in his platoon and, at the time of his arrest, he had a clean conduct sheet. The only problem was that he had no confidence in his platoon commander, 2nd Lieutenant Grice, but he insisted that the other men in the platoon and the NCOs shared his opinion.

The battalion went into action on the first day of the Battle of Passchendaele and it was on that day that an incident occurred that had a profound affect on Tom Kennedy's attitude to his platoon commander. According to Tom, Grice killed two German prisoners 'in cold blood'. When I asked the platoon Sergeant about this, he confirmed that two German prisoners had been killed but added that the platoon commander had had no choice as no one could be spared to take the prisoners back to our lines.

The other men in the platoon were reluctant to talk about this incident but Tom could not put it out of his mind and he admitted that his revulsion at what Grice had done sometimes took the form of wishing the platoon commander dead.

The battalion was withdrawn on 22 August and returned to the line on 1 September. By then everyone knew that Haig's offensive had stalled but Tom's army commander (Gough, I think) insisted that the offensive spirit should be maintained by small scale attacks and raids and it was on one of these raids that the alleged murder took place.

Most raids at this stage in the war were carefully planned but the one in which Tom took part seems to have been an off-the-cuff affair ordered by the battalion commander and carried out by twenty volunteers from D Company under the command of 2nd Lieutenant Grice. The aim was the usual one of capturing German prisoners to identify which regiments were holding that section of the line.

When I asked Tom why he had volunteered when most married men would have kept their heads down, he replied that over the recent rest period Grice had found out that he had been a conscientious objector and had been taunting him ever since in front of the whole platoon. There is little doubt that in the days leading up to the 'murder', the relationship between Tom and his platoon commander was one of intense mutual hostility.

The raid took place in the early hours of Wednesday 5 September. Faces were blackened, some men, including Tom, carried rifles, others had knives, coshes and sharpened bayonets.

Once in the German trench, the raiding party spread out to check the dugouts for suitable prisoners and to snatch what luxuries they could find in the way of wine, coffee and cigars. Grice went straight to one of the deep dugouts signalling to Tom to follow him down the stepladder. Despite the darkness and the blackened faces, Tom claimed that Grice knew who he was selecting to accompany him.

The dugout was lit by two candles and in the flickering light, Tom made out the figure of a young German soldier with his hands raised in surrender. Fearing that Grice might shoot the young German out of hand, Tom gestured to the boy to move over to the stepladder. His intention was to take the German prisoner but before the German moved, Grice ordered Tom to shoot. According to Tom the actual words Grice used were, 'Shoot you bloody conchie'. Tom hesitated and the German, realising what was happening, fell to his knees and held up what looked like a crucifix in front of him. Tom saw Grice with his revolver in his hand take a step towards the kneeling figure. Almost simultaneously, Tom squeezed the trigger of his rifle.

Tom never denied that he had fired to prevent Grice using his revolver. When I put it to him that his reaction to Grice's movement could have been to shoot at the German as he had been ordered to do and that Grice had moved into the line of fire, he shook his head. He had not wanted or intended to kill Grice but he could not pretend it was an accident.

After assuring himself that Grice was dead – according to Tom the bullet struck the side of Grice's head and would have killed him outright – and having exchanged a glance with the German soldier who was still on his knees and still holding the crucifix in front of him, Tom climbed back up the ladder and out of the dugout. The other members of the raiding party were already withdrawing; they had captured two German prisoners and were anxious to get out of the German trench as quickly as possible. Four men were missing, including Grice, but Sergeant Baxendale decided it was too dangerous to wait and led the party back to the British lines. Once there, Tom immediately reported what he had done and Sergeant Baxendale placed him under arrest.

I had no reason to doubt Tom's version of what happened; on the contrary, I was convinced he was telling the truth. I had been at the front long enough to have heard the rumours that British soldiers had got away with murder in the confusion of the battle and I realised that a more unscrupulous man than Tom would never have reported the incident; there was only one witness and he was on the other side of No Man's Land. Tom could easily have told a different version in which Grice had been killed by accident. I am sure some people would say that Tom was his own worst enemy but he was adamant that he had to take responsibility for what he had done and, even if it had not been too late to change his story, I would not have asked him to do so. Where I think Tom was naïve was in his belief that his integrity would count in his favour if it came to a court martial.

When I asked whether Sergeant Baxendale and Tom's friend, Jim Bellringer, could be witnesses to Tom's previous good character, I was told that the battalion had returned to the front line and that both men had been reported missing. Tom himself was held in a cell in the Town Hall at Poperinghe and the Provost Marshal's Department gave strict instructions that, apart from myself, he should have no visitors or contact with the outside world. His guards were forbidden to talk to him and any letters or parcels that arrived for him were not delivered. The reason for these precautions was that the army's hierarchy thought that Tom's killing of 2nd Lieutenant Grice had been an act of rebellion and so went to extraordinary lengths to prevent any details of Tom's offence being known.

By the end of August 1917, the failure of Haig's offensive and the terrible conditions in which the men had been fighting had caused widespread disaffection and some senior officers were afraid that it would not take much to turn disaffection into mutiny. Discipline had collapsed in the Russian army and there were rumours of French soldiers refusing to obey orders. The men in the 12th battalion of the Royal Fusiliers were not rebels or mutineers any more than Tom was but it was Tom's misfortune that his court martial took place at a time when fear of mutiny among British troops was probably more acute than at any other time during the war. When the Divisional Commander asked me to give an undertaking never to reveal the facts of Tom's case, he told me in confidence that he feared there was going to be trouble at the hated Bull Ring in Etaples where Australians and Highlanders were defying authority.

Tom's Field General Court Martial was held on 15 September, well away from Poperinghe at a farmhouse near Abeele. The court met in the large farmhouse kitchen with a grey blanket covering the kitchen table. The members of the court – an infantry major as president and three captains, one of whom was the Court Martial Officer with legal training – sat behind the table with the prosecuting officer at one end. Tom and I sat on kitchen chairs facing the members of the court with two military policemen standing at ease to our left on either side of the door that led out into the deserted farmyard.

Tom and I had agreed that our best hope was to convince the court that Tom's character and record argued strongly against his being a murderer but from the start it was clear that the prosecuting officer, who was the Adjutant of Tom's battalion, had anticipated the line we would take. His case depended less on the circumstances in which Grice had been killed than on his portrayal of Tom as a disaffected soldier who had not wanted to be in the army in the first place, who had developed a grudge against his platoon commander and who had seized the opportunity presented by the raid on German lines to murder him.

I made this summary of the prosecution's case: The fact that Private Kennedy had killed 2nd Lieutenant Grice was not in dispute. He had confessed to shooting Grice on 5 September. His decision to report his crime had been the calculated risk of a clever man. He knew it was almost certain that other members of the raiding party had seen him follow Grice into the dugout and that they may well have heard the shot, so he gambled that no court would find him guilty of murder if he reported the crime himself. But just to make sure, he invented this story of a German soldier on his knees and holding up a crucifix to give himself an apparently selfless motive for firing the shot. Very clever but not clever enough. If Private Kennedy had wanted the court to believe his story, why did he not bring his German prisoner back with the others? He could not, of course, because his German prisoner never existed. The defending officer will seek to portray Private Kennedy as an honest man motivated by a desire to save human life but Private Kennedy's record shows a very different character; a so-called conscientious objector who made common cause with Marxists and anarchists, a soldier who persistently refused orders and was sentenced to Field Punishment and civil prison, a trouble-maker who right at the start of his military career at Mill Hill Barracks was the spokesman for men defying the authority an officer. How far Private Kennedy's murder of 2nd Lieutenant Grice was motivated by personal animosity and how far by hatred of the officer class, we would never know but of one thing we could be certain. This was no unintentional killing but the cold-blooded opportunist murder of a brave officer.

Tom then made a statement on oath, describing to the court, as he had done to me, exactly what had happened on 5 September and insisting he had not intended to kill his platoon commander. He had been warned that his statement could only deal with the facts of the case and could not refer to Grice's killing of the two German prisoners on 31 July. When he had finished, the members of the court had no questions.

It would have been normal practice for the court to consider its verdict before hearing evidence of character but the president said that as Tom's character was central to the question of whether he had intended to kill Grice and whether his version of events could be believed, the court would hear evidence of character first. That decision at least gave me a chance to influence the verdict and I thanked the president for it.

If I were asked now what I thought of the president of the court and whether Tom had a fair trial, I would answer both questions in the same way. There were a number of occasions during the pauses in the proceedings, while the evidence was taken down in longhand, when I caught the president looking at me with a sad and not unsympathetic expression that seemed to say, 'Why are we doing this? It is a foregone conclusion.' Tom's trial may have been fair within the limits of a court martial in the field but in the climate of disaffection that existed in September 1917, a soldier who admitted killing his platoon commander was guilty of murder before he stepped into the court.

Perhaps I am trying to excuse my failure as a defending officer but I don't think so. At the time, I thought I could convince the court that Tom was not guilty of murder or at least that I could persuade them to make a strong recommendation of mercy. A Benedictine monk is not trained in the subtleties of argument but that was probably to Tom's advantage; military men prefer plain speaking. My aim was to persuade the court that the prosecuting officer's portrayal of Tom was wrong in every respect without sounding like a barrister scoring points.

This is a summary of what I said: Tom Kennedy had acted with rare integrity throughout the war, especially in facing up to the conflicting demands of conscience and patriotism. He was a member of the Independent Labour Party but was neither a Marxist nor an anarchist. His ideals were those of Christian Socialism. He had opposed conscription as many patriotic people had because it was an alien imposition and ran counter to our traditional liberties and he was prepared to be arrested rather than compromise. He refused orders, not to undermine military discipline but to remain true to his belief that conscription was wrong. What made him stand out from other men who shared his belief was that once it became clear that the battle to prevent conscription had been lost, he abandoned his conscientious objection and joined the army. He could have continued doing civilian work of national importance but he refused to take that easy way of avoiding the trenches. As a willing soldier he was never in any trouble; on the contrary, his platoon sergeant wanted to recommend him for promotion. He bitterly regretted causing his platoon commander's death. As the court had heard, he was not afraid to take responsibility for this tragic event but he insisted that he acted on the spur of the moment to save the life of a German who had already surrendered and that he had had no intention of killing Mr Grice. Private Kennedy was a married man whose wife was expecting their first child early in the New Year. He was a man of unusual honesty and moral courage who had made a terrible mistake while on active service. He was not a murderer.

Tom had asked me not to refer to his father or to Katherine's work as a nurse in France and Belgium and it was only with difficulty that I persuaded him to let me tell the court that he was married and a father-to-be. He may have been right in thinking that too many personal details would not help his case.

I was allowed to remain with Tom while the members of the court considered their verdict. They took their time and I began to think it was just possible that the verdict was not after all a foregone conclusion. At one point, Tom said 'If I am found guilty, I would like you to be with me at the end' but he did not sound like a man who was resigned to an unfavourable outcome. When we were called back into the court room and the president said the court had 'no verdict to announce at this time' I could tell that Tom, standing beside me, thought that might be good news. He was led away and I was told he was being taken back to the cell in Poperinghe to await the verdict.

When he had left and the others had gone outside to call up our transport, the president and I were left alone. He said he was sorry but it was now 'up to the C-in-C'. Tom had been found guilty and sentenced to death but he could not be told until Haig had decided whether or not to confirm the sentence. I suppose it was the army's way of being merciful; better for Tom to travel hopefully for a few more days while there was a chance the sentence would not be confirmed.

It could take up to three weeks for the papers of a condemned man to work their way up the army hierarchy to the commander-in-chief but Haig must have received Tom's papers within a week because I was summoned back to the Town Hall in Poperinghe on the evening of 22 September.

Tom did not have to endure the public announcement of his sentence in front of his former comrades as happened to some other men condemned to death. He was told in his cell by the battalion adjutant who had been the prosecuting officer. I was there with a medical officer and an assistant provost marshal. When Tom heard that the sentence was to be carried out 'at 0700 hours tomorrow', he flinched as any man would but he stood firm until the adjutant had finished and departed with the other officials. Then he sat down on the bed and said, 'Don't worry, Father, I've been expecting it.' I told him I would be with him now until the end at which he smiled and said in that case, if I didn't mind, he would like to sleep for a while as he hadn't slept for several nights. He took off his puttees and boots and lay on the bed with his knees drawn up to his chest and his face to the wall. He must have been very tired as he slept soundly and did not wake until just before one o'clock in the morning.

The last hours that Tom and I spent together are very clear in my memory. For much of the time, he wanted to talk, especially about his love for his wife Katherine and for the child he would never hold in his arms. There were also periods of silence when I thought I had lost him because he appeared detached and far away as though he considered himself already dead and other rather longer silences when I could tell he was struggling to force down the fear he was determined to control.

Tom was not an easy man to help because he was not an easy man to understand. Of his love for his wife, his intelligence and his moral and physical courage I have no doubt. He was also good company even in those uniquely grim circumstances. But for all his openness and willingness to talk, I was left with the feeling when he had gone that I didn't really know him.

I had given the Last Absolution to men going into battle and Extreme Unction to Catholic soldiers who were dying but Tom was not a Roman Catholic and the Sacraments that would have helped us both were not available. I wanted to comfort him but it was clear he did not want to talk about his religious faith except on his own terms and in his own time. When I asked him whether it would help if we said a psalm and a prayer together, he replied, 'Yes but not yet.'

He told me he had been trying to remember all the verses of a poem by Henry Newbolt called "He fell among thieves". The poem was about a young man of his own age who is ambushed by bandits in a far off country and, because he has killed one of their number in self-defence, is condemned to die at dawn. During a night 'untroubled by hope' he remembers all the good times of his childhood and youth.

Tom said that because there was no more hope, he had been lying awake, free at last to think about all the good times he and Katherine had spent together. He hated the idea of dying when they both had so much to look forward to but he was one of the lucky few who had known what it was to love and be loved. Men were being killed every day who had never experienced that joy. If death was the end, he was grateful to have had the chance to be really alive.

'Death is not the end, Tom,' I said but his response – 'I hope you're right' – indicated that what was uppermost in his mind was not the possibility of Eternal Life but how to face the terrible reality that awaited him. I think he had been seeking and had found a way of seeing his own death in perspective, of diminishing its importance, and that this was giving him courage. I cannot remember his exact words but they went something like this. 'There is life after death, of course there is, not my life but Katherine's and our child's and millions of others. Life doesn't stop just because I am not there. That's what I shall think about at the last moment. Life going on.' And as though he was anxious to put his resolve to the test, he walked across to the small barred window several times to look at the night sky. I glanced at the clock. It was half-past three.

Although I did not wish to thrust religion at him, certainly not in Roman Catholic terms, I wanted to encourage him to make some sort of confession so that he did not remember something on his conscience when it was too late to deal with it. I was considering how best to do this when, still standing by the window, he said it was impossible for him to be sure now what had been in his mind, it had all happened so quickly.

He had not expressed any doubt about his motive before. For a moment I was afraid he was going to confess that he had intended to kill Grice but he went on to say that he could remember clearly in that split second wanting to stop Grice killing the German soldier but that ever since he had been asking himself whether, if it had been someone else, not Grice, he would have fired.

I told him firmly not to torment himself with that question – people's motives were seldom, if ever, simple and I had no doubt at all that he had acted not to take life but to save it. Whatever the court had decided, it was God's judgment that mattered and he should throw himself on the mercy of God. When he looked uncertain about that, I said that everyone had doubts, monks as much as anyone else, which was why Saint Benedict had instructed his followers that they were never to lose hope in the mercy of God.

After a short silence, I suggested this might be the time for us to pray together but he was still not ready to do so. He wanted to tell me how much he had missed his mother who had died when he was only twelve and how sad he was that he would not now have the chance to get to know his father better. He said he had no debts and that his will, leaving all he had to Katherine, was written inside his pay book and had been witnessed by his company commander. He did not blame the members of the court martial for making their decision. He had no grudge against anyone and if anyone had a grudge against him, he hoped they would forgive him now.

At a quarter to six he said he would write his last letter to Katherine; he had been putting it off because he could not bear to say goodbye. He sat at the small wooden table and started to write. When he had finished he folded the letter and gave it to me and I promised it would reach Katherine safely.

Then, at last, he said, 'I am ready to pray, Father'. We knelt together on the stone floor. At his request, I prayed for the family of Rupert Grice and for the families of all the men on both sides who had been killed in the war. He asked God to forgive him for what he had done and I gave him a form of Absolution asking God to forgive any past faults though not using the Sacramental formula. He prayed for Katherine and their child, asking God to look after them in the years to come. Then we said the Our Father together and I gave him my blessing. We were about to stand up when he remembered that he wanted to ask God to protect the young German soldier whose life he had saved.

Soon after six, breakfast was brought in. Tom ate a roll and sipped the steaming coffee but declined the tot of rum. I explained what would happen when the Assistant Provost Marshal arrived. I had checked the details because I did not want Tom's resolve to be undermined by the necessary preliminaries to an execution. He heard me without comment but he had not lost his nerve or his sense of humour. When I had finished –

'You look tired, Father.'

'I shall rest later.'

'So shall I.'

I had not intended to write any more but because Katherine has read some accounts of executions during the war which are rather highly coloured, I am adding this brief description of Tom's execution.

Soon after six-thirty, the Assistant Provost Marshal entered with the medical officer and two military policemen. One of the policemen tied a bandage over Tom's eyes, fastened his hands behind him and cut of the buttons on the front of his tunic. Forewarned, Tom made no protest, but when the medical officer, pinning a small square of lint over Tom's heart, felt something in the top pocket, Tom said, 'It's just a photograph. Please leave it.' The medical officer looked at the Assistant Provost Marshal who nodded and the photograph was allowed to remain.

We were driven the short distance to the outskirts of Poperinghe and there Tom was helped down from the back of the truck and led across a small field to a wooden post. The firing party of twelve men was drawn up about twenty-five yards from the post facing the dawn with their backs to Tom. Tom's arms and legs were secured to the post and I was allowed to stand beside him for a few moments. I grasped one of his hands to say goodbye. 'Goodbye Father, thank you', he replied quite calmly. I said 'God bless you, Tom, I shall pray for you.' Then the Assistant Provost Marshall motioned me to stand aside.

The firing party received no spoken orders. At a sign from the officer in charge, they turned about and, six standing, six kneeling, they took aim. Tom was quite still and I could not help wondering whether he was, as he had intended, thinking about the future, about life going on.

Tom died instantaneously, the medical officer reporting five bullets through the heart, so there was no need for anyone to deliver the coup de grace. A grave had already been dug in a corner of the field and the military policemen carried Tom's body there. When they had filled the grave and pressed the earth down, they walked away carrying their spades, which caught the first rays of the morning sun. I signed the label on the identifying peg which I placed at the head of the grave, and then I prayed aloud: 'Eternal rest grant unto him O Lord. Let perpetual light shine upon him. May he rest in peace.'

CHAPTER THIRTEEN

When Father Peter returned after Vespers, I was in a defiant mood. I told him that if Brodie ever learnt the truth, he would be proud of what his father had done. My reactions to the account of Tom's court martial and death were dominated by an immense sense of relief that my faith in Tom's innocence had been vindicated. He was not a murderer and he had done nothing of which his family need ever be ashamed, just as he had written in his last letter. But my relief and my deep sadness that his life had been taken in that way could not hold back for long my anger at such a blatant injustice. Grice was the murderer, not Tom, but Grice was an officer and well connected while Tom was an ordinary soldier. The officers of the court martial had stood on their own. The President had refused to accept any evidence that an English officer would callously kill a German prisoner and so had sent an innocent man to his death.

Sitting in the convent parlour on that summer evening, I had no idea what might be involved in overturning the court martial's verdict and obtaining justice for Tom but that is what I intended to do. When I told Father Peter, he raised objections. He had let me read his account of Tom's court martial on the understanding that I did not share my knowledge with anyone else, he said, and there were anyway no grounds for overturning the verdict. The court had been conducted correctly and there could be no new evidence to justify a review of Tom's case. If I tried to obtain justice for Tom, I would experience only disappointment and I might do harm by bringing Tom's execution into the open.

'What about the German boy?' I asked him. 'He is the one person who really knows what happened.'

Father Peter tried to persuade me that I should be satisfied with knowing the truth about Tom's court martial. Even if the court had believed Tom's story of the young German soldier, it would not have changed their verdict. Once Tom admitted killing his platoon officer during a raid on the German trenches, the verdict and the sentence were bound to follow.

'Then you think Tom was guilty?' I asked, making no attempt to hide my frustration.

'Tom was guilty under military law, Katherine, but I believe he had no intention of killing Grice. His impulse to save life stemmed from all that was good in him but it had tragic consequences, not only for himself and for you and Brodie but for Grice and his family too.'

'What will I tell Brodie?' I asked.

'If Brodie ever has to know, he can read the account for himself and make his own judgement,' he replied.

He had lived with the truth for years and knew his way round the arguments but I was not ready to accept there was nothing I could do to clear Tom's name. We talked on that evening until it was time for Compline. Our relationship was based almost entirely on correspondence as we had only met twice in ten years but I trusted him as Tom's friend and I understood why he wanted to discourage me from thinking I could change what had happened in the past by finding new evidence. He thought I should be content with what I had learnt and when I mentioned again the young German soldier whose life Tom had saved, he shook his head; I would be looking for a needle in a haystack and when I didn't find him, would I then be able to stop myself wondering whether Tom had been telling the truth?

During a restless night in a strange bed that question was my constant and unwelcome companion, so much so that I suspected that Father Peter had planted it deliberately, not just to deter me but to tell me that all along he had had doubts about Tom's version of Grice's death. At dawn, I dismissed that idea as ridiculous and disloyal to Tom but I could not dismiss all together the thought that unless we knew for certain that the young German soldier had existed, there would always be for me and eventually for Brodie and for his children, the shadow of a doubt.

In the morning, Father Peter made another attempt to convince me that it would be impossible to prove Tom's story was true; we had to have faith in the man we knew. I thanked him for all he had done for Tom and for me and then I said that as the young German soldier was the only witness, I was determined to find him. I was prepared for disappointment but I wanted to try.

He sighed and smiled. 'I predict a great future for Brodie,' he said. 'If he has inherited the characteristics of both his parents he will go far. I still think you are making a mistake, Katherine, but I will use what contacts I have in the army to see if there is any way of finding that German soldier.'

We continued to correspond regularly but it was a long time before he had definite news for me. Meanwhile, Brodie started at the grammar school and I returned to nursing part-time at Kendal Hospital. I needed the money and the satisfaction of doing the job for which I had been trained. I would have loved to have had other children because Brodie was growing up so fast and, although we were still close, he sometimes showed an independence that made me think that my role as his mother would soon be over.

I was thirty-eight and a war widow and I wondered whether I would consider marrying again if anyone asked. Some women felt trapped by an obligation to honour the memory of a fiancé or husband killed in the war but I did not; I believed that Kitty had been right when she said Tom would have wanted me to live a full life. I was reconciled to having no more children but not to spending the rest of my life alone, though I feared that what had happened to Tom might always be a barrier to a new relationship. And it was because of this fear that removing any doubt about Tom's story of the young German soldier became the key to my own future as well as to Brodie's chance of one day being proud of his father.

In the autumn of 1929, Brodie underwent a sudden conversion. His almost total indifference to the war in which his father had been killed was transformed when Tom's father sent him a copy of All Quiet on the Western Front. I did not take much notice at the time as I was used to Tom's father sending books to his grandson but Brodie read this novel over the weekend and by the Sunday evening he was asking me whether his father had died in hospital or in No Man's Land where the doctors could not reach him.

I had long ago worked out that if Brodie asked about the circumstances of Tom's death, I would say that I had not been told where he died but that from my experience, I thought it likely he had died in a Casualty Clearing Station where there were doctors and nurses and drugs to take away the pain. This answer seemed to satisfy Brodie's curiosity on this occasion but I was sure he would now want to know more about Tom's life in the war and to read his father's letters for himself. Tom's last letter and all the letters from Father Peter and the War Office I had hidden safely away.

At home, I could deal with Brodie's new enthusiasm for reading about the war but when the time came for our next visit to Cambridge in the Easter holidays in 1930, I was afraid that Tom's father, pressed by Brodie to talk about where Tom had died, might say something that would arouse Brodie's suspicions. The Professor had given no hint during our many visits over the years that he knew how his son had died but I believed that he did at least know Tom had not died of wounds and his obvious determination to encourage Brodie's interest in the war made me wonder whether he was trying to force the subject of Tom's death out into the open.

On the day we arrived, he gave Brodie Edmund Blunden's new edition of Wilfred Owen's poems and the following evening he took us to the Arts Theatre to see Journey's End, R C Sherriff's play about life in the trenches. When we returned from the theatre and Brodie had said goodnight, he told me the Americans were making a film of All Quiet on the Western Front and that he would take Brodie to see it when it opened. Unwisely perhaps, I said I thought Brodie could have too much of the war.

'What are you afraid of, Katherine?' Tom's father asked and in such a way, looking directly at me with his eyes searching my face, I was in no doubt that he was asking me how much I knew. Twelve years ago we had let slip an opportunity to be frank with one another and I would have loved to have told him now that his son was innocent of murder but I dared not take the risk. If I was wrong and he knew nothing, I would destroy whatever peace of mind he had arrived at to comfort his old age, so I replied that I was just anxious that Brodie should not spend all his time reading about the war. 'His father was reading Macaulay at his age,' the Professor said.

I had to wait nearly another year before Father Peter at last identified someone who might be able to help me find Tom's German soldier. He apologised for the delay, he had been over-optimistic about his contacts, but he thought Captain Victor Rockeby at the Imperial War Museum would be worth writing to 'along the lines we agreed'. He had been a contemporary of Father Peter at Downside School and was now engaged in creating an archive of the German army for the Museum.

I wrote at once, giving Captain Rockeby details of Tom's battalion and the date of the raid on the German trenches and saying that I wished to contact the German soldier whose life my late husband had saved on that occasion.

His reply was not encouraging.

Imperial War Museum
Lambeth Road
London

23 February 1931

Dear Mrs. Kennedy,
Thank you for your letter. I cannot hold out much hope of being able to help you.

Even if the German soldier survived the war or his story was well known in the regiment, there is no guarantee he could be identified. Identifying the German regiment holding that sector of the line on 5 September 1917 is relatively straightforward but a German regiment is equivalent to a British brigade and contains at least three thousand men.

Some German regiments have published regimental histories in recent years and our library has copies but they are printed in the old Gothic script and without an index so that even a German speaker such as myself would not have the time to search for a reference to an incident such as the one in which your late husband may have been involved. Stories of chivalrous gestures and miraculous escapes were commonplace during the war and most of them bore no more relation to the truth than the Angel of Mons, so they are unlikely to appear in regimental histories anyway.

Some German regiments have a Veterans Association and that would be a possible line of enquiry, though the largest Veterans Association, the Stahlhelm, currently refuses to respond to requests for information from this country.

Please convey my greeting to Dom Peter Quinn. As he suggested that you should approach me, I will see whether there is any realistic way to take the matter forward but I strongly urge you not to anticipate a favourable outcome. Nor should you expect further correspondence for some time.

Yours sincerely,
Victor Rockeby

I resigned myself to another long wait but I did not lose hope and with Brodie approaching puberty and adolescence and my work at Kendal Hospital, I had plenty to occupy me. When he was about fourteen and a half, Brodie plunged into adolescence with the impatience of a swimmer who is determined to reach the far bank as quickly as possible. Whereas other boys took their time to become young men, he chafed at the delay and seemed to be trying to accelerate the process. My mother and I took the strain of his unpredictable behaviour – his disappearing for the day when he should have been at school and his all too noticeable walking out in the middle of my father's sermon. The headmaster of the grammar school called me in on several occasions to tell me there was a limit to the school's forbearance. 'Brodie needs a father,' he said as though it was my responsibility to acquire one as soon as possible.

If Brodie and I were alone together, he was not an angel, more like a devil resting between performances, but at least we could talk to one another. His latest enthusiasm was the No More War Movement, a consequence of the books Tom's father had encouraged him to read. He subscribed to the journal No More War and he pointed out to me the name of the editor. It was Fenner Brockway.

'He was a friend of Daddy's, wasn't he?' he said.

'Yes, they were good friends in the early part of the war.'

Brodie said he would write to Fenner to introduce himself as Tom Kennedy's son and to tell him he was going to start a branch of the No More War Movement at his school. Remembering the limit to the school's patience, I suggested he should ask the headmaster's permission first.

That was the cause of our first real quarrel, which ended with him shouting angrily at me that I always sided with the school and storming out of the house, banging the front door behind him. It was dark when he returned and I asked him if he wanted anything to eat. He shook his head. 'I want to read all my father's letters,' he said. Much later, when the house was quiet, I saw the light under his bedroom door but I resisted the temptation to go in. Instead, I lay awake for a long time in case he wanted to talk about his father but it was several days before he referred to the letters and then only to say that Fenner Brockway had done the right thing by staying in prison. And if Tom had stayed in prison, I thought, he would be alive today.

The timing of Harry Melrose's letter was fortuitous but I could not help thinking it was typical of him that he had written just when

I needed distracting from the job of coping with Brodie's adolescent moods.

Brigadier H C R Melrose
Quetta
Baluchistan
India

20 August 1932

Dear Katherine,

Will you forgive me writing again when your silence made it abundantly clear last time that you did not want to meet? My only excuse is the entirely selfish one that I would so much like to see you again. It is fifteen years since we said goodbye in Boulogne and while you, I am sure, are as lovely as ever despite your great sadness at the loss of your husband, I am becoming more of an old soldier every day and fear that if I leave it much longer you will not recognise me.

I have decided to retire from the army next year. I have gone as far as I can go in the terms of promotion and frankly I am tired of trying to keep the Hindu and the Muslim from killing one another; I did not cheat death at the Somme – thanks to a nursing sister who was at pains to be correct and professional, I remember – to end up as a glorified policeman. Besides, our rule in India is coming to a close and I would rather not be part of the retreat.

My wife and I have divorced, without rancour I'm glad to say, and she has married a cavalry officer eight years younger than herself, so I shall put the house in Worcestershire on the market and buy a flat in Kensington. I don't fancy living in London but I have to earn a living and friends have offered to give me introductions in the City. Can you imagine me setting off each morning with a bowler and a rolled umbrella? I can't but army chums who have taken that route tell me it is not so difficult once you have made up your mind it is time to move on.

Is it too much to hope that you may come to London from time to time? If not, I can easily come to Kirkby Londsdale but it would give me so much pleasure to take you to dinner in one of the best restaurants in London to make up for that rather mousy French place near the docks in Boulogne. Please say 'yes' this time as there is so much I would like to talk to you about.

With my very affectionate good wishes,

Yours sincerely,
Harry Melrose

At first, I went through the same anxiety as before, thinking Harry might know about Tom's court martial, but I persuaded myself that he would hardly have invited me to dinner in London if he knew I was the widow of a man who had been executed for murder. How Brodie would react concerned me more but Harry was not returning to England until next year, by which time Brodie should have reached the far bank and be grown up enough to understand that I was not being disloyal to his father if I enjoyed the company of other men.

I replied to Harry that I would be happy to dine with him again when he had settled in London and, as an afterthought beneath my signature, I wrote, 'Brigadier Melrose sounds very grand,' hoping he would catch the echo.

Chapter Fourteen

In our correspondence, Father Peter and I had agreed that the chaos in Germany probably accounted for Victor Rockeby's silence, so that when in the spring of 1933 Adolf Hitler came to power and restored law and order, I assumed Rockeby's enquiries would now be much easier. Yet still the weeks went by and I heard nothing. It was not until the autumn of that year that Rockeby sent me the letter I had begun to think would never come.

Imperial War Museum
Lambeth Road

21 October 1933

Dear Mrs Kennedy,

I regret that my enquiries have taken so long and that the only information I have obtained will be of limited interest.

The German regiment opposite the 12th Royal Fusiliers at the beginning of September 1917 was Infantry Regiment 371. That regiment was recruited for the most part in Berlin and it has a Veterans Association there with which I have been trying to make contact for well over a year. Last week this letter arrived from a Herr Anton Meyer who describes himself as the Secretary of the Association. I have translated this letter for you and you will see that after making his excuses and providing some unnecessary background information, Herr Meyer claims to have heard of an incident that occurred on or about 5 September in which his friend, Martin Schneider, was saved from death by a British soldier.

Before you jump to the conclusion that this is the information you were seeking, I must tell you that in my view the story lacks credibility. The most likely explanation is that Schneider witnessed an accidental shooting and decided to embellish the story with himself at the centre so he would have something interesting to tell his family when he returned home. There is no evidence that your late husband was involved in whatever incident did take place.

I regret that I cannot help you any further and my advice is that you should now let the matter drop. Your late husband gave his life for his country and his sacrifice needs no embellishment. I should warn you that the present regime in Germany would not take kindly to any attempt to contact Schneider who, from what Herr Meyer says, may well be in protective custody or have fled the country.

Yours sincerely
Victor Rockeby

Translation of Herr Meyer's letter of 1 October 1933
As General Secretary of the Veterans Association of Infanterie-Regimenter 371, I am replying to your request for information about an incident on 5 September 1917 during the 4th Battle of Flanders. I apologise for the delay. For many months, all office work has been put on one side as Veterans Associations have been playing an active part in helping the new Chancellor, Herr Hitler, to build a united Reich.

I know of an incident that may be the one to which your correspondent refers. A former friend in the regiment, Martin Schneider, claimed that his life had been saved by a British Tommy during a raid on our trenches in early September. Dr Schneider is no longer in Berlin and neither I nor this Association has any knowledge of his whereabouts so I can only tell you what he told me.

Martin Schneider and I were school friends before the war at the Freidrichs-Werdersche College in the Berlin suburb of

Charlottenburg. In November 1916, shortly after our 17ᵗʰ birthdays, we received an order to present ourselves at the armoury of the Elizabeth Guarde Regiment for physical examination and were passed fit for infantry training. We were very proud when we were told, 'You have been chosen to protect the Kaiser and the Fatherland, our homes and our women.'

We spent three months training in Baden before being sent to the Western Front to join Infanterie-Regimenter 371. When we arrived in the trenches we were given a 'Tommy's Greeting' of heavy shellfire but throughout our time at the front we had only respect for the English. We were afraid of the Scottish regiments because they did not take prisoners and we hated the French because we had been told that, if they won the war, they would give our German women to their black African troops.

Martin Schneider and I served together in the same rifle company until the end of the war. On the night in question, we had been ordered to evacuate our trench but for some reason a small number of our platoon did not receive the order and were left behind. One of these was Martin Schneider. He was alone in one of the deep dugouts when two British soldiers entered. Fearing he was going to be killed, he fell to his knees and held up a crucifix. We all carried a small crucifix or a pocket New Testament with a gold cross on the cover for just such an occasion as this. According to Schneider, the two soldiers were arguing about whether they should kill him when one of them stepped forward and pointed a revolver at Schneider's head. Schneider heard the shot but felt nothing. The soldier with the revolver was knocked off his feet and fell across a table. Still afraid he was about to be killed, Schneider glanced at the other soldier who was standing only a few feet away. To Schneider's astonishment, this soldier walked forward to see whether his comrade was dead and then left the dugout without saying a word.

Naturally, we did not believe Schneider's story at first because he was already in trouble for failing to withdraw with the rest of us but when we returned to the trench Sergeant Krueger went to inspect the dug-out and there was the British soldier with half his head blown off by the bullet fired at close range. He had no badges of rank but a letter from his mother revealed that he was an officer and on Sergeant Krueger's instructions he was given a Christian burial.

Schneider and I had been studying civil engineering before we joined the army but after the war he said he wanted to do something humanitarian because his life had been spared, so he trained to be a doctor. Unfortunately, Dr Schneider chose to work in the poorest districts of the city where he came under the influence of Marxists who are the worst enemies of the German people and that was what brought our friendship to an end.

I was triumphant. Martin Schneider's story was the same in almost every respect as the story Tom had told at his court martial and that had been dismissed as the invention of a clever man trying to hide his guilt. Four years ago, when I read Father Peter's account, I thought my faith in Tom had been vindicated. Now I was sure. It might never be possible to have the court martial's verdict overturned but I could hand on to Brodie and to future generations a memory of Tom they would be able to live with, not one they would have to shut away as a dark secret.

There was a final step I had to take before I would feel free to move on in my own life.

'You will not be surprised to hear that I do not intend to take Captain Rockeby's advice,' I told Father Peter when I wrote to give him the news. 'If I can find Martin Schneider and hear the evidence direct from him, I shall have done everything that it is possible for me to do for Tom and for the future of our family. So at the very least I must try. You have helped me for so long, dear Father Peter, sometimes against your better judgement, I know, but please stay with me for this last part of the journey. Then we shall both be able to put the past to rest.'

Downside Abbey
Stratton on the Fosse
Near Bath
Somerset
1 November 1933

Dear Katherine,

I was very glad indeed to receive your news. Hans Meyer's letter confirms what we have both always believed and that is that Tom was telling the truth about the German soldier. Although it does not prove that Tom had no intention of killing Grice, it tips the scales firmly in favour of his not being guilty of murder but of a tragic mistake inspired by his generous impulse to save life. I'm afraid the military mind is no more likely to recognise that distinction now than it was in 1917 but we know that our faith in Tom was entirely justified.

I am not at all surprised that you want to find Martin Schneider; having come this far, it would have been unlike you to be satisfied with evidence that is convincing but second hand.

If I can help, I will. There is a Benedictine Congregation in Bavaria – I stayed in one of their monasteries just before the outbreak of the war – and I will see whether they know of any way to trace a Berlin doctor who may have been arrested. Meanwhile, I suggest that you contact the British Medical Association in London to ask if a Dr Martin Schneider is among the refugees from Germany who are seeking permission to practise in this country. It is a long shot but worth trying.

Forgive me for reminding you that when you make your enquiries you cannot share with anyone your knowledge of Tom's court martial.

Let us compare notes from time to time. I am due to give Lenten talks in Whitehaven, one of our Benedictine parishes not far from you, next year, so we should be able to meet then.

May God bless you and Brodie. I always remember you both with Tom in my prayers.

Yours very sincerely in Christ,
Peter

By this time, I had become accustomed to the way my hopes rose and fell at each stage in my search for the truth about Tom's death but I had triumphed against the odds and was not disheartened by further set-backs. Our initial enquiries produced nothing. The British Medical Association had no record of a Dr Martin Schneider and the Benedictine Congregation in Bavaria regretted that they judged it too dangerous 'in the present climate of hostility towards monastic communities' to ask questions about individuals in protective custody. Neither of us knew where to turn next and my life was so disrupted by other events that I had little time even to think about where Dr Martin Schneider might be.

In March 1934, Tom's father died after a short illness and Brodie and I went down to Cambridge for the memorial service in Trinity College. My Viking son was sixteen and six feet tall. His foothold on manhood was still rather insecure but he obviously enjoyed being my escort and he took my arm as we walked into the college chapel. The address was given by the Master who praised Professor Kennedy's distinguished contribution to Hellenic studies but made only a passing reference to Tom as the only son 'who gave his life in the recent conflict' and made no mention at all of Brodie or myself. These omissions were noticed by other members of the congregation. After the service, Edgar Adrian, who had met Tom early in the war, apologised on behalf of the college and invited us to tea in his rooms.

Although I did not know it at the time, Adrian had won the Nobel Prize for medicine two years before, yet he happily spent an hour that afternoon listening as Brodie put the case for out and out pacifism as a way of preventing war. 'I recall my conversation with your father very well,' Adrian said at one point. 'I think he represented all that was best in the anti-war movement at that time.' On the way home, Brodie reminded me that Tom, in one of his letters, had said of Adrian that he had the humane, enquiring mind of the true scientist which was a contrast to the narrow pedantry of some classical dons and he asked me whether when Tom wrote that he had been thinking of his father. 'Your father and your grandfather never really understood one another,' I replied. 'They could have been much better friends than they were.'

Tom's father left a small bequest to his housekeeper, Mrs Danby, and a sum in trust to pay for Brodie's university education. The remainder of his estate, together with the house in Grange Road, he left to me. His generosity was not unexpected but I was deeply moved by it because our relationship, which had started so well when we had recognised one another as allies with Tom's interest at heart, had become less close over the years. This was partly because I resented his attempts to monopolise Brodie on our visits to Cambridge but principally because the unacknowledged truth about Tom's death made us cautious about showing too much warmth of feeling towards one another. Whether he did know how Tom had died was a secret he kept to the end but it is my belief that he did.

The possibility of moving to Cambridge and living in the house in Grange Road now became the subject of much family discussion. My mother was in favour. They had been in the parish for thirty-one years and she had confided to me often that she dreaded my father dying in harness and the family having nowhere to go, but my father, now that there was a real prospect of leaving, found reasons for staying on. Thirty-one years was not a long incumbency for Kirkby Lonsdale, he said, one of his predecessors in the eighteenth century had stayed for sixty-one years.

When I talked with Brodie about the possibility of moving to Cambridge, I thought it was characteristic of him that he was unconcerned about packing up and moving on. He would miss friends but he would make new ones and he would miss the valley and the fells but he said he had always thought of Cambridge as his second home. As for schools, if Edgar Adrian recommended that he should take his higher certificate at the Cambridge and County High School, that was good enough for him.

I was undecided. Cambridge had many happy memories for me but, unlike Brodie, I could not pull up my roots in Kirkby Lonsdale just like that. The Rectory had been my home since childhood, my father's church was where Tom and I had been married and the beautiful valley and its surrounding hills were where Tom and I had walked as young lovers and where, after his death, I had often walked alone with his memory. I was afraid that if we moved to Cambridge, I would be weakening the ties that held Tom and I together. In the end, I made the decision on the purely practical question of where I could find a job.

When I wrote to Addenbroke's Hospital, they had no job to offer but the matron suggested I should write to the Royal College of Nursing in London which kept a record of vacancies in senior posts. The General Secretary of the College, Frances Goodall, replied to my letter straight away. The College was looking for a deputy director of education who had had experience of nursing during the war and who would be interested in arranging courses for qualified nurses on aspects of war-time nursing such as the treatment of 'shell shock' and the nurse's role on active service.

Organising courses sounded to me like a poor substitute for working in a hospital but I was sufficiently interested to make the long trek to London for an interview. I was won over by the friendly charm of Frances Goodall and by the fact that the College was on the corner of Cavendish Square, not far from Brown's Hotel and Bloomsbury where Tom and I had spent our honeymoon.

So it was decided that we should all move to Cambridge at the end of Brodie's summer term. I wrote a note to Harry Melrose to say that if his offer of a better dinner than the one in Boulogne was still open, I would be working in London from the beginning of September. I saw nothing inconsistent in wanting to hold on to every memory of Tom and yet looking forward to seeing Harry Melrose again. And if Kitty asked, 'Who is the forward hussy now?' I would reply that I was only following her advice.

Father Peter, too, was on the move. The new Abbot was sending him to be parish priest of Beccles in Suffolk, a Benedictine parish for which Downside Abbey was responsible. 'As the crow flies, we shall not be far apart', he wrote. 'And there will always be a bed for me at Benet house in Cambridge.' He was following events in Germany more closely than I was and he warned me that the chances of Martin Schneider looking for work in England were small. Even if he had succeeded in escaping the Nazis, most refugees fleeing Germany were heading for France or the Netherlands and those who did come to England were probably in transit to the United States. I was not discouraged. Tom had once said that he was absurdly optimistic about the future and that is exactly how I felt. I had identified the German soldier whose life Tom had saved and soon or later we would meet face to face.

Cambridge can be a Siberian town in January and February with an icy wind blowing across the Fens and the windows of the coffee shops white with steam but on the day we moved in August 1934 it was so hot and still that we left the doors and the windows wide open at Grange Road in the hope of attracting a breeze. While the removal men sweltered under their heavy loads and my mother and I sorted out where the crockery and cutlery and linen should go, my father and Brodie disappeared as men do when there is domestic work to be done. And with them both out of the way, I broke down.

I was asking Mrs Danby whether she would be willing to come in twice a week to help with the housework as I would be going to London every day and when she replied that she would be glad to do so, I burst into tears. I was ashamed to be weeping in front of the removal men but their foreman, without a word, collected a wicker chair from the van and, carrying it into the garden, placed it under the copper beach so that I could sit down in the shade for a while. Poor Mrs Danby, who, unlike Mrs Bickersteth, was a quiet wisp of a woman, thought she had said something wrong but it was just chance that all my sadness at leaving Kirkby Lonsdale should have chosen that moment to ambush me.

I started my new job at the Royal College of Nursing on 1 September. The transition from hospital nursing was made much easier for me by my friendship with Frances Goodall, a friend-ship that at first was based on what we admired and envied in one another. She wished she had had my experience during the war and I wished I had half her elegance and sophistication. She was tall and always beautifully groomed, with luxuriant auburn hair, and she was so vivacious and knowledgeable about books and music and the theatre, she would have made me feel like a country cousin if she had not been so completely lacking in any form of vanity. No one could play the same role in my affections as Kitty had done but Frances had a more subtle worldly wisdom and I was soon talking to her freely about personal things and especially about my feelings for Harry Melrose.

I had never taken Harry's flirting seriously and was intrigued to know whether his invitation to dine with him at the Café Royal was for old time's sake or something more. 'Why don't you stay the night with me?' Frances suggested – she had a flat over the office – 'then he won't be tempted to make sure you miss the last train.'

We were sitting in the soft autumn sunshine in Cavendish Square during our lunch hour discussing Harry's motives for want-ing to see me again. We were agreed that a divorced, fifty year old retired brigadier was not looking for romance – sex, perhaps, of a not too demanding kind but not romance – and that more than anything else he was probably looking for someone to come home to, someone to turn the light on and light the fire and cook the supper.

'He will need you more than you will need him,' Frances said. 'It is always that way with a middle-aged man!' I told her that I would have a look and see what was on offer but I had nothing suitable to wear. So the next day she took me to Liberty's which had recently opened a model dress department and there, after trying on two or three that were far too expensive, I chose a dress in ivory satin and pale green silk velvet with diamante buckles and a low v-shaped back. Standing in front of the long mirror, with Frances nodding approvingly at my shoulder, I was pleased to see how well the dress showed off my figure.

Harry was waiting for me just inside the main entrance. 'You look wonderful,' he said. 'People will think I'm a millionaire.'

He was not at all the retired brigadier of Bateman's cartoons – no scarlet cheeks or bulging waist but looked much the same as when we had said goodbye eighteen years before. His hair had receded a little and he may have put on weight but in his evening clothes it did not show. He had reserved a table in the Grill Room, where the ornate gilded mirrors made me think of the casino that had served as a base hospital in Boulogne. Once we had sat down and chosen from the menu, we slipped easily into memories and confidences. Perhaps it is just for old time's sake, I thought, but Harry is a very agreeable companion. When he ordered champagne, he looked at me in mock anxiety as though he feared I was going to ask about his wife and when, later, I did ask, he spoke frankly about his wife's infidelities – the young cavalry officer she had now married had not been the first though he had been arrogant enough to assume that he was – and said that whatever love there had once been between his wife and himself had not survived the war.

'Our love did survive the war,' I said.

For a moment, Harry was puzzled but then he said, 'I'm very sorry about your husband.'

I asked him how he had heard.

'I called at your headquarters in London when I was last on leave.'

'And what did they tell you?'

'That your husband had died of wounds in 1917.'

'I shall always love Tom,' I said, satisfied that he knew nothing of the circumstances of Tom's death.

I wanted Harry to know that while I was open to the possibility of a relationship, I was not a lonely war widow looking for love but he behaved so impeccably throughout the dinner and when he walked me home up Regent Street to Cavendish Square, not even asking if could kiss me goodnight as he had done in Boulogne, that I feared I might have gone too far. But in the morning, a dozen red roses were delivered to the office with a note suggesting that as we were making up for lost time, we should meet again as soon as possible.

I had imagined that if a relationship with Harry developed, I would have time to accustom Brodie to the idea, so I resisted for several weeks Harry's suggestion that I should stay with Frances on a regular basis. He still contrived to meet me once a week, hurrying across London from the City to take me to lunch or leaving his office early so that I would find him waiting for me at the end of the day. He was playing the role of the ardent young lover and I was amused by his performance but I began to take him seriously and to ask myself what I wanted from the relationship. I enjoyed his company and companionship was something I had missed. But I wanted more than that. If I was to give up my freedom, I wanted him to love me. He insisted that he had fallen in love with me the first time he saw me and that I had been wrong to think it had just been a wartime flirtation but I thought, 'if he fell for a stranger when he was already married, I have no guarantee that the same thing will not happen again.'

I decided to invite him to Cambridge for the weekend to meet Brodie and my parents. I was more than just very fond of him and yet not, I thought, in love with him and I wanted to see whether his visit to Cambridge would tip the scales one way or the other.

Brodie took the news of Harry's impending visit in his stride. 'Are you going to marry him?' he asked.

'No darling. At least, I don't know. These are early days.'

He put his arm round my shoulder, my older brother rather than my son. 'It's seventeen years since Daddy died. You're not exactly a fast mover.'

My father seemed pleased that I had found a male companion at last and dropped hints about the sands of time like an elderly parent who is anxious to get an unmarried daughter off his hands. My mother was more cautious and I understood why. Our conspiracy to hide the truth about Tom's death had long ago ceased to require either of us to explain what we were afraid of. If Harry ever discovered that my first husband had not died of wounds but had been executed for murder, my happiness might be snatched away as brutally as before.

I could not tell my mother what Father Peter had revealed to me about Tom's death or that I was so close to confirming that Tom had laid down his life to save a German prisoner but her anxiety made me question my certainty that Harry knew nothing. According to Father Peter, the army had gone to great lengths to prevent the details of Tom's court martial from being known, yet I remembered that Harry had been returning to the Salient to rejoin his regiment and that one battalion of the Worcesters had gone into action alongside the Royal Fusiliers. Even if the names were not known, the fact that a Royal Fusilier officer had been killed by one of his own men during the battle would surely have leaked out.

I did not immediately come to the conclusion that if Harry proposed, it would be better to tell him the truth so that whether he already knew or not, there would be no secrets between us. Nor did I think it was necessary to alert Father Peter to the possibility that I might marry again. In my next letter to him, asking if he had any news, I just mentioned that I had met one of the badly wounded officers I had nursed in the Casualty Clearing Station during the Battle of the Somme and that he had taken me to dinner at the Café Royal.

The Presbytery,
St. Benet's,
Beccles,
Suffolk

20 January 1935

Dear Katherine,
No news I'm afraid but a lead that might be worth following.
One of my parishioners, who has recently retired from a senior post in the civil service, has told me that he thinks the Cabinet agreed some time ago to give priority to those refugees from Germany who

can make a contribution to British society, especially doctors and research scientists. The Cabinet's policy has not been made public because they don't want it to be known that we are only taking the 'best' refugees, so Whitehall will deny all knowledge. But my parishioner thinks there must be some organisation that is helping to place these doctors and research scientists in jobs and universities. Is there someone in Cambridge of whom you can make discreet enquiries, not mentioning Schneider by name?

You are fortunate to meet your badly wounded officer again. Occasionally in Beccles I pass a man in the street and think I remember him from the war but not well enough to go up to him and say, 'Weren't you with me at Passchendaele?' And I am invited to regimental reunions every year but the Abbot, having sent me to Siberia, does not think I should be attending dinners in London.

God bless you

Yours very sincerely in Christ,
Peter

I did know someone of whom I could make discreet enquiries. I wrote a note for Edgar Adrian asking whether he knew of such an organisation and, taking it round to the college, left it at the Porter's Lodge.

CHAPTER FIFTEEN

The Society for the Protection of Science and Learning had an office in Gordon Square, close to the main buildings of London University and an easy bus ride for me from Oxford Circus.

'We cannot give out information about individual refugees without their permission,' Tess Simpson, the Society's secretary explained to me. 'But Professor Adrian has been a very good friend of the Society so if you can tell me why you wish to meet this man, I will pass on your request. It will then be entirely up to him. What is his name?'

'Dr Martin Schneider,' I replied, hoping for a reaction but Tess Simpson's expression gave nothing away. We were sitting in her office, a large high-ceilinged room that looked out onto the square and I had prepared and rehearsed exactly what I was going to say.

'I believe my late husband, Tom Kennedy, saved his life during the war. Tom died of wounds at Passchendaele and I was told that shortly beforehand, during a raid on the German trenches, he saved the life of a young German soldier. A friend of Schneider's, who now runs the regiment's veterans association in Berlin, told me the story and, if what he says is true, I would like to meet the man whose life Tom saved.'

'Schneider is usually but not always a Jewish name,' was her only comment. 'That would explain why he left Germany.'

'Do you know him?' I asked.

She shook her head. 'I'm sorry Mrs Kennedy. All I can say is that if Dr Schneider has registered with us, I will pass on your request. Please give Professor Adrian my kind regards.'

By skirting round my question, Tess Simpson convinced me that she knew Martin Schneider and where to contact him, so that on the bus back to Oxford Circus, I was already excited at the prospect of coming face to face with the man whose testimony would bring to an end the years of not knowing for certain that Tom was the innocent man I believed him to be. I never doubted that Schneider would agree to see me; the only question was how soon. Harry was coming to Cambridge for the first time at the weekend and I did not want my new life and my old life to become entangled.

I had warned Harry that Brodie, like his father, was impatient with small talk, and that at the age of seventeen, he liked nothing better than arguing a political case he did not believe in, so Harry was prepared when, as soon as we had sat down for lunch, Brodie challenged him on the subject of Mussolini. Wouldn't England be better off with a strong leader like Mussolini, Brodie want to know, rather than the second-rate men who made up the National Government? Whatever his private thoughts, Harry had the wit to disagree so that they locked horns in an argument which was friendly but a trial of strength nevertheless and which moved on from Mussolini to Hitler and eventually to disarmament as a way of preventing another European war.

'Did you ever meet my father?' Brodie asked when Harry said something about the last war being a tragedy that need never have happened.

'I think we were in the same brigade at one time,' Harry replied. 'So we may have come across one another without knowing it.'

They were getting on well. Brodie respected someone who was prepared to take him on in an argument and Harry, an older and wiser adversary, was content to score enough points to let Brodie know that he was not someone who could be taken for granted. Watching and listening to Harry, I realised that I was beginning to fall in love with him. I did not think I would ever love him in the same compulsive way that I had loved Tom but enough to want to live with him and to be happy surrendering some of my independence.

After lunch, Brodie offered to show Harry round Cambridge and they were still discussing disarmament when they returned an hour later. Regular army officers did not always take kindly to clever young men but on our way to the station, Harry said he had enjoyed talking with Brodie and that he was sure they would become good friends.

'Is that important to you?' I asked him, realising too late that I had probably thrown away my last chance of being proposed to in a romantic setting. On a dull February afternoon, the road to the station was one of the least attractive parts of Cambridge. But I had underestimated Harry. He did not propose then but waited until the following week when we were having lunch in a small restaurant off Bond Street.

'I think you know my answer, Harry,' I replied. 'But I would like a little more time, just a week or two.'

I was not free to say yes until I had Martin Schneider's testimony safely in my possession so I was relieved when on the morning after Harry had proposed, Frances greeted me with a message from Tess Simpson. 'If you are free in your lunch hour, I have some news.'

Martin Schneider was willing to meet me at the Society's office but he wanted a third party to be present at the meeting. 'He speaks English very well but as a refugee he is naturally cautious,' Tess Simpson explained. 'I would be happy to sit in but you may prefer to bring a friend.'

'I have a good friend who knows the situation. He is a Benedictine monk who was an army chaplain in the war.'

Tess Simpson smiled. 'Well that should satisfy Dr Schneider's concern though I must say he doesn't strike me as the anxious type.'

She told me that Schneider had been working in one of the poorest quarters of Berlin when Hitler came to power. His mother was a German protestant from Lower Saxony but his father was Jewish and, although he had been brought up as a Christian, he thought it was only a matter of time before he was barred from practising medicine or beaten up by Nazi Storm Troopers who had marked him down as having communist sympathies. He crossed the border into Poland and then worked his way to England via Danzig and Rotterdam, arriving in the summer of 1934. He had hoped to be allowed to practice medicine but the British Medical Association, fearful of competition from too many foreign doctors, had refused to recognise his qualifications so he was waiting for a place on the German quota for refugees wishing to enter the United States. To make ends meet, he was working as a hospital porter during the day and washing corpses in the mortuary by night.

'Which hospital?' I asked.

'The London Hospital in Whitechapel. He has a room somewhere in the East End.'

It was of no consequence where he was working but that it should be the London Hospital strengthened my sense that the different phases of my life were gathering to this point and that once I had met Schneider, I would be ready to start a new phase where the past was not forgotten but mattered less.

On the day set for the meeting, I met Father Peter at Liverpool Street Station and persuaded him to let me pay for a taxi to Gordon Square. He seemed more nervous than I was, twice urging me not to expect any dramatic revelation from Schneider and twice reminding me not to give away what I knew about Tom's death.

'If it had not been for you, Father, I should never have known about Schneider,' I said. 'And to the end of my life I should have gone on thinking that the man I loved might have been capable of murder.'

Tess Simpson suggested we should use her office and when Dr. Schneider arrived, she would make the introductions and then disappear. We did not have to wait long but even so the sound of the doorbell made me start. I heard Tess Simpson's voice in the hall and a man's voice responding. The door opened and a tall, athletic man with lively, intelligent features and a mass of curly black hair walked in. Before Tess Simpson had a chance, he introduced himself.

'I am very pleased to make your acquaintance, Mrs Kennedy, and yours Father. I am Martin Schneider.'

We shook hands and took our seats at the table and Tess Simpson withdrew, closing the door quietly behind her. As Father Peter had suggested, I gave Schneider the translation of Hans Meyer's letter so that he could see what we had been told.

I said, 'I don't have the German original, I'm afraid.'

He was a disconcertingly attractive man who appeared to radiate energy even when he was sitting quite still and I had the fanciful thought that by saving his life Tom had released in him an extraordinary zest for living. When he had finished reading, he looked up at me and said, 'You have gone to a lot of trouble to fine me.'

'I believe it was my husband who saved your life.'

'And killed Second lieutenant Grice?' he asked.

I had not anticipated that question and I did not know what to say. Schneider took an envelope from the inside pocket of his jacket and pushed it across the table towards me, saying, 'Sergeant Krueger told me to keep this but I am going to America and I think this letter belongs in England. Perhaps you would like to have it.'

The envelope was addressed in a copperplate hand to 'Second Lieutenant Grice, 12th Royal Fusiliers, BEF' and, as I drew the letter out I realised that this must be the letter found on Grice's body.

Lady Grice
21 Cornwall Gardens
S.W.

22 August 1917

My own dearest Rupert,

We know that fierce fighting has been going on for days and darling we fear you must have been in the thick of it. Oh! That we may hear you are safe and well.

Frank Walton set forth yesterday fully equipped and I hope he will turn up in time for your birthday with letters and cards from us – also a waistcoat from Father, lined chamois and a very soft blanket from me. It does not seem possible that it is nineteen years since you were born; the time had gone far too quickly and I remember that day so well.

Your Father is going to see a specialist on Thursday as I am not happy at his having got so thin; he is absolutely skin and bone. He eats well and sleeps well – I cannot understand it.

Archie is working hard and came with us to see Frank off for Southampton. The station was crowded with soldiers of all sorts going back from leave and it made us realise the risks you and all our soldiers are running hourly so close to home. Well, I hope the Kaiser will have had his fill soon.

It will be such good luck if you are able to celebrate your birthday out of the line. Write soon and tell me all about it. Your Father says I shouldn't ask you to write so often but I cannot help it. You are never out of my thoughts and I long for news of you more than I can express.

Archie and Father send loads of love. God bless you and keep you safe my own beloved son.

Ever your devoted Mother,

Edith Grice

I passed the letter to Father Peter. I resented Grice's intrusion into my meeting with Schneider, all the more so because in my search for the truth about Tom's death, I had given no thought to Grice's family and I suspected that Schneider had guessed as much.

When Father Peter had read the letter, he said to Schneider, 'The family were told he had been killed in action.'

'I shall always be very grateful to your husband, Mrs Kennedy', Schneider said. 'I am only sorry that my life should have been spared at the cost of others.'

'Others?'

'Grice's and your husband's, I think.'

There was a short silence. Then Father Peter asked how long he had known.

'From the beginning,' Schneider replied. As soon as Sergeant Krueger discovered that the dead man was an English officer,

Schneider feared that the soldier who had saved his life would be court martialled and shot. 'In the German army too,' he said. 'What your husband did, Mrs Kennedy, would be a Kapitalverbrechen, a capital offence. I am very sorry.' When Tess Simpson asked whether he would be willing to meet an English war widow and explained why, he had realised at once who I was.

'We did not want to deceive you, Dr Schneider,' Father Peter said. 'But Mrs Kennedy is anxious that as few people as possible should know what happened to her husband. Her son does not know.'

Schneider turned to me and I explained that Brodie had been born three months after his father's death and was now a young man of seventeen. 'One day he will have to know that his father was executed for murder,' I said. 'When that day comes, I want him to know the truth about what happened when Grice was killed and you are the only witness.'

Schneider appeared to hesitate so Father Peter said, 'What you tell us will only be for the family. I give you my word.'

'Then I will write down for you, Mrs Kennedy, as much as I can remember,' Schneider said. 'I hope it will help you when you talk to your son about his father.'

Father Peter took a sheet of paper from a drawer in Tess Simpson's desk and I walked over to the window. I must have stood there for almost half and hour while behind me Father Peter and Dr Schneider were talking quietly and I imagined that Father Peter was helping Schneider with his written English. Eventually, Father Peter said, 'Katherine, would you like to read this through before I witness Dr Schneider's signature?'

I took the paper from Father Peter and sat at the table.

Martin Schneider's Account
My name is Dr Martin Schneider and I am a refugee from Germany registered with the Society for the Protection of Science and Learning in Gordon Square, London.

I am writing this because I am the only surviving witness of the death of a British officer, 2nd Lieutenant Grice, during a raid on our trenches on the night of 5/6 September 1917. At that time, I was 17 years old and a member of Sergeant Krueger's platoon in Number 3 Rifle Company of Infantry-Regiment 371.

On the night in question, the platoon was ordered to evacuate the trench but I did not receive the order so I was alone in one of our deep dugouts when the enemy attacked. Two men entered the dugout, one carrying a revolver, the other holding a rifle. Their faces were blackened and they had no badges of rank but I now know that the two men were 2nd Lieutenant Grice and Private Kennedy of the Royal Fusiliers.

I expected them to kill me and I had no means of defending myself but there was a chance that the raid was to take prisoners so I knelt down and held up a crucifix. I am not a Catholic but many of us carried a crucifix for good luck and because we had been told that British Tommies were superstitious.

2nd Lieutenant Grice shouted an order at Private Kennedy but almost immediately took two steps towards me himself and pointed his revolver at my forehead. I heard the shot but felt nothing and it was Grice who fell sideways across the table we used for our meals. I did not at first realise what had happened but I think I assumed that Grice had been shot by accident as he was so close to me and that Kennedy would now kill me. He was standing about fifteen feet away, holding his rifle in both hands in front of his waist with the muzzle pointing to his left away from me. He walked forward, keeping the rifle in that position, and, ignoring me, bent over Grice. When he straightened up, he gave me a brief glance, walked over to the ladder and climbed out of the dugout. In that brief glance, I had my only human contact with the man who had saved my life.

I remained on my knees for some minutes shaking uncontrollably. When I stood up, I saw that Grice could not be alive and I was tempted to take his revolver as a souvenir but German soldiers can be superstitious too and I did not wish to 'push my luck' as the English say.

I cannot possibly know what was in Private Kennedy's mind when he fired but, as the only witness, I would say that the most probable explanation is that he intended to fire a warning shot to stop his officer killing a man who had already surrendered. It was clear from the way Private Kennedy was holding the rifle that he must have fired from the hip. German soldiers knew that the British Lee Enfield was the best rifle in the world if you had time to take aim from the shoulder but that it could be very inaccurate if fired from the hip because it was so difficult to control. The bullet from Private Kennedy's rifle could just as well have hit me as 2nd Lieutenant Grice.

In my opinion, 2nd Lieutenant Grice's death was an accident of a sort that can occur easily in war.

Martin Schneider.

When I read the last sentence, my feelings of joy and relief were so overwhelming that I was unable to speak but after a few moments I managed to say, 'Thank you. That is all I wanted.' However inadequate that sounded as an expression of my gratitude, I was sure that Martin Schneider understood how much his testimony meant to me.

Our business was complete and Schneider said he had to be back at the hospital. I was reluctant to let him go because I thought it unlikely we would ever meet again but he wrote down Father Peter's address at Downside and promised to let us know where he settled in the United States.

'Tell me one last thing, Dr Schneider,' I said. 'My husband's expression, when he looked at you, what was it like?'

'You know, I'm not sure, it was only a glance,' he replied. 'He was probably checking that I did not have a gun, otherwise he would not have turned his back on me.'

We shook hands.

'Goodbye Mrs Kennedy. When your husband saved my life, I was the same age as your son. If I have a son, I shall tell him that we owe our lives to a brave English soldier called Kennedy.'

Father Peter went with Martin Schneider to the front door and when he returned, we stood at the window without speaking as the short day began to fade and the lights came on in the houses across the square. Then Father Peter said, 'It's time to let Tom go now, Katherine, you have done everything it is possible to do.'

He was right and I was ready to move on but I did not think I would ever be able to let Tom go, if by that Father Peter meant that I should try to forget. Tom would be mine for ever in God's sight and I had never doubted that one day we should be together again.

I thanked Father Peter for sharing the long journey with me and I asked him to say a prayer for Tom, which he did, ending with the words he had said over Tom's grave.

'Eternal rest grant unto him O Lord. Let perpetual light shine upon him. May he rest in peace.'

Chapter Sixteen

'The last chapter'

Harry and I were married at the Cambridge Register Office on 31 May 1935. My mother was there and Brodie and Frances Goodall were our witnesses. Sadly my father and Father Peter had to stay away because Harry had been divorced and Harry's only close relative, a younger sister, was living in what was then called Nyasaland, where her husband was a colonial officer.

Our honeymoon was spent touring the highlands of Scotland and making a trip by steamer to the Western Isles. Harry was a Macleod on his mother's side and wanted to see the clan's ancestral home. When we returned to London, I moved in to Harry's flat in Kensington and we spent most weekends at my house in Cambridge. Frances thought we were unwise not buying a new home of our own but I could not sell Grange Road while Brodie and my parents needed it and there seemed to be little point in moving from one London flat to another.

Our marriage was not without some difficulties but we overcame them because we both wanted to make the best of our second chance. It helped that we shared memories of the war but the more we grew to know and love one another, the less we wanted to dwell on the past. We both had to adjust, I more than Harry because I had been on my own for so long and was unfamiliar with the white lies and compromises needed to sustain the long haul of married life but Harry was sensitive to this and to my need to keep some privacy and independence. He encouraged me to continue with my job at the Royal College of Nursing and to have my own bank account into which my salary could be paid. Although he always declined to come with me and gave the impression that he thought it curious that I had a friend who was a Benedictine monk, he never objected to my visiting Father Peter at Beccles. Above all, Harry was good company. He was amusing, attentive and had the wonderfully redeeming quality at being able to laugh at himself, especially at the retired brigadier he tried hard not to be.

We thought of ourselves as a thoroughly modern couple but we loved one another too much not to be jealous of the past. Harry never gave the slightest hint that he was thinking of his first wife and the flat in Kensington was his not theirs, which was one reason I was happy to move in, but I could not resist looking in the drawers to see whether he had kept any letters or photographs. I had a photograph of Tom in the drawing room at Grange Road which it had never occurred to me to hide and I found it oddly disquieting that I did not know what Harry's first wife looked like. The result was that I speculated more than I need have done about their relationship. According to Harry, she had been free with her favours and I wondered how long Harry had known and why he had not divorced her sooner. I thought the answer might be that he had been too much in love but Frances dismissed the idea. 'Some men are too proud to admit that their wives have been unfaithful,' she said. 'Others just don't care.'

I did not ask Harry about his first wife and he never asked me about Tom but I suspected that he was jealous of the fact that Tom still had a place in my heart. There was nothing I could do about that except show Harry that I loved him. My two loves existed in different worlds and were not in competition with one another but I did not try to explain that to Harry because I did not think he would understand.

Much more important to me than occasional unspoken jealousy was Brodie's readiness to accept Harry. As Harry had predicted, they became good friends. When Brodie won a scholarship to read law at Trinity College, it was Harry who sent him a bottle of champagne and when, the following year, Brodie was allowed to have a guest at dinner in hall, it was Harry he invited. I was sure Brodie did not think of Harry as a substitute for his father but he needed a man to talk to and I was only too happy that Harry should fill that role.

Their enthusiasm for political argument was undiminished. As an undergraduate at Trinity, Brodie abandoned pacifism in disgust at the government's failure to stand up to Mussolini and Hitler and, along with many of his Cambridge contemporaries, he became an ardent anti-fascist. Harry shared Brodie's contempt for Neville Chamberlain but while Brodie flirted with the Cambridge branch of the Communist Party, Harry argued for rearmament and support for Winston Churchill, so that their friendly disagreements were a feature of our weekends. Just like his father, Brodie assumed that I needed educating in political matters and I tolerated his lectures because they were part of the process whereby Harry became a full member of the family.

The only threat to the happiness of our marriage lay in the secret that Father Peter had insisted I could not share with Harry. He was adamant that the chances of Harry finding out the truth about Tom's death were negligible and that if I broke my word, I would be putting my marriage at risk and probably my relationship with Brodie too. I had no choice. However much I hated deceiving Harry and living with the fear that he would discover the truth by accident, I could not defy Father Peter. For my sake, he had gone against the advice of his abbot and had broken the oath he had taken at Tom's court martial. We still corresponded and once or twice a year I made the journey by train to Beccles but he and Harry never met. They belonged to different parts of my life.

When the war broke out in 1939, Brodie had just completed his three years at Cambridge and had been accepted as a member of the Middle Temple but he was of military age so his training as a barrister had to be postponed for the duration. This time there was no argument about conscription – Tom and Fenner had fought and lost that battle in 1916 – and when Brodie was called up he went willingly. Harry did his best to stop me from worrying but I needed Tom beside me because this was our son going to war, just as his father had done, and the thought that Brodie, too, might not return was unbearable. He said he would like to try for a commission in the Royal Fusiliers, his father's regiment, but to my relief, Harry persuaded him that a good county regiment like the Worcesters would suit him better.

Brodie was commissioned in January 1940, two weeks after his twenty-second birthday, and was sent to join the 8th battalion which was part of the British Expeditionary Force. I followed the fortunes of the BEF in the columns of the newspaper as I had done before but this time the war was very different and I read the accounts of the swift German advances with foreboding. In May, Brodie's battalion was overrun by Rommel's Panzer Division and Brodie was taken prisoner. After the war, he told me how lucky he had been in his captors; on the same day and only a few miles to the north, the SS Adolf Hitler Regiment had murdered eighty British prisoners in cold blood.

Brodie spent five years as a prisoner of war, frustrated and bored but with the foresight to continue his legal studies and to become fluent in German. For over a year I was not told where he was being held and had no idea whether my letters sent through the Red Cross were reaching him but he was out of the battle and Harry assured me that even Hitler's Germany would abide by the Geneva Convention.

With Brodie a prisoner in German hands, my thoughts turned to Martin Schneider. He had not, as he had promised to do, written to Father Peter to let us know where he had settled in the United States. Then one Sunday when Harry and I were walking along the Backs in Cambridge, I saw Tess Simpson coming towards us. She knew nothing of the true reason for my wanting to meet Martin Schneider but I feared she might say too much and make Harry wonder why I had never mentioned to him or to Brodie that Tom had saved the life of a young German soldier. She could not be avoided but as soon as I introduced Harry as my husband she must have grasped the need for discretion because she said nothing about Martin Schneider and did not ask after Father Peter. At Professor

Adrian's suggestion, the Society's office had moved to Cambridge for the duration and I would be welcome to call at any time.

I told Harry that I had met Tess Simpson in London before we were married which was true and, because I knew he would ask, I explained that Tess's Society was responsible for finding university jobs for German scientists who had fled from the Nazis. 'Interesting,' he said, which was Harry's code for 'Thank you – I don't want to know any more.'

It was several weeks before I had a chance to ask Tess Simpson if she had any news of Martin Schneider. He was using the English version of his name, she told me, and as Dr Martin Taylor, he had qualified at Chicago University Medical School and was now in his last year of training to be a consultant paediatrician. I was not surprised that Schneider had wanted to break his ties with the old world and I was glad that he was doing something worthwhile with the life Tom gave him. If the man Tom had saved had become a Nazi, that would have been a bitter pill to swallow.

Harry and I continued our jobs in London throughout the war though at the height of the Blitz we spent more nights in Cambridge than in Kensington. When there appeared to be a real danger of a German invasion, I tried to persuade my mother and father to stay with friends in Kirkby Lonsdale but they got no further than packing a trunk and having it ready in the hall. They were both in their seventies and very reluctant to leave Cambridge, which they now regarded as their home.

The war brought me new responsibilities at the Royal College. I was appointed deputy director to Frances Goodall and for a short while in 1940, I was an adviser to Ernest Bevin, the Minister of Labour, on the recruitment of nurses. I liked Bevin. His directness and his refusal to give himself airs reminded me of Kitty. At our meetings he always treated me with respect, listening carefully to my suggestions. I was flattered to be consulted by a member of the War Cabinet but even when my work was at its most absorbing, it did not distract me for long from my anxiety about Brodie. Through Harry's contacts at the War Office I knew that his prisoner of war camp – Stalag 1Va – was near the German city of Dresden, far away from the industrial centres that were being so heavily bombed but in the direct line of the Russian army's advance and, like other wives and mothers, I feared that as the Germans faced defeat they might take revenge on allied prisoners.

Brodie's camp was liberated by the Red Army in March 1945 but it was several weeks before these prisoners were released by the Russians and handed over to the British navy at the Black Sea port of Odessa for the long journey home. Harry and I went to Waterloo to meet the boat train and when I caught sight of Brodie, striding down the platform and waving, I left Harry and ran towards him thanking God for his safe return.

I should have known that Brodie would be impatient to get on with his career. He was twenty-seven, he said, and had no time for a holiday. On the day after he returned to England, he went round to the Middle Temple to see when he could begin his pupillage. He was not interested in talking about his years as a prisoner of war and I had the impression that he had left them behind as easily as he had left behind the years he had spent in Kirkby Lonsdale. But one weekend in the September after his return, when we were alone together in the garden in Grange Road, he told me that something had happened not long before his camp was liberated that had profoundly affected him and made him feel more acutely than ever before the absence of his father.

In February 1945, the British had bombed the city of Dresden and the prisoners of war had been marched from their camp in the suburbs to the city centre to help clear the debris. They knew it had been a heavy raid but they were not prepared for what they saw. On every street and every square there were piles of corpses, mostly women and children, waiting to be taken away for burial.

'The German guards did not have to order us to search the cellars for survivors,' Brodie said. 'We did it willingly.'

He went down with a guard into one cellar and was surprised to see people still sitting there, old men, women and children, twenty-four hours after the raids had ended. But then he realised they were all dead, the firestorm had starved them of oxygen. When he looked at his German guard, he saw that he was crying. Other prisoners were called to help bring the bodies up onto the street. Brodie did not know how many thousands of civilians had been killed but later that day as the prisoners were being marched back to the camp, there were angry crowds shouting at them, 'Murderers, murderers.'

When he had finished telling me this, Brodie was silent and I did not know what to say. Then he said, 'That night I couldn't sleep. I wanted to talk to my father because I thought he was the one person who could make sense of it but all I could hear was my own voice reading the parts of his letters that I had remembered.'

If there was a time when I could, and perhaps should, have been honest with Brodie about his father's death, this was it but the years of keeping the secret from him as Tom had wanted me to do had created a barrier that I did not have the strength to move.

In 1948, Brodie married Victoria Faulkener, a girl from Belfast who was already established as a barrister while he had only just completed his pupillage. I eyed this ambitious young woman warily but when their first child was born and they asked my permission to call him Tom, I was delighted and I pressed the young family to stay at Grange Road whenever they could. But it was with their second child, Julia, that I had a special bond. Her gypsy darkness reminded me of Tom and from her earliest, tottering days she attached herself to me. Harry was not used to having young children around but he did his best to join in their games and I have a picture in my mind of him standing in the garden in his plus-fours, throwing a ball for Tom and Julia to chase as though they were puppies. They called him uncle.

My father did not live to see his first great-grandchild. He died a few weeks after Brodie's wedding. Before he died, he asked me to forgive him for opposing my marriage to Tom and although I did not think there was anything to forgive, I set his mind at rest. My mother died two year later at the age of eighty-three. She had been a wonderful mother and a constant friend and she had shared the agony of Tom's execution and the burden of secrecy, never once complaining. To the end, she worried that our secret would one day destroy my marriage to Harry and I tried to reassure her without revealing how much I knew. She died peacefully in her own bed in Grange Road.

The year after my mother died, Harry and I decided to retire from our jobs and to make Cambridge our home. I insisted that he should bring his favourite pieces of furniture from the flat in Kensington and I moved the photograph of Tom from the mantelpiece in the drawing room to the small sewing room which became my sanctum but I need not have worried. Harry made himself at home in Grange Road and our years there were the happiest of our marriage. We had time for one another. Harry was never going to be a domesticated man, there had always been a batman or servant on hand, but he kept the garden in order, launching vigorous campaigns against the encroaching weeds as though they were tribesmen on the North West Frontier, and each evening he read to me as I was preparing supper. We took it in turns to choose the book. Harry liked adventure, especially Henty and Buchan, and I like the Brontes, whose books had been banned at the Clergy Daughters School, so that Through the Sikh Wars was followed by Jane Eyre which was followed by Greenmantle. When Harry was reading his adventure stories, I remembered how young he had looked in the Casualty Clearing Station and I thought that part of him had never grown up.

Then one day, Harry said he would like to visit India again to see how things had changed since independence but it was the year of the Suez Crisis so we had to postpone our trip until 1957. We were all set to go in two weeks time when Harry told me his doctor had sent him to Addenbroke's Hospital for a check-up before we sailed; he had not mentioned his symptoms to me because he did not want to worry me unnecessarily.

Harry's cancer was inoperable. At first he was for going to India anyway and 'damn the doctors' but we both knew that was impossible so he became, and remained to the end, quietly philosophical. 'I have faced death before,' he said. 'And I am a very lucky man because I have the same nurse.'

The doctors let me look after him at home. When Brodie came to say goodbye, he brought half a dozen bottles of champagne to see Harry through the final days and they talked politics for an hour until Harry was too tired to continue. Towards the end, I could tell that Harry was impatient to be gone and I did not blame him; for a man like Harry, a gunshot wound to the chest was vastly preferable to slow decay. On the evening before he died, he took my hand and said that although I had not taken him seriously, he had fallen in love with me at first sight. 'We love each other now darling,' I said, 'that is all that matters.' His last thoughts were about the war and at the end, when his mind was wandering, he seemed to be trying to tell me something about having done his duty but he lost the train of thought.

After Harry's death, I thought of selling the house in Grange Road which was too big for me living on my own but it held too many memories so I offered rooms to postgraduate students from the women's colleges and, for the last ten years, I have had a succession of young women engaged in research of one sort or another. They fend for themselves and sometimes I do not see them for days on end but I enjoy having them around and occasionally I entertain them to tea. Some of them think I have led a sheltered life but others are more perceptive and, seeing the picture of Tom on the mantelpiece and the one of Kitty and I in the Easter sunshine at Gournay-en-Bray, they ask me questions about the Great War. It is then that I realise the Somme and Passchendaele are as remote to them as the Charge of the Light Brigade was to us.

Even the more perceptive are puzzled that a Benedictine monk comes to stay and I suspect that when they see Father Peter and I talking for a long time in the garden, they assume that I am taking instruction in the Roman Catholic faith. But I am not. Father Peter and I talk about all sorts of things but especially about how we can make sure that someone we can trust gives my manuscript to Brodie before, but not too soon before, the court martial papers are made public in 1992. We also have to consider my grandchildren, Tom and Julia. They are grown up now and before long they will have children of their own, so the question of revealing the truth to Brodie in the right way and at the right time is of the utmost importance.

I shall be seventy-eight next month. I am in good health and sound mind but I think it would be wise to finish this last chapter here. I am not afraid to die because I know there is another life after this one where Tom and Harry and all those I have loved will be waiting for me and the thought of our reunion fills me with great joy.

EPILOGUE

I finished reading Katherine's manuscript shortly after midnight. The monastery was silent. The monks had retired after Compline and as far as I was aware there were no other guests. When I drew back the curtains and pushed open the window, the warm summer night flowed in and I was tempted to escape to walk in the grounds and breathe the country air after being shut in my room for six hours but the Notes for Guests informed me that the outside doors were locked and that if I tried to open them I would set off an alarm. The thought of setting off an alarm in a monastery in the middle of the night appealed to the mischievous in me and I imagined a scene that I felt sure Father Peter would have enjoyed of monks emerging from their cells, slightly dazed like the figures in some depictions of the Resurrection, to be confronted by the local police.

Reluctantly, I went to bed, relying on my hours of reading to send me to sleep and on the bell for Mattins to wake me in time for the first office of the day but Tom Kennedy was too much on my mind. At half past five, in the grey morning light, I hurried along the cloister, unshaven and un-refreshed, overtaking two elderly monks so as not to be the last into the abbey Church. The vastness of the building dwarfed our small gathering. About twenty monks were already sitting in the choir stalls and, as the only outsider, I chose self-consciously to sit in the second row of the nave and waited for the office to begin.

The monks wore their hoods up, presumably to shield themselves from distraction, but I thought I could recognise the Abbot at this end of the back row. He was looking straight ahead, as were the other monks, and at no time during the service did anyone glance in my direction. I listened to their plain chant, their readings and their prayers for deceased brethren. I thought of Captain Peter Quinn returning from the war to this cloistered life, still a young man, bringing memories with him that the older monks did not share and would not have been able to understand; and of all those memories, the one that would surely have been most difficult to live with, even here in seclusion from the world, was the memory of Tom Kennedy. Fifty years later, when he met me at Tyne Cot, it was at Tom Kennedy's grave that he was saying his prayers. For forgiveness? No, there was no need of that. He must have been praying, as he would have prayed every day since Tom's death, for Tom's soul to rest in peace. And now he was asking me, an agnostic, to play my part.

'Shall we walk outside?' the Abbot suggested when I caught up with him after the service. His hood down, he was again the rather austere scholar who, if I remembered correctly, had spent some years in Rome as Procurator of the English Benedictine Congregationand had about him the air of someone who, however humble, had been close to the corridors of power.

The sun was touching the top of the buildings as I followed him through a small formal garden to an avenue of trees that led up a gentle slope away from the monastery. When we were walking side by side, he glanced at me once or twice as though surprised to note that I had not shaved but he said nothing and I did not think it was for me to initiate the discussion of Katherine's manuscript.

'Have you come to a decision?' he asked eventually.

I told him I was willing to do what Father Peter had asked but that I thought I should meet Katherine first to make sure that she was happy with my being the person who would give her manuscript to Brodie.

The Abbot nodded. 'Katherine will be very grateful,' he said. Then he walked on a few paces before adding, 'When you give the manuscript to Brodie Kennedy, there is something you will have to tell him, something that Katherine does not know and that Father Peter decided not to put in his letter to you.'

I jumped to the conclusion that I knew what he was going to say. Tom had confessed to Father Peter at the last moment that he had after all intended to kill Grice and Father Peter, for pity's sake, had never told Katherine. But the Abbot was not the sort of man you interrupted, so I kept my thought to myself.

He said, 'Harry Melrose was the President of the court martial that sentenced Tom Kennedy to death.'

Taken completely by surprise, I had difficulty disentangling the implications of what he had said. I seized on one.

'Harry Melrose married Katherine without telling her?'

'Yes.'

I was astonished. 'But Father Peter knew. Why didn't he tell her?'

At the end of the avenue of trees, a gate leading to a public road marked the limit of the monastery's land. Here the Abbot stopped and turned to face me. I cannot remember his exact words or capture his rather legalistic way of speaking but I believe this is an accurate summary of what he told me:

Father Peter had had no contact with Harry Melrose since the court martial in 1917 but he remembered him well and so faced a terrible dilemma when Katherine wrote to tell him who it was she was going to marry. Should he tell Katherine and risk destroying her marriage before it had begun or say nothing and risk an even greater blow to her happiness if she found out later? He decided to meet Harry and explain the whole situation to him, even though it would mean admitting that he had broken the oath of secrecy they had both taken before the court martial. Needless to say, Harry Melrose was surprised to be contacted by the Roman Catholic padre who had been Private Kennedy's defending officer and, at first, he was angry that Father Peter had told Katherine so much but he soon recognised that what they both wanted was to protect Katherine's happiness. After a long discussion, in which they worked through all the consequences, they agreed it was better to say nothing.

Of course, Father Peter had misgivings but he was won over by Harry Melrose's sincerity. Harry told him that he had not proposed to Katherine out of pity or guilt but because he had loved her ever since their first meeting. And he felt no moral obligation to tell her the truth. The fact that he had been the President of the court martial that had sentenced her husband to death was a coincidence he had only discovered after the war. At the time, he had not known there was any connection between the soldier on trial and the nursing sister he had met in the Casualty Clearing Station. No officer liked serving on a court martial but the Divisional Commander had appointed him and he had had no choice but to do his duty.

'I tell you this sub sigillo,' the Abbot said in conclusion. 'To this day Katherine knows nothing about Harry Melrose's role in Tom Kennedy's death.'

There was something about the way he put that, a Vatican bureaucrat closing the file, that made me say Katherine would never have forgiven Harry, or Father Peter either, if she had discovered what they had kept from her.

The Abbot looked at his watch. 'We have time before Lauds to see where Father Peter is buried, if you would like to do that.' So we retraced our steps, the sun flashing between the branches, and it was not until we were approaching the small cemetery that the Abbot turned to me again, and said, 'They were happily married for over twenty years.'

Three weeks later, on a hot August afternoon, I was sitting in the shade of a magnificent copper beach in the garden of Katherine's house in Cambridge.

'It is very good of you to take on something that should have been my responsibility,' Katherine said. 'But when the court martial papers are released, I shall be long gone. Will you try the ginger cake? I made it this morning.'

I had looked forward to meeting her and she was much as I had imagined she would be. At the age of eighty-one, she was full of life, with a lovely, eager face in which her clear, intense blue eyes were the most striking feature. Below her high cheekbones, her lightly mottled skin had sunk a little and her once golden hair, drawn back and tied in a bun, was grey but she was still a very attractive woman.

I told her how I had met Father Peter Quinn at Tyne Cot and how, in a short time, he had become a good friend of the family, which was why I would be glad to do what he had asked. Katherine was very business-like. She wanted to discuss how we should keep in contact without alerting my wife or colleagues and whether I thought it would be wise for her to find a pretext for me to meet Brodie so that when the time came, the manuscript would not be handed over by a complete stranger. She asked whether I was aware that a future government might set aside the Judge Advocate General's ruling and release the court martial papers early and I assured her that I was and that the Department of War Studies where I worked would be among the first to know, so she could trust me to see that her manuscript reached Brodie in good time.

I must have sounded a little put out that she had thought it necessary to ask that because she smiled at me, a smile of apology and amusement, and I understood then how easy it had been for Tom and Harry to fall in love with her at first sight. To cover my thoughts, I asked her about Brodie.

'Well you know he is married with two grown up children,' she replied. 'He is a successful barrister at the commercial bar. For a short time after the war, he wanted to work for the United Nations but the commercial bar held greater attractions for him. He's a good lawyer so he may try to have Tom's conviction overturned.'

'Is that what you want?' I asked.

She shook her head. 'All Tom would have wanted is that his son should understand that he had to make a choice. Either he let Grice commit murder under the cloak of war or he tried to prevent him. I think Tom was right, morally right, I mean, and I am proud of the choice he made but I no longer think his death was a miscarriage of justice.'

It was as well that I had not made the mistake of underestimating her. Her mind was sharp and, although she joked about remembering odd things from the distant past like the pudding she had chosen as her treat on her fifth birthday, she had no difficulty recalling the facts that mattered to her. And far from being reluctant to talk about Tom's death, she used the fact that I was a lecturer in War Studies as an opportunity to tell me what she had learnt about the killing of prisoners. After Harry's death, she had obtained a reader's ticket for the University Library which was nearby and had read all she could find about the rules of war. She could not believe, she told me, that Tom was the only soldier who felt so strongly about the killing of prisoners that he tried to prevent it. After all she had been through and at an age when most people would have been content to leave the past alone, she was still trying to understand what Tom had done and to put the killing of Grice into some sort of perspective. I do not believe in a life after this one but I knew that she did and I thought that she was probably determined to have all the arguments straight in her own mind before she saw Tom again.

When it was time for me to leave for the station, she made me promise to come back soon, which I was glad to do. We walked to the front gate together and said goodbye. A short way off, I turned to wave but she had already gone back into the house. The more I thought about her on my journey back to London, the more I admired her. If all went according to plan, when I gave her manuscript to Brodie, he would discover not only the painful truth about his father's death but also what a very remarkable woman his mother had been.

Printed in Great Britain
by Amazon